Curious
Notions

Tor Books by Harry Turtledove

(writing as H. N. Turteltaub)

Curious Notions

Crosstime Traffic—Book Two

Harry Turtledove

TOR®

A Tom Doherty Associates Book

New York

CURIOUS NOTIONS: CROSSTIME TRAFFIC—BOOK TWO

Copyright © 2004 by Harry Turtledove

This book is printed on acid-free paper.

A Tor Book
Published by Tom Doherty Associates, LLC
175 Fifth Avenue
New York, NY 10010

www.tor.com

Tor® is a registered trademark of Tom Doherty Associates, LLC.

Library of Congress Cataloging-in-Publication Data

Turtledove, Harry.
    Curious notions / Harry Turtledove.—1st ed.
        p. cm.—(Crosstime traffic; bk. 2)
    "A Tom Doherty Associates book."
    ISBN 0-765-30694-8
    EAN 978-0765-30694-4
    1. Germans—California, San Francisco—Fiction. 2. San Francisco (Calif.)—Fiction. 3. Undercover operations—Fiction. 4. Fathers and son—Fiction. 5. Retail trade—Fiction. 6. Time travel—Fiction. I. Title.

    PS3570.U76C87 2004
    813'.54—dc22

                                                                            2004048034

First Edition: October 2004

Printed in the United States of America

0 9 8 7 6 5 4 3 2 1

Curious
Notions

One

Every now and then, Lucy Woo could pretend San Francisco was a great city in a great country. Sometimes, when she hurried south toward Market Street, the fog would be just starting to lift. Through the thick, wet, salty mist, the big buildings on Market would look as fine as if they were new and in good repair. They loomed up like dinosaurs, grand and imposing.

And dead. When the sun came out, it pricked pretense. It showed the long-unpainted bricks, the peeling plaster, the broken windows. Some of the buildings still had cracks from the quake of 1989, and that was more than a hundred years ago now. Here and there, vacant lots and piles of rubble showed where buildings had been pulled down or fallen on their own. Lucy stayed as far from the rubble as she could. Squatters built shacks and caves from it. Some of them were harmless. Some weren't.

Traffic was a swarm of people on foot and on bicycles. You made your own path and you pushed ahead. If you didn't, you'd never get anywhere. Trucks and rich people's cars crawled along. They couldn't go anywhere in a hurry, either. Even ambulances got stuck. People died on the way to the hospital because they couldn't get there soon enough.

Only one kind of car horn made everybody jam onto the sidewalk and get out of the way. That particular shrill scream was reserved for German cars alone. If Americans didn't clear a path in a hurry, the Kaiser's men were liable to start shooting. They didn't always, or even very often, but you never could tell.

This morning, Lucy had to move aside for the occupiers three times in the space of four blocks. She was furious. She was also frightened. If she was late to her job at the shoe factory, they might let her go. That would be awful. Her family really needed the money she brought in, even if it was only eight dollars a week.

A Mercedes rolled by. Bigwigs in high-crowned caps and fancy uniforms sat inside. Bodyguards in steel helmets with ornamental spikes rode shotgun. That was what people called it, anyhow. But they didn't carry shotguns. Assault rifles were a lot more deadly.

The big blond man who scowled down at Lucy wasn't mad at her. "I hate those so-and-sos," he said. "They think they own the world. Well, they do, near enough, but they don't have to act like it."

"Yes," Lucy said, and let it go at that. Her own features were almost as Chinese as her name. One of her great-grandmothers had been Irish. That made her nose and chin a little sharper than they might have been otherwise.

Even saying yes to the man was taking a chance. He might have belonged to the *Feldgendarmerie,* the Kaiser's secret police. And if he didn't, he was taking a chance talking to her. A sixteen-year-old Chinese girl wasn't a likely snoop. The Germans looked down their noses at what they called Orientals. Again, though, you never could tell.

Horn still screeching, the Mercedes plowed forward. The blond man looked daggers after it. As people unsquashed and started moving, he said, "I'm late. It's their fault. It's not mine. You think my boss will care?"

"Not if he's like mine," Lucy said. "I've got to hurry, too." She dived into the crowd. Being short had few advantages. Disappearing easily was one of them.

He didn't follow her. She made sure of that. And he couldn't know who she was. San Francisco was full of Chinese faces. She hurried on to the shoe factory. If she stepped on a few toes, well, some other people stepped on hers, too. And if she stuck an elbow in the side of a fat woman who blocked her way, she wasn't about to let that fat woman make her late. She wouldn't let anybody make her late.

She punched in just barely on time. Punching in wasn't good enough. She had to get to her machine on time, too. The foreman was a bald man named Hank Simmons. He was so mean and strict, he might have thought he was a German. But Lucy didn't— quite—give him an excuse to yell at her. A couple of women who came in right after her weren't so lucky. They got scorched.

Lucy's job was to sew instep straps onto women's shoes. That was what she did, ten hours a day, six days a week. Other women in the big building had other jobs. Some nailed on heels. Some stitched soles to uppers. Some sewed on decorative trim. They all did the same thing through the whole shift, over and over and over again.

Some of them were younger than Lucy. A few couldn't have been more than eleven or twelve. Some were gray-haired grandmothers. Some were Chinese, some white, some Japanese, some Mexican, some black. San Francisco held a few of just about every kind of people under the sun. And the Kaiser's officials treated them all just the same way: lousy.

When Lucy's foot hit the button, the sewing machine snarled to life. She guided the strap and the upper through the machine. The vibration made her hands tingle. She shook them a couple of times. She always did, first thing in the morning. After that, she forgot about it.

Other sewing machines buzzed, too. Nail guns clacked. Off in the back, electric leather cutters made what was almost a chewing noise. Lucy wouldn't have wanted that job for anything. They had their own foreman back there, and he screamed at you if you wasted even a scrap of leather.

"How's it going?" asked the sandy-haired woman on the machine next to Lucy's. She was twice Lucy's age. She'd been making shoes in here since she was fourteen. She'd go right on doing it till she couldn't any more.

"I'm okay, Mildred. How are you?" Like Mildred and most of the others in the factory, Lucy could work without looking at what she was doing. Her hands did it whether she watched or not. She was sure she could sew straps in her sleep.

Everybody said the same thing. Every so often, though, someone would stop paying even the little bit of attention she needed to do the job. The shriek of pain that followed would make everyone jump. After that, people would be careful . . . for a little while.

Mildred's thin face was always sour. She looked even more unhappy now. "My boy is sick with something," she said. "Haven't got the money for a doctor. Haven't got the time, neither." Grimly, she went on sewing.

Lucy tossed a finished upper into the bin by her station. She started to sew another one at the same time as she asked, "Who's watching him, then?" It wouldn't be Mildred's husband. He was a longshoreman, and worked even more hours than she did.

"My kid sister," Mildred answered. "She just had her own baby, you know, and she can't go back to work yet."

"Sure," Lucy said. Mildred and her family were better off than some, even if she didn't realize it. At least she and her husband *were* working. And her kid sister was able to stay home for a while after she had a baby. Not that staying home with a brand-new one was any vacation—Lucy had helped her own mother with her brother, though she'd been little then. But plenty of women in the USA couldn't afford to stay home at all. As soon as they could stagger out of bed, back to work they went.

"It's not fair," Mildred whined. "It shouldn't ought to be like this."

Lucy only shrugged. "Tell it to the Germans," she said, which meant, *You can't do anything about it, so forget it.* Life was the way it was. She couldn't do anything about it herself. Mildred couldn't do anything about it. Nobody could do anything about it. You got by as best you could. What other choice did you have?

Whenever her bin filled up, a boy carried it off and brought her an empty. A quality inspector came by in the middle of the morning. He spoke to a couple of women, but left Lucy alone. If he spoke to you too often, you found yourself on the street. He hadn't bothered Lucy for weeks. She knew what she had to do, and she did it. She didn't do any more than she had to, not one single thing. It wasn't as if she were in love with her job. They paid her as little as they could get away with, and she worked as little as she could get away with. That was how things went, too.

She got twenty minutes for lunch. Some women bought food at the factory cafeteria. That made the bosses extra money, and the place never had anything good. Lucy brought rice and vegetables and a little fish from home. She'd be hungry before she went back there for supper, but she couldn't do anything about that.

"Back to work!" Hank Simmons yelled three or four minutes before the lunch break ended. "I don't want you dilly-dallying around, now. You hear me?"

What he wanted was to cheat them out of some of the little break they got. Lucy made sure she was working when she was supposed to. She also made sure she didn't get busy *till* she was supposed to.

15

She would have had to if Simmons came by. But he didn't, not today, and so she didn't, either.

She hardly remembered the rest of the afternoon. That happened sometimes. Your hands would do the work, and your brain just sort of went away. You would look up in amazement and discover hours had gone by and you'd never even noticed. Sometimes that was nothing but a relief.

Sometimes it scared Lucy half to death. It was a little like dying. You weren't *there*. Where were you?

She came back to herself half an hour before her shift finally ended. She shook herself as if she were coming out of a cold bath. The world was back. If she could get home fast, she'd be able to spend a little time with her family before she got so tired she'd have to fall into bed. That little while was what she looked forward to— unless she was squabbling with Michael. He had more bounce than she did. He didn't have to work so much.

"See you tomorrow," Mildred said when they went to clock out.

"Oh, yes," Lucy said in a hollow voice. "You sure will."

"This is one of the alternates where we need to be especially careful," Paul Gomes' father warned him for what had to be the fiftieth time.

"Yes, Dad. I know that. Thank you." Paul sounded more sarcastic than patient, though he wouldn't have thought so. He'd graduated from high school the month before. He planned on going to UC Berkeley, but not till he'd spent a couple of quarters in the alternate San Francisco his father had been warning him about.

However much Paul tried not to see it, the two of them were much alike. They were both of medium height, with swarthy skin, dark hair, and dark eyes. They were both stocky, with square faces and eyebrows that would quirk up when they thought something was funny. Lawrence Gomes wore a bushy mustache that made him look like a bandit. Paul wouldn't have been caught dead with such a horrible thing on his upper lip.

"We can get into real trouble here," Dad persisted. "We can get Crosstime Traffic into real trouble, too."

"I know, Dad. *Jawohl.*" Paul hoped throwing in a little German would persuade his father he took this seriously. "We've been over it before, you know."

He might as well have saved his breath. Dad went on as if he hadn't spoken: "This is one of those alternates where, if they find we can travel across timelines, they can probably start building their own transposition chambers. And if they do—if anybody does— we've got a lot of trouble on our hands."

Paul started to tell him he knew that, too. He decided not to bother. How much good would it do? None—he could see that. He felt as if he were back in a high-school history class. Dad thought he thought he knew more than he did. He thought Dad thought he knew less than he did.

About fifty years earlier, not long before Dad was born, the home timeline was a mess. It was running out of food and energy at the same time. Then Galbraith and Hester figured out how to travel not through space but across time, to visit other Earths where history had taken different turns from the way it had gone here. There were alternates where the Roman Empire never fell. There were others where the Armada conquered England, or where the South won the Civil War, or where the Communists won the struggle with capitalism. There were alternates where no one from Europe discovered America, and the Native Americans were still going through the early

Bronze Age. There were others where the Chinese colonized the New World. And there were some where man never evolved at all.

The home timeline began trading with the inhabited alternates. It began taking what it needed from some of the empty ones. That trade probably saved the world from collapse. Inside a very few years, it made Crosstime Traffic even bigger than Microsoft had been at the end of the twentieth century.

So far as anybody knew, the home timeline was the only one where people had figured out how to travel from one world of if to another. But quite a few alternates with fairly recent breakpoints had the technology to do it, if the idea occurred to them. Crosstime traders had to be doubly careful in places like those. Dad was right about that, even if he did go on and on about it. But they couldn't stay away from worlds like those. If they did, somebody might find the secret while they weren't looking. That wouldn't be good, either.

The alternate where Paul and his father were going was one of those. Its breakpoint was 1914, less than two hundred years in the past. In the home timeline, Germany was stopped short of Paris in the opening days of World War I. Four years of trench warfare followed. In the end, the Germans lost. A generation later, Hitler and the Nazis tried again—and lost again, even worse than before.

Things were different in this alternate. The Russians had moved against eastern Germany more slowly than in the home timeline. The Germans had been able to put a few more divisions into the attack on France. Their Schlieffen plan had worked here, where it failed in the home timeline. They'd wheeled around beyond Paris, not in front of it, and they'd knocked the French Army and the British Expeditionary Force clean out of the war. Then a lot of them had climbed onto trains and headed east. When they met the Russians, they smashed them, too.

After that, everything looked different. The Kaiser ended up sitting on top of the world. France and England were humbled—France more so, because it took a worse beating. When they tried to get their own back at the end of the 1930s, Germany beat them again. It didn't need to worry about Russia this time around. Russia had fallen to pieces in a long civil war, and a lot of the pieces—Poland, Finland, Courland, the Ukraine—were German puppets.

Once Germany won that second war, it dominated Europe the way no one had since the days of the Roman Empire. It looked west across the Atlantic. The United States looked east—nervously. It hadn't fought in either European war. It didn't believe in getting tangled up in the affairs of foreign powers. It paid for its mistake.

In the home timeline, the USA got the atomic bomb first. One of the reasons it did was that a lot of scientists had fled Hitler's Germany. Quite a few of them, like Einstein, were Jews. Others couldn't stand what the Nazis were doing.

Again, things were different in this alternate. The Kaiser didn't persecute Jews. Those talented scientists stayed in Germany. They were happy to work for the German Empire, because it wanted them. And, here, the Germans got the bomb first.

They got it—and they used it. War between Germany and the United States broke out in 1956. The Germans had the bomb, and they had airplanes to deliver it. A dozen American cities went up in smoke the first day (the only reason San Francisco didn't was that both bombers aimed at it got shot down). The war lasted a couple of months, but most of it was just mopping up for the Kaiser's men.

In this alternate, imperial Germany had run things ever since, for close to a century and a half now. The United States was a second-rate power now, and had to do what the Kaiser's officials said. Technology wasn't as far along here as it was in the home timeline. It wasn't that far behind, though. If the locals ever got

19

their hands on a transposition chamber, for instance, they might be able to build one of their own.

Dad said, "We need to keep an eye on them. And we need to buy produce from them. No matter what timeline you're in, the Central Valley turns out some of the best produce in the world."

"Are we smart, trading them some of our gadgets?" Paul wondered.

"If you don't give, you can't get," his father said.

"I know—but if we give them things they haven't seen, won't they want to know where that stuff comes from?" Paul asked. "And aren't they liable to come up with the right answer once they ask the right question?"

Dad only shrugged. "I don't set policy—and neither do you," he added pointedly. "But Crosstime Traffic isn't there for their health. They're there to show a profit. So we trade. We trade carefully, but we trade. Where would we be if we couldn't visit the alternates?"

Paul had no answer for that. He knew where the home timeline would be without the alternates. Up the famous creek without a paddle, that was where. Still, *trade carefully* reminded him of *all deliberate speed*, a phrase he'd run across in a history class. It wanted you to do two things at the same time, and they pulled in opposite directions. If that didn't mean trouble, what would?

"Are you ready to go crosstime?" his father asked.

"Oh, I'm ready, all right. All I have to do is put on my costume. We don't even need a new language through our implants, not for San Francisco in that alternate. They speak English there, too."

"Yes, but it's not quite our English." Dad was just full of good advice. Paul would have been more grateful if he'd heard it less often. Dad seemed convinced he was eight, not eighteen. "You have to remember. You have to be careful."

"Right," Paul said. His father sent him a sour look, but they left it there.

They changed clothes before they got into the transposition chamber. Paul put on a pair of Levi's not too different from the ones people wore in the home timeline. They were a little baggier, a little darker shade of blue. Chambray work shirts like the one he tucked into the jeans had been popular in the home timeline a hundred years ago. He'd seen pictures. Only the pointed-toed ankle boots and the wide-brimmed derby seemed really strange.

His father wore a similar outfit. He had on a double-breasted corduroy jacket with wide lapels over his shirt. In the home timeline, he would have looked like a cheap thug. The style was popular in the alternate, though. So was the wide leather belt with the big, shiny brass buckle. It said he was somebody solid and prosperous.

The woman who ran the transposition chamber snickered at them when they got in. Paul would rather have worn a toga or a burnoose or a flowing Chinese robe. Those would have been honestly weird. This way, he just looked as if he had no taste in clothes. It was embarrassing.

He and Dad got into their seats and put on their belts. He didn't know what good the belts did. Transposition chambers didn't run into things. They didn't move physically, only across timelines. The seats were like the ones in airliners, even to being too close together. That was probably why they had belts.

For that matter, he didn't know what good the operator was, either. All she did to start the chamber was push a button. Computers handled everything else. Operators were supposed to navigate the chambers if the computers went out, but what were the chances if that happened? Slim and none, as far as Paul could see.

He couldn't tell when the chamber started across the alternates toward the Kaiser's America. It would seem to take about fifteen minutes to get there. When he left the chamber, though, it would be the same time as it had been in the home timeline when he left. Duration was a funny business in transposition chambers. Even chronophysicists didn't understand all the ins and outs.

"We're here." The operator caught him by surprise. He hadn't felt the arrival, any more than he'd felt the motion across the timelines.

His father stood up and stretched. When he did, his hands brushed the ceiling of the transposition chamber. It wasn't very high. Paul got up, too. If he hadn't, Dad would have said he was dawdling. He didn't feel like banging heads over that. He and his father banged heads often enough anyway.

The operator closed the door. The subbasement here had exactly the same position as the one in the home timeline from which the chamber had left. The air smelled a little different: a little smokier, a little more full of exhaust, and a little more full of people who didn't take baths as often as they might have.

Paul and his father left the chamber. Silently and without any fuss, it disappeared. Was it going back to the home timeline or on to a different alternate San Francisco? Paul knew he would never know.

Bare bulbs lit the chamber. Iron stairs led up to a trap door in the ceiling. A plump man came through. He waved. "Hello, Lawrence," he called to Paul's father. A moment later, as an afterthought, he added, "Hello to you, too, Paul."

"Hello, Elliott," Dad answered. "How's business?"

"Tolerable," the plump man said. "This station makes a profit. The company isn't going to close it down any time soon." He laughed. "If we can't make a profit so close to the Central Valley, we'd better shut up shop."

"Shh." Dad put a forefinger in front of his mouth. "Don't let Crosstime Traffic hear you." He laughed, too. He got along fine with people his own age. He seemed to get along fine with everybody except Paul, in fact. The two of them were water and sodium. That made Paul wonder if there was something wrong with *him*.

Elliott said, "Come on upstairs, and you can see for yourself." Up they went. Their boot heels clanged on the iron risers. Once they got out of the subbasement, Elliott closed the trap door behind them. Then he rolled a file cabinet that didn't look as if it could roll over the door. That subbasement wasn't supposed to be easy to find. He suddenly looked worried. "You've got your *Kennkarte?*"

"Oh, yes." Dad reached into the back pocket of his Levi's and pulled out his identity papers. Paul did the same. Elliott nodded, obviously relieved. If you didn't have papers in this alternate, you might as well not exist. Theirs were forgeries, of course, but they were forgeries made with all the skill of the home timeline. They were at least as good as the real thing. They just happened not to be genuine.

The German word for identity papers seemed right at home in the English Elliott used, the English of this alternate. Paul had no trouble following it, but it wasn't the English he spoke at home. It was slower, the vowels flatter, some of the consonants slightly guttural. It was, in fact, an English that had had German rubbing off on it for a hundred forty years or so.

Elliott led Paul and his father into the front room of the shop, which stood on Powell Street between Union Square and Market. The name of the place was Curious Notions. From inside, it looked to be spelled out backwards in gold letters on the plate-glass window opening on the street. Toys and gadgets, most of them from the home timeline, filled the shelves.

"Nobody's wondered about any of this stuff?" Paul's father asked. He didn't hesitate to steal Paul's idea. Maybe he didn't know he was doing it. Maybe.

23

"Not that I've heard," Elliott answered. "And if I can't find out here, it's a good thing I'm leaving town."

Paul looked out the window. Men wore the same kind of clothes he and Dad—and Elliott—did. Women mostly had on linen blouses, sweaters, and skirts that came down below the knee. The women wore pointed-toed shoes, too. Misery loved company. White and black women wore their hair in fancy curls. Those whose ancestors came from Asia mostly didn't bother.

Cars and trucks slowly picked their way past pedestrians and people on bicycles. They looked like those from more than a hundred years earlier in the home timeline. All of them burned gasoline or diesel fuel. The Kaiser's men didn't seem to worry about global warming. Of course, they'd had to dodge a nuclear winter in this alternate. It wasn't so crowded here as in the home timeline, either.

A truck driver leaned on his horn. That could have happened in the home timeline, too. Paul wished the noisy idiot would cut it out. It did no good, and only annoyed everybody in earshot. That was probably why the trucker did it.

Snarling motorcycles with sidecars rolled past. The sidecars had machine guns mounted on them. The German soldiers who rode in them didn't believe in taking chances.

"You know what this is?" Dad said. "This is an alternate that never heard of Adolf Hitler. That's not bad."

"It's still not a very pretty place," Paul said.

Elliott looked from one of them to the other. "You're just a big, happy family, aren't you?" he said. "Will you be all right here after I go back to the home timeline?"

"We'll be fine," Dad answered. "Paul's a little wet behind the ears, that's all. It's nothing to worry about."

"Thanks a lot, Dad," Paul said.

"Any time." His father seemed to think he meant that for real thanks.

Elliott plainly knew better. He also plainly knew better than to try to step into the middle of a quarrel between father and son. The only thing that happened when you did that was, you got shot at from both sides. The departing shopkeeper just said, "Well, you know the drill here. To the authorities, we sell these little gadgets and we deal in produce on the side. I've told our people in the Central Valley that the two of you would be taking over for a while."

"Sounds good," Dad said. "We'll manage. Don't you worry about a thing. We've been here before. They know us. They know we'll treat 'em right." He nudged Paul. "Don't they?"

"Huh?" Paul said, taken by surprise, and then, "Uh, sure, Dad." He couldn't argue with his father about that. As far as the local merchants went, Lawrence and Paul Gomes were some of the most reliable people in the world.

Dad laughed. "Dealing here is fun, too. When I think I can get an enormous trailer full of garlic from down in Gilroy for twenty-five dollars . . ." He laughed again, louder.

So did Paul, without any hesitation. Prices here *were* a joke if you came from the home timeline. A dollar there was a little aluminum coin, worth nothing in particular.

A dollar for your thoughts, people said. Even a benjamin wasn't worth all that much. Things were different here. You could buy more, much more, with a dollar here than with a benjamin back home. Even cents were real money here: bronze coins, not aluminum. And the phrase this alternate used was *a penny for your thoughts.*

Somewhere off in the distance, a fire engine roared through

the streets, bell clanging. Police cars here used bells, too. They were painted red, not black and white like the ones in the home timeline.

Dollars, not benjamins. Bells, not sirens. Red, not black and white. Those were the small differences, even if they were the ones you noticed first after crossing the timelines. Occupation, not freedom. Poor people, not prosperous ones. Those were the differences that really counted.

As things went in Chinatown, Lucy Woo's family wasn't badly off. They didn't have a television—they weren't rich. But they did have a radio and a small refrigerator. The money she brought home from the shoe factory helped pay for luxuries like that. Plenty of their neighbors got by with less.

"So long," her younger brother said. Michael hurried out the door. He was ten, and had a summer job as a grocery delivery boy. He'd go back to school when fall started. He needed to learn as much as he could—he'd take over their father's business one of these years. Lucy would have liked to stay in school, too. It hadn't worked out. They needed the money. And sons got breaks like that more often than daughters did.

Lucy hurried to finish her own bread and jam. She drank tea with breakfast. It helped her forget how tired she was when she first got up in the morning. Dad was already gone, opening up the shop. He bought, sold, and repaired anything that ran on electricity, from lamps to large adding machines. He was teaching Michael, too, all the time. Lucy's brother was already getting pretty good with a soldering iron.

"Got to go," Lucy said, and grabbed her lunch pail. She was tempted to open it and see what was inside, but she didn't. Mother tried to surprise her every day, at least with something. It wasn't always easy, but she usually managed.

Mother blew Lucy a kiss when she went out the door. Lucy yawned in spite of the tea. She really wished she could go back to bed. But no such luck. She had to head for the shoe factory.

Down the stairs. Other people in the apartment building were going to work, too. She nodded to some. With others, she didn't bother. They were as bleary-eyed as she was. Out the front door, turn left. Down Powell toward Market. She yawned again. If she couldn't have more sleep, she wished for more tea, or maybe coffee. Coffee, she decided. It was stronger.

The morning was nice and clear. San Francisco wasn't foggy all the time, just often enough to be annoying. Gulls soared overhead. They mewed like cats. On the cracked sidewalks, pigeons paraded underfoot. They cocked wary orange eyes at passing people. Sometimes they got handouts. Sometimes they wound up in pigeon stew. They couldn't tell which ahead of time. No wonder they were wary.

Newsboys waved papers and shouted headlines. Divers had found the skeleton of the *Hindenburg* where it crashed off the coast of France almost a hundred fifty years earlier. That was interesting, but not interesting enough to get Lucy to part with two cents for a newspaper.

Some shops were opening up as she walked by. Shopkeepers called out to passersby in English and Chinese and Spanish—and, if the passersby looked rich, in German. People in San Francisco sold anything that moved. If you stepped away from your shadow for a minute, they'd pry it off the sidewalk and try to sell it back to you. Lucy heard men and women hawking pork, clothes, jewelry, watches, vegetables, secondhand books, medicines, radios, slide rules, bicycle tires, and everything else under the sun.

27

She'd grown up here. She knew the "fine gold jewelry" would turn your arm green if you wore it very long. The "Swiss watches" were cheap copies sold at not-so-cheap prices—either that or they were stolen. The black-and-orange Seals shirts and beige ones for Missions backers would come apart at the seams sooner than they should have. The bicycle tires were liable to be retreads. Sometimes the medicines were what they claimed. More often, they were sugar pills. If you bought from somebody you didn't know, you took your chances. If you came expecting wonderful things at rock-bottom prices—well, that was what people here wanted you to do. Truth was, you got what you paid for, here as anywhere else.

A few places showed OPEN signs but didn't have people out front telling the world about how wonderful they were. Those quiet places were the ones where you could get good stuff . . . if you knew what you were looking for, and knew what you were looking at. Fine gold jewelry was for sale—for those who could afford it. Some "antiques" hadn't been made day before yesterday in a room behind the shop where they were for sale. Not all radios had their original innards replaced by junk that would wear out in weeks. Because of what her father did, Lucy knew some of the tricks of that trade.

And there was Curious Notions. Lucy's father was curious about that place. She couldn't blame him. They had phonographs smaller than anyone else's that sounded better than machines costing five times as much. They had radios you could put in your pocket and listen to with earphones. They had battery-powered games that were like nothing anyone else sold.

They could have been millionaires, selling what they sold. By all the signs, they weren't interested in being millionaires. What they sold here in San Francisco was almost an afterthought. People said they did most of their business with the grape growers and produce farmers in the Central Valley. Lucy knew how much—or rather, how little—what people said was often worth.

As she often did, she stopped in front of the window. The stuff in Curious Notions *looked* different. It didn't pretend to be wood even when it wasn't. It wasn't ornamented to pieces. Everything was just *there,* there to do a job and not make a fuss about it. It wasn't stylish. It didn't have to be stylish. It worked, and worked well.

Lucy had got used to the chubby man who bustled around inside the place. She didn't see him there this morning. Instead, two other men, plainly father and son, stood talking behind the counter. She didn't recognize them, but they acted as if they had every right to be there. The father, whose big mustache made him look tough, banged the countertop with his fist to make a point. The son might have been Lucy's age, or maybe a year or two older. He nodded in a way that said he'd heard it before and wasn't much impressed.

Though Lucy could see that, the man with the mustache couldn't. He went on talking. The younger one started tidying things up inside the shop. Every so often, he would nod again. He was polite, but he wasn't interested.

He looked out the window and saw Lucy. He smiled at her. She found herself smiling back. Did he know she'd been standing here watching him for a minute or so? She couldn't tell. She couldn't stay here watching him all day, though. She couldn't be late for work.

Down to Market she went, and then south and west along it toward the factory. She wished she weren't going there. She wished she could do something she enjoyed instead. She didn't want to spend most of her waking hours tending a sewing machine. Only a crazy person would.

But only a crazy person would want to go hungry, either. You couldn't always do what you wanted to do. Sometimes it was what you had to do. Maybe, one of these days, she wouldn't have to go to the factory every day. She could hope. She could dream. Meanwhile . . . she could work.

Some German businessmen came through the place in the middle of the shift. One of them wore a top hat, something she'd seen only in movies before. They all looked fat and pink and rich. They paid more attention to the machines in the factory than to the people working in it. Lucy understood that. They could always replace the workers. The machines would be much more expensive to change.

Even Hank Simmons had to fawn all over the Germans. Seeing the petty tyrant of a foreman humble made Lucy smile again, this time in a nasty way. She kept her head down so nobody else would notice her doing it.

Two

The bell over the front door at Curious Notions tinkled. Paul looked up from his bowl of shrimp and rice. He'd been eating lunch as fast as he could, hoping to finish before another customer came in. No such luck. He shoved the bowl under the counter and put what he hoped was a businesslike smile on his face. "Hello. How can I help you?"

"I am Inspector Weidenreich," said the customer, who turned out not to be a customer after all. "You will show me your *Kennkarte* and your permit for doing business here. At once." *I'll close you down if you don't,* his manner declared. His German accent wasn't thick, but you could hear it. That made him an imperial official, not just one who worked for San Francisco or California. It also made him more dangerous.

But papers were not a problem, or Paul hoped they weren't. "Certainly, sir," he said. He took his identity papers from his hip pocket and laid them on the counter. "Here is the *Kennkarte.*" The permit was framed, and hung on the back wall. He set it beside his papers.

Weidenreich examined the business permit first. Paul wasn't worried about that at all. The permit was genuine. The tall, somber-looking inspector—his expression said someone in his family might have died not long before—took the permit out of the frame. He held it in front of a light so he could see the watermark. Finding it was there only made him grunt.

Then he looked at Paul's *Kennkarte*. He took a jeweler's loupe out of one of his jacket pockets and peered at the papers through it. The forgery was supposed to be perfect. Paul hoped it was.

With another grunt, Inspector Weidenreich shoved the identity papers back at Paul. He gnawed on his underlip as he stowed the loupe once more. "Everything appears to be in order." He sounded as if he hated to admit even that much. "Appears, I say."

"What's going on?" Paul did his best to seem innocent and ordinary. And so he was—in the home timeline. Here, he counted for neither.

"I ask the questions," the German said.

"Yes, sir." Plainly, this was no time to be rude. As plainly, Elliott hadn't known what he was talking about—and had left town just in time. Paul went on, "We haven't done anything wrong. We have our permit. You see that. We pay all our taxes. I can show you the receipts, if you want."

Weidenreich waved that away. "No, no. I knew as much before I came here. I know who you are. The Kaiser's government knows who you are. What we do not know is *what* you are."

"I don't understand," Paul said, understanding much too well. No, Elliott hadn't known what he was talking about, not even a little bit. Or had he covered things up on purpose? Too late to worry about that now.

Inspector Weidenreich's wave took in the whole shop. "Then I will make myself very plain, very clear. Where do you get your goods? We have examined them. We have done this with great care, in fact. We have never seen anything like them from any other shop. This makes us wonder. Can you blame us?"

For being nosy? Of course I can. Paul didn't suppose hearing that would make Weidenreich any happier. He said, "We're just lucky that we've been able to set up good connections in Chinatown."

"Aha!" The inspector rubbed his long chin. China was far, far away from Germany. The Chinese said they admitted the Kaiser ruled over them, too. In a certain sense, he and the Germans did. They could nuke China back to the Stone Age if they ever decided to do it. The Chinese couldn't hit back. They didn't have the bomb.

But China was too big a place to be easy to rule. It had too many people for the Germans to keep an eye on all of them, or even very many of them. Almost anything could come out of China. No one would be especially surprised if it did. By Weidenreich's face, he had no trouble believing these electronic gadgets might spring from there.

He took out a small notebook and a fountain pen. "You will provide for me your sources of supply," he said. "Immediately." If a German was going to know any five-syllable word in English, that was likely to be it.

"I'm sorry, sir, but I can't. I don't know." Paul looked as dumb as he could while still breathing. "I don't handle any of that side of things. I just sell stuff. My dad buys it."

"Where is your father?" Weidenreich asked, scribbling.

"He went out a while ago. I don't know when he'll be back," Paul said, which was true. He knew Dad wouldn't thank him for this, but he didn't see what else he could have said. And Dad hardly ever thanked him for anything.

More scribbles. The inspector said, "I shall return to inquire of him. You may be sure of it. For now, good day." He clicked his heels and marched out. Paul had never seen anyone do that before except in some ancient and very bad movies.

Dad came in a few minutes later. He was chewing on something: he'd gone out for lunch. Seeing Paul's expression, he swallowed. "What's up?" he said. "You look like a goose just walked over your grave."

"It wasn't a goose," Paul answered. "It was a German inspector named Weidenreich."

That got Dad's attention, all right. He said something pungent. Then he said something downright incandescent. Paul just nodded. He felt the same way. But swearing at the Germans—and at Elliott—wasn't going to change anything. His father needed a little while to figure that out. He finally did, and asked, "What did he want?"

Paul shrugged. "About what you'd expect. To see if our permits and papers were in order, to start with. If they weren't, he could have done anything he wanted. My *Kennkarte* passed a really good inspection. And to find out where we were getting our stuff." He waved at Curious Notion's stock in trade, hardly any of which came from this alternate.

Dad did a little more swearing. "What did you tell him?"

"That we got it from some Chinatown merchant or other—I didn't know who—and that *he* got it from China."

"Hmm." His father gnawed at the skin by the edge of one thumbnail. "That's not bad. What did he say?"

That's not bad was about as much praise as Paul's father gave. Paul basked in it for a moment. But then he had to say, "He didn't like it a whole lot. He was going to come back here and get all the details from you."

Dad exploded for a third time. This one made the other two seem tame. "What am I supposed to say to him?" he howled after the Big Bang cooled down enough to allow ordinary speech once more.

Paul shrugged again. "I don't know. I couldn't very well tell him the truth, so I gave him the best lie I could come up with. He jumped like I stuck a pin in him when I started going on about China."

"Terrific," his father said sourly. "The problem is, we only know a few people in Chinatown, and we don't do a whole lot of business with any of them. Inspector What's-his-name can find that out pretty quick, too."

That was part of the problem. It wasn't all of it. The other part was that the merchants in Chinatown might be as curious about Crosstime Traffic's goods as the Germans were. What would they say if Weidenreich started poking around there? Paul didn't know. He hoped he wouldn't have to find out.

"You'll come up with something, Dad," he said.

That could have been sarcasm. Part of it *was* sarcasm. Part, but not all. When Paul's father chose to use it, he had the gift of gab. He was liable to find some way out of this fix, right there on the spur of the moment. Paul could never do that sort of thing. He was just glad he'd survived with Weidenreich. Dad might do a lot better than surviving.

Or he might not. The gift of gab didn't come through all the time.

"We're liable to have to get out of this alternate altogether. That would be terrible," Dad said, and then, "What are you doing?"

"Finishing my lunch. I was halfway done when Weidenreich came in. He didn't spoil my appetite. I don't know why, but he didn't." He dug into the shrimp and rice again. For once, he had the last word.

"Oh," Lucy Woo's father said heavily. "*Those* people."

"They don't look so bad," Lucy said. "They just look like . . . people."

"Well, I suppose they are just people," Father said, and paused for a big forkful of rice and vegetables. The family ate with fork and knife more often than chopsticks, though Lucy could use them. Her ancestors had been in the United States since they helped build the transcontinental railroad—almost 250 years now. They were as American as anybody else. They thought so, anyhow. The Germans sometimes had trouble believing it. After Charlie Woo swallowed, he went on, "But they're people who've got things nobody else has. They've got things nobody else knows how to make. I wish I knew how they did it."

"Why? Could you do the same?" Lucy yawned. She couldn't help it. She came home from the shoe factory beat every night.

Her father scratched at the thin, scraggly mustache he wore. "I never had a fancy education," he said, and Lucy nodded. He took another bite of dinner. "I wish I did, but I didn't. I'm just a guy with a soldering iron and a lot of practice taking stuff apart and putting it back together and making it work again."

"You're good at it." Lucy spoke with family pride.

Now Charlie Woo was the one who nodded. "Yeah. I am. Everybody who comes to me knows it. And so I've seen some of the things that Curious Notions place sells."

"And?" Lucy knew she was supposed to ask. If she didn't, her snoopy brother would have beaten her to it.

Her father looked very unhappy. "I can't tell for sure, but I've got the feeling I could know everything there is to know about electric goods and it wouldn't help me a bit if I needed to fix one of those things."

"How come?" This time, Michael beat Lucy to the punch. She couldn't get too mad at him. He'd probably end up running the shop one of these days down the road.

"How come? I'll tell you how come." After another bite, Charlie Woo did: "Because I don't think even one of the big brains could understand some of what I see in the guts. Circuits are tinier and neater than anything anybody else builds. They're more powerful, too. They can do things I wouldn't have figured you could make anything electric do. They almost think for themselves." A bottle of beer sat by his plate. He took a swig from it.

"Why do they have them when nobody else does?"

"You find that out, you win the prize," her father answered. "I don't know. I can't even guess. All I know is, they make me feel stupid. I don't like feeling stupid. I don't like it at all."

Lucy paused to do some eating, too. There was a little pork mixed into the rice and vegetables, more for flavor than anything else. She smiled when her teeth came down on a chunk bigger than most. After savoring it, she asked, "Do you think they make the Kaiser's men feel stupid, too?"

Her father paused with a forkful halfway to his mouth. "That's a good question. The Germans know all kinds of things Americans don't."

"Well, sure." Michael sounded surprised anybody needed to say that. One of the ways Germany stayed on top was by keeping the rest of the world ignorant. That wasn't fair, but it worked.

After dinner, Lucy helped her mother do dishes. They both yawned while they worked. As soon as they finished, they got into pajamas and went to bed. When Lucy's mother wasn't watching Michael, she took in laundry and did housework for people who were too rich and too lazy to take care of their own houses. That left her exhausted at the end of every day. The way it looked to Lucy, anyone who wasn't tired all the time didn't work hard enough.

She did have Sunday off. That meant she got to run around trying to do all the things she wanted to do during the week. When she finally caught up—or finally decided she just couldn't catch up this week—she got to see her friends. They were all working, too, and as tired and busy as she was.

"There has to be a better way," Peggy Ma said as they rode the bus to Golden Gate Park. Busfare was only a nickel. They could wander around the park for as long as they wanted without spending anything except maybe a little on snacks. Peggy's family was no better off than Lucy's.

"A better way." Lucy sighed. "You'd think so, wouldn't you?"

Instead of wandering very far, they sat down by Stow Lake, spent another nickel on a bag of bread crumbs, and started feeding the ducks. The park birds were fat and pampered. They charged this way and that after the crumbs, quacking loudly and bumping one another out of they way. They had the crazy selfishness of a three-year-old without the brains.

Lucy kept eyeing them, not just because they were pretty and funny. "They'd taste good, wouldn't they?" she murmured. She'd had duck only a couple of times, but she liked it a lot.

So did Peggy. "I was thinking the same thing," she said. "I bet they do disappear every now and then."

Signs in the park warned, IT IS FORBIDDEN TO HARM THE ANIMALS HERE, UNDER PENALTY OF LAW. But the ducks were friendly and tame. If you were hungry enough, and thought you could get away with it . . .

Some coots squabbled with the ducks over bread crumbs. Lucy had never heard of anybody eating coot. The black birds with the red-and-white beaks looked tough and stringy. Screeching jays with dark blue crests hopped in and out, stealing from ducks and coots alike.

Off beyond the fragrant pine trees, music started playing. Lucy remembered a band shell stood over there. By the thumping drums and blatting tuba, that was a German military band performing. "Do you want to go over and watch?" Lucy asked.

Peggy shook her head. "I'd rather stay here. If I just listen to them and don't see the uniforms, I'll enjoy the music a lot more."

"Okay." Lucy was happy enough to sit on the bench. The sun shone warm on her face, but the breeze blowing in off the ocean kept it from being too annoying. She said, "You'd think we could take care of ourselves without the Germans around, too, wouldn't you?"

"You'd think—" Peggy broke off. A policeman strolled up the path. He was plump and well fed, and twirled his nightstick by the leather thong. Tipping his hat to the two girls, he walked on.

"You'd think we could speak our minds without worrying about whether some dumb flatfoot heard us," Lucy said when he'd got out of earshot.

"He might not have done anything," Peggy said. Lucy nodded. That was true. On the other hand, the cop might have run them in if he'd heard. You never could tell. Peggy knew as much, too. Otherwise, she wouldn't have shut up when he came by.

Thinking about the police only made Lucy blue. "I wish everybody would just leave us alone," she said. She wasn't sure whether *us* meant her and Peggy, all the Chinese in San Francisco, all of San Francisco, or all of the United States. All those things at once, probably.

"Maybe we ought to go home," Peggy said. Seeing that cop had taken the fun out of her day, too.

"Maybe we should." Lucy scattered the last of the bread crumbs. The ducks didn't care who ran the world. All they cared about was getting fed. Up till now, Lucy had never wondered whether ducks were smarter than people. Suddenly, though, that looked like a pretty good question.

Paul wandered through Chinatown. He didn't look as if he was going anywhere in particular. Truth to tell, he wasn't. He also wasn't much impressed. Just as this San Francisco as a whole seemed a sad, shabby imitation of the one in the home timeline, this Chinatown wasn't much, either. A lot of the shops were marked with Chinese characters as well as ordinary letters, but most of the people inside them spoke only English. In this alternate, Chinese immigration had stopped a long time ago. People in this San Francisco went through the motions of being Chinese, but plenty of them had forgotten what it meant.

WOO'S ELECTRIC REPAIR, a sign said. Below it was a dragon whose tail ended in a plug. That was cute, but it wasn't much more than cute. Would somebody who really felt Chinese have used such a sign? Paul hoped not, anyway.

He went into the little café across the street and ordered spare ribs and fried rice. The spare ribs came slathered in a sweet pinkish purple sauce. The fried rice was greasy enough to lube a car. Paul sighed. Chinese food here wasn't what it was in the home timeline, either.

While he ate, he kept an eye on Woo's Electric Repair. It was one of the places Dad had named for Inspector Weidenreich. He'd got the names out of a city directory, but the inspector wouldn't figure that out for a while. Maybe Weidenreich wouldn't figure it out at all. He was looking for plots, after all. If these people denied doing business with Curious Notions, wouldn't he think they were lying and trying to hide something?

That would be too bad for the locals. Paul supposed he ought to feel sorry for them. He had a hard time doing it, though. They weren't from his world. That made them seem a little less real to him.

No policemen burst into Woo's shop while he ate and watched. He hadn't really expected that they would. He had hoped so, though. It would have livened up his day.

When he left the café, he checked to see if he was being

followed. He couldn't be sure what Weidenreich might have in mind. Paul didn't spot anybody who looked out of place.

He wished for a cell phone to call Dad and make sure everything was okay back at the shop. They existed in this alternate, but they were supersecret, superfancy German military gadgets. You couldn't walk down the street with one plugged into your ear, the way people did in the home timeline.

Space travel and satellites here had got off to a much slower start than they had back home, too. There, World War II had given them an enormous boost. Here, they'd stayed toys for hobbyists for years and years. It was well into the twenty-first century before they'd got good enough to make the Kaiser's government sit up and take notice. The first man to fly to the moon in this alternate was still alive. There hadn't been a second man. The flight was nothing but an enormous stunt.

A few high-tech alternates worked hard at exploiting the Solar System. They were running out of resources on Earth, the same way the home timeline had been fifty years earlier. They didn't know about crosstime traffic, so they had to do the best they could with what they had.

Trouble was, it wasn't very good. The Solar System turned out to be a less inviting place than people had thought back in the middle of the twentieth century. No oceans full of dinosaurs on Venus. No canals on Mars, and no Martians, either. Savage radiation belts around Jupiter. No decent real estate anywhere.

One alternate was terraforming Mars: crashing huge icy asteroids from the outer Solar System into it to give it oceans and enough oxygen to breathe. But that would take years and years to finish. Even after it was done, it wouldn't solve Earth's problems. It would just give people the chance to have problems somewhere else.

"Can you spare a quarter, sir, or even a dime?" The tired,

hopeless, whining voice brought Paul back to the here-and-now. A woman had her hand out. At her feet, a toddler slept on a grimy wool blanket. If not for the little girl, Paul would have walked on. You couldn't help everybody. You'd go crazy if you tried. That was one of the first lessons crosstime travel taught.

But sometimes you could help some people. A toddler didn't deserve to go hungry. Paul dug in his pocket and pulled out a quarter. In the home timeline, twenty-five cents was too small an amount to worry about. So was twenty-five dollars, come to that. Here, though, a quarter was worth five or six benjamins: enough for a meal, if not for a fancy one.

The woman's face lit up. How many people had walked by pretending she wasn't there? "God bless you, sir!" she exclaimed.

Paul nodded and walked on. He hoped other beggars wouldn't notice what he'd done. But they did, of course. They always did. He had men and women follow him along the street. When he didn't give to them the way he had to the woman with the toddler, they got angry. They shook their fists and called him names. He'd been afraid that would happen. It made him sorry he'd given anything to anybody. Then he was ashamed of feeling that way.

A policeman with a large wart on his nose pointed to the beggars with his billy club. "Break it up, you bums!" he boomed. "Leave the gentleman alone!" Still grumbling, they obeyed. They knew he would have used the club if they didn't.

"Thank you," Paul called to the cop. He knew why the beggars had come after him. He even sympathized with them. But he couldn't help them all. And he wanted the policeman to see that he was grateful. No matter what he thought of the authorities here, he had to stay on good terms with them. That helped Curious Notions stay in business.

With a tip of the cap, the policeman answered, "My pleasure, sir." Just as Paul was polite to him, so he was in return. He had no idea who Paul was—Paul didn't think he did, anyhow—but he'd seen that Paul was somebody beggars followed. That made him prosperous. Cops often figured prosperous people were the ones they should be guarding.

Prosperous people did nothing to discourage that notion, here or in any other timeline.

Newsboys on street corners waved copies of the *San Francisco Chronicle*. They shouted out the headlines. The lead story was the Kaiser's visit to Paris. Germany had dominated Europe for more than a hundred fifty years in this alternate. Kaisers often visited Paris. They usually said it was for reasons of state. Had Paul had a choice between Berlin and Paris, he knew he would have visited pretty often, too.

He gave one of the newsboys a nickel. The kid handed him a *Chronicle* and three cents. Paul waved away the change, saying, "Keep it."

"Thank you, sir." The newsboy really was grateful. Three cents would buy something here: gum or candy or something like that. Back in the home timeline, Paul couldn't think of anything you could get for three dollars. This alternate hadn't known inflation, the way his world had.

It hadn't known a lot of things. He walked along reading the paper. It went on and on about what the Kaiser was doing, and the Emperor of Austria-Hungary, and the Sultan of the Ottoman Empire, and the King of England, and the King of Portugal, and even the Emperor of Brazil. It said that the latest rebellion in India had been put down. *When crowds refused to break up,* the story went on, *it became necessary to open fire with machine guns. Native casualties were heavy. Only three white men were hurt, none seriously.*

In the home timeline, that sort of attitude had pretty much

disappeared after the Second World War. It was alive and well in this alternate.

An okay place to visit, if you've got money, Paul thought. *You can be comfortable enough. It's not like Agrippan Rome, say, where they still think bad air causes disease. Even so, I wouldn't want to live here.*

Lucy knew something was wrong even before she went in the door after her day's work at the shoe factory. Just the way Mother was yelling at Michael told her that. Her mother sounded not just angry but afraid.

"What's going on?" Lucy asked when she went inside.

"Your father hasn't come home from work," Mother answered in a flat voice that tried to hide fear but couldn't.

"He's working late," Lucy said. Father sometimes did that, though he usually brought work home with him when it was past closing time.

But Mother shook her head. "No. Old man Lin said the Germans were in the shop this afternoon."

Ice ran up Lucy's back. "Why?" she exclaimed. "He hasn't done anything to get the Germans mad at him. All he does is fix radios and record players and toasters and things. What's wrong with that?"

"Nothing," her mother answered. "You know it, and I know it, too. But if the Germans don't know it . . ."

She didn't go on. She didn't need to go on. The Germans could do whatever they pleased. A lot of the time, they stayed in the background while U.S. officials did their dirty work for them. But when they wanted to, they came out in force.

What Lucy couldn't understand was why they would want to

here. She loved her father, but she knew he was an ordinary man. He ran an ordinary little business. Once a month or so, he would play cards with some friends, and sometimes he'd have a little too much to drink before he came home. If the Germans started arresting everybody in San Francisco who did things like that, they'd empty the place in a hurry.

She couldn't put all that into words. What she did say was, "They must be crazy." She spun a finger by the side of her head.

"I should hope so," Mother answered. "I just don't know if that will do Father any good, though." The fear came out in the open. People dreaded the Germans exactly because they could do whatever they wanted. They didn't need to be right. They could ruin your life just as easily if they were wrong.

No sooner had that thought crossed Lucy's mind than someone knocked on the door. It wasn't a cheerful, hello-there-here's-your-friend kind of knock. No. This was an open-right-now-or-I'll-kick-in-the-door knock. Whoever knocked like that would be wearing boots to kick better, too.

Bam! Bam! Bam! There it was again, echoing up and down the hallway. "What do we do?" Michael squeaked.

"We answer it," Mother said. "What else can we do?"

Lucy right behind her, she opened the door. Four enormous German *Feldgendarmerie* men stood in the hallway. They all wore identical green trench coats—and, sure enough, polished black jackboots. One of them had had his fist raised to knock some more. He lowered it.

"You are the Woos?" he asked in good if accented English. Then, because there were lots of Woos in Chinatown, he added, "This is the home of Charles Woo, the repairer of electrical goods?"

"That's right," Mother said. "Where is he? What have you done with him?" She didn't say, *What have you done* to *him?* Lucy admired her for that. She went on, "Why do you want to know?"

"Charles Woo has been detained for interrogation. If he is innocent, nothing will come of it." The secret policeman didn't sound as if he thought that was likely. He turned to his pals and spoke a few words of German.

Figuring out what the phrase meant didn't turn out to be hard. The *Feldgendarmerie* men went ahead and turned the place inside out. They threw things on the floor. They opened anything that might be hollow. They didn't care what they smashed. They even took pictures off the wall and looked behind them.

"What do you want?" Mother wailed as one of the Germans flung clothes out of drawers, "We haven't done anything!"

"Ha! Now tell me another one," the *Feldgendarmerie* man said. "Nobody's ever done anything, not in all the history of the world. But things keep getting done anyway. Maybe it's a miracle, eh?" He laughed some more.

"But we haven't!" Lucy exclaimed. "What do you *think* we've done?"

"Oh, yes. You don't know. Of *course* you don't." The big man's mocking tone filled Lucy with despair. He wasn't going to believe the Woos, no matter what they told him. He went on, "I suppose you'll say you haven't had anything to do with that Curious Notions outfit, too."

Lucy looked at her mother. Mother looked as surprised as she felt. "But we haven't!" they both said at the same time.

Sure enough, the man from the *Feldgendarmerie* didn't believe them. "A likely story! And isn't your husband one of their big suppliers? Of course he is." He liked that *of course.* He already knew all the answers.

"He is *not!*" Lucy shouted. She was too angry now to be scared.

Besides, she had the feeling she couldn't make things much worse than they were already. "He was just talking the other night about how he doesn't know where the place gets what it sells, because everything they have is so strange."

"How neat. A built-in alibi. Very clever. But it won't work," the secret policeman said. "And do you know why it won't work? Because the people at Curious Notions have already admitted your father's part in the scheme. So if you deny it, you must be lying, eh?"

Now the look Lucy and her mother shared was one of horror. "No, they're the liars!" Lucy said. She tried to imagine why the people at Curious Notions would tell that kind of lie. What did they have against her father? He wasn't competition. He didn't sell what they did. He couldn't even fix what they sold. It made no sense.

"Don't you worry," the German said cheerfully. "We'll get some answers out of him, even if we don't get them out of you." He spoke to his own men: "Well? What about it?"

They shrugged. "Doesn't look like anything, boss."

"You see?" Lucy's mother said. "We're innocent. We haven't done anything, and neither has my husband."

"No, that is not how it seems to me," the *Feldgendarmerie* man answered. "I will tell you how it seems to me. It seems like this. We have found no evidence—*ja,* this is true. But does this mean you are not guilty? That I find very unlikely. So it must mean you are very clever. You think you have outwitted us. For the time being, you may even be right. We shall see, though, what further questioning of *Herr* Charles Woo will bring."

"You're nuts!" Lucy burst out. "Can't you see that no evidence means we haven't done anything?"

"Everyone has done something." The *Feldgendarmerie* man spoke with great assurance. "My job is finding out what it might be."

A slow, happy smile crossed his face. "I am very good at my job, too."

After that, he clicked his heels, of all things, as if Lucy and her mother were German noblewomen. He and the goons he led stamped out of the apartment. Lucy stared at her mother. Her mother was staring back. Again, they both said the same thing at the same time: "What are we going to do?"

"Hire a lawyer?" Lucy asked, trying to answer the desperate question.

Her mother laughed. The sound was so high and shrill, it wasn't far from hysteria. "Where would we get the money? And even if we had it, why would the Germans pay any attention to what a lawyer says? It sounds like they think we're some kind of spies. How's that for ridiculous?" She laughed again, sounding even wilder than before.

"I'll tell you what's ridiculous," Lucy said grimly. "What's ridiculous is the people at Curious Notions saying they got their stuff from Father. Why would they do that? It's a lie. Father wants to know where they get it himself."

"Who knows if they even did?" her mother said. "That German might have made it up just to confuse us."

Lucy hadn't thought of that. After a few seconds, she shook her head. "No, that's too crazy, Mother. There *is* something funny about Curious Notions. Father noticed. Would it be any big surprise if the *Feldgendarmerie* noticed, too?"

"What difference does it make?" Bitterness filled her mother's voice. "They've got your father. That's the only thing that matters. If we had the money, we might pay them to let him go. But they'd just laugh at the sort of bribe we're able to give. They'd throw us in jail for insulting them."

She was bound to be right. If you had enough money, you could get away with anything. The Woos had never had enough money. There were Chinese moneylenders who might give them enough this once. Lucy knew why her mother hadn't said anything about them. Better to be in trouble with the Germans than with the moneylenders. The Germans would kill you, and without a second thought. The moneylenders would kill your children, gloat about it, and then kill you. Father wouldn't deal with them no matter what.

But did *no matter what* really stretch this far?

"They just look like ordinary people." Lucy knew she sounded bewildered. "We're ordinary people, too. Why would they want to pick on us?"

"Who cares what they look like?" her mother answered. "They've got some scheme going. We must have got in the way. If you're little, that's all it takes. People who are big think they can step on you, and they're usually right."

How could you argue with that? Everything that went on proved how true it was. "It's not fair," Lucy said.

"What is?" her mother replied, another question without an answer. Mechanically, she started picking clothes up off the floor, folding them, and putting them back in drawers. Just as mechanically, Lucy helped her. Lucy's hands knew what to do with sweaters and undershirts and unballed socks. As long as her hands were busy, the clamor in her head eased a little.

It eased, but it didn't go away. The same questions kept gnawing at her. Why had Curious Notions lied about her father? Where *did* the shop get the gadgets it sold? Why were the Germans so interested in it?

And, above those, the one that really mattered: what would the *Feldgendarmerie* do with—do to—Father?

Three

Curious Notions stayed open on Sundays. It did a lot of its business then. People who were too busy the rest of the week came in to spend their money. Paul wondered if he would have enough game sets and portable stereo players to last till the next shipment from the home timeline came in.

Not everybody who walked through the door could afford to buy. Merchandise stayed in cases or firmly fastened to walls till customers showed cash. Things got stolen every now and again even so. That annoyed Paul, but less than it would have had the store been his personal source of income. As things were, theft was Crosstime Traffic's worry, not his.

An Asian girl not far from his own age walked up and down the aisles. She paused now here, now there. Her clothes were neat but shabby. Paul didn't think she could afford to get anything, but she didn't seem to want to leave. She kept looking around at the other customers. He began to wonder if she was there to pick pockets, not to look at fancy electronics. But she didn't get near anybody else. In fact, she shied away from other people.

After a while, Paul discovered she was watching them hoping they would go away. That took some time. Finally, though, she was the only person in the place besides him. Even then, she needed a moment to get up the nerve to come to the counter.

Maybe she wanted to buy something after all. "What can I help you with today?" Paul asked in his smoothest tones.

The answer he got was not what he expected. The Asian girl glared at him as if she'd just found him on the bottom of her shoe. In a fierce whisper, she said, "What have you done to my father?"

Paul blinked. Was she nuts? Did she think he was somebody else? "Miss, I haven't done anything to your father," he said carefully. "Why do you think I have? No offense, but I don't even know who he is."

"He's Charlie Woo, that's who," she said, as if he ought to know who Charlie Woo was. His expression must have shown he didn't. That only made her angrier. She pointed a forefinger. "Don't try to pretend you don't know about him, either. You can't fool me. When the *Feldgendarmerie* arrested him, they said you people said you got your stuff from him. That's a lie, and you know it!" She was quivering with fury.

And then the name did ring a bell. He'd had his lunch across from Charlie Woo's little shop. Yes, Woo was one of the men Dad had fingered for Inspector Weidenreich. He'd been nothing but a name in the phone book to Paul. But names in the phone book didn't have angry teenage daughters. Charlie Woo, on the other hand . . .

"You *do* know something!" the girl exclaimed. "Don't try to tell me different, either. I can see it in your face."

Paul had never been a very good poker player. "I—" he began, and stopped. He didn't know where to go from there.

"Why did you do it? Why?" Charlie Woo's daughter demanded. "The Germans have him in jail, and they won't let him go. What are we going to do? I've got a little brother. How are we supposed to make ends meet without Father? What can we do?" She looked ready to burst into tears—either that or take a gun from her purse and start shooting.

And the strange thing was, he didn't see how he could blame her. Right before his eyes, she stopped being somebody from an alternate, somebody who mattered to him no more than a character in a video game, and turned into a human being. He still understood why his father had done what he did. Now, though, he also understood what that had done to Charlie Woo's family. Till this girl came in, he hadn't cared. Curious Notions' troubles with the Germans had counted for more. Things suddenly looked different.

"I'll do what I can," Paul said. "I don't know how much that will be, but we'll find out."

Now she stared at him as if she couldn't believe her ears. "You will?" She sounded astonished, too.

"I said so, didn't I?" Paul answered, and wondered how much trouble he'd just let himself in for. "Uh, I'm Paul. What's your name?"

"Lucy," she said, and then, "Why did you get my father in so much trouble if you're willing to help him now?"

That was a good question. He wished he had a good answer for it. Since he didn't, he said, "It was a mistake, that's all. I'll see if I can fix it." That seemed better than telling her, *My dad and I didn't think of your father as a human being at all. We just needed to get Inspector Weidenreich out of our hair for a while.*

"What will you do?" Lucy asked. She wasn't quite giving him a my-hero look, but she wasn't measuring him for a coffin, either.

There was another question for which he wished he had a good answer. Again, he did the best he could: "I don't think the Germans will listen to me all by myself. But I've got some pretty good connections with American policeman and officials, people the Germans will pay attention to."

He waited to see if that would surprise her. It didn't. She just nodded. "You'd have to, to stay in business, wouldn't you? If you need bribe money, we can give you . . . some." By the way she bit her lip, the Woos didn't have a lot.

"I think it'll be all right," Paul said gently. The home timeline could give him as much of this America's money, real or counterfeit, as he wanted. He couldn't tell that to Lucy. He couldn't tell her anything about the home timeline. He was just glad small-time—and sometimes not so small-time—corruption was a way of life here. When he said he had connections, she believed him.

"When will I know if you've done anything?" she asked. "When will I know you aren't stringing me along?"

She had a good notion of the way the world could work, all right. "Meet me in the Japanese garden in Golden Gate Park day after tomorrow, about three o'clock," he said.

"I'll be at my job," Lucy said bleakly. "I can't get away. I especially can't get away with Father locked up."

She looked too young to have a full-time job. In the home timeline, she would have been. Things were different here. Paul said, "What time do you get off?"

"Six o'clock," she answered.

"Can you meet me there at six-thirty, then?" he asked. She nodded. He held out his hand. She shook it. They had a bargain—what sort of bargain, Paul didn't know yet.

Lucy thought her shift at the shoe factory would never end. She often felt that way, but it was especially bad tonight. At last, the whistle blew. She got to her feet, stretched, and headed for the clock to time out. She stuck the card in the slot, got it stamped, put it back in its place on the wall, and left the building.

When she waited at the bus stop down at the corner instead of just walking home, Mildred asked her, "Where are you going?" Any time you broke routine, people noticed. They wondered why.

"I've got to meet somebody about Father," Lucy answered. That satisfied the older woman. She probably thought Lucy meant a lawyer or somebody like that, but what she thought wasn't Lucy's worry.

The nickel that went into the fare box was. She hated to spend money. Her family never had enough of it. She didn't know anybody who did, either. But she couldn't walk to the park, not if she wanted to get there by half past six.

The Japanese garden there was one of her favorite spots. Gardeners kept it beautifully landscaped. When it wasn't too crowded with tourists, it was one of the most peaceful places she knew. The big bronze Buddha, green with age, stared out tranquilly over the flowers and ferns and shrubs. And there was the bridge across the stream. It was no ordinary bridge, but a great arc of a circle. You had to climb it to get to the top.

Lucy climbed it for a reason, not just for the fun of it. She could see farther from there than from any other spot in the garden, and Paul Gomes hadn't told her exactly where he wanted to meet. The Japanese garden didn't seem very big . . . till you were in it.

She met him, all right—he was climbing up the other side. She reached the top before he did. "Hello, there," she said.

"Hello, yourself," he answered, scrambling up to stand beside her on the brown-painted planking. "I came up here to look for you."

"I did the same thing," Lucy said. In a strange way, that pleased her. But such pleasures were just that—small. She stabbed out a forefinger. "What do you know about Father?"

"I don't *know* anything," Paul said. Lucy wanted to hit him, or to push him over the rail into the stream. That would surprise the colorful carp swimming down below. He went on, "I do know I've got an American police captain and an assistant district attorney asking the Germans questions about him."

"Talk is cheap," Lucy said. "We want him back. We miss him. We need him." Had Paul really done anything at all? Or was he just talking to make her feel better? She couldn't tell, and not knowing was a torture in itself.

He said, "I did find out your father's okay. They're holding him, yeah, but they haven't hurt him or anything."

"That's good," Lucy said. Again, she wondered if she could believe him. She wanted to. She wanted to very badly. That only made her more suspicious. Angrily, she demanded, "How do you know?"

"Captain Horvath found out for me," Paul answered. Now Lucy took him seriously. Everybody in Chinatown knew, or knew of, Fatty Horvath. Paul Gomes went on, "It's about even money whether the Germans come after my father and me next."

"You?" Lucy stared. Up there on top of that funny bridge, the idea seemed even more ridiculous than it would have somewhere else. "Why would they want to come after you? With the stuff Curious Notions has, you must be the goose that laid the golden eggs for them."

"Yeah, right," Paul said tightly. Lucy hadn't heard that slang phrase before, but she had no trouble figuring out what it meant. Her cheeks got hot. Paul added, "You remember what happened to the goose that laid the golden eggs, don't you?"

Till Paul reminded her, Lucy *hadn't* remembered. Now she did. They'd killed the goose, trying to figure out where the eggs came from. She said, "Is that why you people named my father? To get the *Feldgendarmerie* off your own necks?"

Paul nodded. He looked out across the garden, not at her. "That's right," he said, and then, after a small but noticeable pause, "I'm sorry."

By the way he said those last two words, they were an enormous gift to Lucy—a gift she probably didn't deserve. But he *had* said them. And, by the look on his face, he knew he couldn't take them back. Lucy said, "Sorry doesn't do anything. You talked to this lawyer fellow, and you talked to Fatty Horvath. But what happens if they can't get Father loose?"

"What do you want us to do then?" Paul asked. "Bust him out of jail?"

He plainly meant it for a joke. But Lucy found herself nodding. "Yes. That seems fair, doesn't it? He's in there on account of you." She studied him carefully. She didn't think she'd ever looked at anyone like that before. And she found herself nodding again. "I think maybe you can, too. With all those strange things you sell in that shop, who knows what else you've got in there?"

Now Paul's eyes snapped back to her. What was on his face was shock—shock and maybe fear to go with it. "You don't know what you're talking about," he said slowly.

The way he said it convinced Lucy he was lying. "Oh, don't I? What would happen if the Germans really tore that place apart? What would they find? How much trouble would you people be in?"

Paul turned white. Lucy had heard people talk about that, but she'd never seen it herself till now. She knew she'd made a hit. She just didn't know where. He hung on to the rail for a moment to steady himself. "We wouldn't be," he answered. "We'd jump in a hole and pull it in after us."

"What's that supposed to mean?" Lucy asked. "There's nowhere in the world the Germans can't come after you. Well, maybe the middle of China, but you wouldn't fit in there very well."

He only shrugged. He didn't say anything more. By his sour, unhappy smile, he'd already said too much. Somehow, though, Lucy didn't think he'd been bragging or just plain lying. If he said he had a way to get free of the Germans, he probably did. But she couldn't imagine what it was.

"Who are you, Paul Gomes?" But that wasn't the right question. Lucy realized as much as soon as she asked it. What she really wanted to know was, *What are you?* On the other hand, she didn't get an answer even to the question she asked.

"You know what you are, Paul?" his father said. "You're an idiot."

Paul gave back a sour smile. "I love you, too, Dad."

"An idiot," his father repeated, relishing the word. "You think this local girl is cute, so you're ready to move heaven and earth to get her out of a scrape. If that doesn't make you an idiot, kindly tell me what would."

Do I think Lucy Woo is cute? Paul wondered. He shrugged. He probably did. She wasn't gorgeous or anything, but she wasn't bad. *Is that why I'm trying to help her, though?* That was a different question. He shook his head. Not a chance. He said, "You're the one who got her into this scrape, remember. You can't just treat the locals like a bunch of movie characters. If something bad happens to them, it happens. They're people, too, same as we are."

"Very pretty," his father said. "You'd win points for your high-school debating team. But I need to remind you of something. This alternate is also full of people who want to nail our hides to the wall. It's full of people who want to squeeze our secrets out of us. Keeping them from doing that is more important than anything else we do here. If we don't, if we mess up, we could ruin Crosstime Traffic and put the home timeline in a lot of danger. Next to keeping our secrets, what happens to the locals *doesn't* matter, not for beans. Have you got that?"

If Paul didn't have it, that wasn't because they'd ignored it in training. They'd hammered away at it, in fact. The home timeline came first. Nothing else counted next to keeping the home timeline safe and secret. In the training sessions, that seemed to make a lot of sense. Here in this alternate, this might-have-been San Francisco, the differences between *us* and *them* felt a lot smaller.

"It's not as simple as you make it sound, Dad," Paul said.

His father rolled his eyes. "The devil it's not," he said. "You're behind the counter. That Weidenreich comes in and starts grilling you. If you don't give him some kind of answer, what's he going to do? Haul you off to jail and start ripping answers out of you, that's what. So, Mr. Not-As-Simple, what do you tell him?" He folded his arms across his chest and waited.

Paul opened his mouth. Then he closed it again. He didn't know what to say. He knew what the *Feldgendarmerie* often did to people who didn't care to talk. The Germans in this alternate had the same sort of attitude as Crosstime Traffic wanted its people to show. They came first, and everybody else could look out for himself.

"Well?" Dad wasn't shy about rubbing it in. Dad wasn't shy about anything. That made him good at running this operation. But there were too many times when it made him a real pain to be around.

"Well, all right, we had to tell the inspector something. I can see that," Paul said at last. "But that doesn't mean we shouldn't try to fix the damage. If we do it so we don't get noticed, where's the harm?"

His father looked at him—looked through him, really. "Okay," he said. "If we don't tip our hand, it's not so bad. But that's not the way you were acting. You sounded more like you wanted to charge right out there, slay the dragon, and rescue the fair maiden. And that's not a good idea—*not*, you hear me?"

"I hear you, Dad. I always hear you," Paul said wearily.

"Yeah, you hear me. But do you listen?"

Instead of answering, Paul turned away. Neither one of them was going to change the other's mind. Paul already knew the only way to reach his father was to hit him over the head with a two-by-four. Dad still hadn't quite figured out that Paul was just as stubborn. It didn't show so much in Paul, because he was quieter about it. But if he saw something he thought needed doing, he'd do it, and he wouldn't let anything or anybody—his father included—get in his way.

Or maybe Dad had figured out more than Paul thought. He said, "Look, son, what you do on your own is fine, as long as nobody can trace it back to Crosstime Traffic. This is one of those alternates we want to keep quarantined. The Germans here hold down everybody else's technology. We have to hold *theirs* down. We don't want them thinking about transposition chambers."

He wasn't wrong about that. An Imperial Germany that could rampage across the alternates was the last thing Paul wanted to see. But Imperial Germany already oppressed the Americans in this world. For people from the home timeline to oppress them, too, added insult to injury.

When Paul said as much, his father only shrugged. "You can't make an omelet without breaking eggs," he said. He seemed to think answering one cliché with another meant winning the argument. Paul gave it up. He would do what he would do. If Dad turned out not to like it, he was welcome to try to do something better.

Lucy waited for several days to see if her father would come home. When he didn't, she decided to visit Curious Notions again. She was tired after a long day at the shoe factory. She didn't even know if the shop would be open when she got there. She only knew she had to try.

Curious Notions hadn't closed. But when Lucy looked in the front window, she saw Paul Gomes wasn't there. That was his father writing something behind the counter. The big, black, bushy mustache he wore did nothing to cut the resemblance.

A bell rang when Lucy opened the door. The man who looked like Paul put down his pen and nodded to her. "Hello. How can I help you today?" He sounded pleasant enough. "We have some things here you won't find anywhere else, at prices most people can afford."

Maybe the people he usually dealt with could afford those prices. Lucy couldn't come close. She said, "I'm Lucy Woo. Do you have my father? What kind of price do I have to pay to get him back?"

The man's face changed. Not even that big mustache could hide his frown. "I think maybe you'd better come back another time," he said, and all of a sudden he didn't sound nearly so pleasant.

"Why? So you can have the *Feldgendarmerie* waiting for me?" Lucy pronounced the hard *g* and the guttural *r*'s without a bobble. *Feldgendarmerie* was a German word most Americans used too often to get it wrong.

"No." The man shook his head. "So you can talk to my son. He's the one who's taking care of that."

Taking care of it how? Lucy wondered. *Really trying to get Father out? Or just pretending till I give up and go away?* She said, "I've already talked with Paul. He said he'd help. He hasn't yet."

Paul's father shook his head. "That isn't true. He's done stuff, all right. He's done more than I would have, as a matter of fact. It just hasn't paid off yet. Do you see the difference?"

Lucy would have expected to think he was lying. Oddly, though, she found herself believing him. She wondered why. Probably because he looked so disgusted when he talked about what Paul had done. She would have bet anything she owned that he wouldn't have done it himself.

She said, "When do you think it will pay off?"

"*I* don't know." Paul's father sounded disgusted, too. No, he wouldn't have lifted a finger to help Charlie Woo. When he saw his answer didn't satisfy Lucy, he let out a long, put-upon sigh. "If I had to make a guess, I'd say things would start happening in maybe another week or so. But I'm only guessing. I'm not promising."

"Another week?" Lucy said in dismay.

"It's not such a long time," Paul's father said.

He wasn't sixteen. He didn't have a father locked up in a German jail. But, again, Lucy didn't think he was trying to pull the wool over her eyes with his guess. He meant it, even if he didn't have the faintest idea how hard it was on her. Reluctantly, she nodded. "A week," she said. "But if he's not out by then . . ."

Paul's father leaned across the counter toward her. His face didn't change. His voice didn't change, either, unless it got a little softer. But when he said, "You don't want to threaten me, Miss Woo. You really don't want to threaten me. Have you got that?" she nodded before she even thought about it. She'd always known the Germans could do dreadful things. What American didn't know that? Could Paul Gomes' father be just as dreadful, or maybe worse? Right then, she didn't doubt it. He smiled, seeing that he'd made her afraid. "Anything else?"

"No, I don't think so." Lucy gathered herself. She couldn't just slink out of the shop, no matter how much her feet wanted to do exactly that. She made herself look Paul's father straight in the face. "I wasn't kidding about what I said. If my father doesn't come home, there *will* be trouble."

61

She'd surprised him. She could tell he hadn't thought she'd have the nerve to answer back. He said, "Go on. Get out. It's closing time here."

Now she did leave. She left with her back straight, and she didn't look behind her. She thought about slamming the door as she went out, but she didn't do that, either. She wouldn't let Paul's father see he'd upset her. He had to know he had, but she refused to let him see it. That felt very important to her just then.

An American cop in a baggy uniform of cheap blue cloth nodded to her. He looked tired—maybe a little hungover, too. His shoes needed shining. He had bad teeth. He was just a man doing a job, trying to get along as best he could. Lucy didn't have anything against that. She was trying to do the same thing herself.

She walked on. A couple of blocks closer to her home, she saw a German officer. His field-gray uniform fit perfectly. His jackboots were polished black mirrors. He strode along as if he owned the sidewalk—and didn't he? People scrambled to get out of his way. If they hadn't, he made you think, he would have walked right through them. He was proud to be what he was. How many Americans were proud these days? What did Americans have to be proud of? Not bloody much.

From behind the German, someone yelled, "Go home, you stinking—!" He finished with great sincerity and even greater fury.

The officer whirled. His Luger was in his hand even before the motion stopped. But dozens of people were walking along back there. Who'd cursed him? How was he supposed to tell?

And now, with his back turned in a different direction, somebody else told him where to go and how to get there. He spun again—he was quick as a cat. That quickness did him no good at all. As soon as he faced a new direction, another American in back of him called him a vile name.

Most people would have figured that out faster than he did. He kept jerking this way and that, like a puppet with four or five people fighting over the strings. He finally got the idea. He threw his hands in the air and stuck the pistol back in its holster. "Have your sport, American pigdogs!" he shouted in accented English. "You think you are funny, *ja?* See how funny you are when it comes time to pay taxes! Until then, bark as you please!" He tramped on.

It was a good comeback. Even Lucy, who despised him, knew as much. It would have been better if he'd thought of it sooner, but how much could you expect from an officer? The Germans had got where they were at least as much by being stubborn as by being quick.

I'll be stubborn, too, Lucy thought. *If it works for them, it can work for me.* She sighed. The Germans also had money and soldiers and scientists going for them. What did she have? Stubbornness, and that was about it.

When she got home, her brother set up a chant: "Lucy's back! Lucy's back! Lucy's back!"

Her mother came running out of the kitchen to give her a hug. "Thank heavens!" she exclaimed. "I was afraid the *Feldgendarmerie* had taken you away, too."

Lucy shook her head. "It didn't have anything to do with the *Feldgendarmerie.* I stopped at Curious Notions to see if they were doing what Paul Gomes said they would." She made an unhappy face. "I still don't know if they are or not. His father told me to wait another week, and I guess I will. But I'm not going to wait any more than that, and you'd better believe it."

"You'd better be careful, so you don't end up in trouble," Mother said. "What can you do, anyway? You're only a girl."

"I don't know what I can do," Lucy said. "Get *them* in trouble, maybe, or more trouble than they're already in, because I think they're in some. But I think they are trying to do something for

63

Father, too, and nobody else is, and they're doing it on account of me even if I am just a girl." She took a deep breath. She hadn't quite expected all of that to come out at once, but there it was.

Her mother looked startled, too. She didn't say anything, not right away. She just squeezed Lucy again, harder than ever. She didn't seem to want to let her go. When she did, Lucy was amazed to see tears gleaming in her eyes. "At your age, you think you can do anything," she said. "And sometimes you're right—and sometimes you're not. But you won't believe you're not, not yet you won't."

That Lucy didn't believe it went a long way toward proving her mother right. She didn't think of it that way, though. But she didn't feel like arguing with Mother, either. All she said was, "I'm home, and I'm fine. What needs doing now?"

She helped her mother with dinner. It wasn't very exciting: noodles and cottage cheese. But enough noodles made hunger go away, and there were enough. Then she did the dishes. After that, she yawned and listened to music on the radio while she darned socks. Pretty soon, she'd go to bed.

At the top of the hour, the radio played five minutes of news. Lucy would have got up to change the station to find more music, but she was too tired. She wondered what her brother did to socks. Did Michael have little hole-eating animals inside his shoes? She wouldn't have been surprised.

"Today, the Imperial German government announced a new campaign against terror and subversion," the newsman said. "Suspicious persons will be questioned and punished. Disloyalty will not be tolerated. Examples will be made of those foolish enough to resist the rightful authority of the German government."

Lucy's mother was sewing a patch onto one knee of Michael's jeans. She looked up at that. Her eyes met Lucy's. They shared a silent moment of worry. What would happen to Father if the Germans were talking tough like that?

"There are reports of new scientific advances in Berlin," the announcer went on. "Details are not available. The Kaiser's officials know how important it is to keep scientific progress secret."

That kind of story just made Lucy yawn. She heard one like it about every other week. The Germans always wanted to prove they were smarter than anybody else. Lucy thought that made them dumber than anybody else, but nobody cared about her opinion.

The radio played a commercial for a local bakery. Lucy's mind went back to the first piece the newsman had read. Slowly, she nodded to herself. If she had to, if Paul Gomes and his father didn't do what they'd said they would, she had a chance to make them pay. *Would I use it?* she wondered, but she didn't wonder long.

A truck pulled up in the alley behind Curious Notions. Two big, burly, suntanned men got out of the cab. They both wore overalls. One had on a shapeless, low-crowned cloth cap, the other a straw hat with a wide brim. Neither had taken a bath any time lately. But the odor of garlic wafting out of the crates in the back of the truck did a good job of covering that up.

Paul Gomes opened the back door to the shop. "Let's bring it in," he said, and pointed to the waiting storage room. The farmers up from Gilroy had dollies with them. That made moving their fragrant cargo easier. Paul counted off the loads. If they'd brought a third dolly for him, he would have pitched in. He'd done it before.

Panting at the end, the fellow in the cloth cap said, "That's all of it, kid."

That *kid* grated on Paul. He didn't let it show, though. "Here you are," he said, and handed the man a twenty-dollar bill and a five.

"Thank you kindly," the farmer said. "That's a . . . real good price." It was at least five dollars more than he could have got at the city markets. Curious Notions didn't worry about money so much, and aimed to keep the people they dealt with happy.

"My pleasure, Mr. Mouradian," Paul said. "You've got good garlic. We're glad to get it from you."

"I expect you must sell to just about every Italian and Greek restaurant in the whole Bay Area, the way you buy," Mouradian said. Paul only smiled. The garlic here traveled a lot farther than the local could imagine. The farmer went on, "Well, you know your own business best, and I'm no snoop. I do want to tell you, though—that movie player your dad sold me works great."

They had CDs and DVDs here—not quite the same as the ones in the home timeline, but pretty close. They weren't on the civilian market, though. Anything that had anything to do with lasers was an Imperial German military secret. Even VCRs that played tapes were fairly new here. In the home timeline, VCRs were as obsolete as typewriters. But, before they'd gone obsolete, they'd grown a lot more bells and whistles than the local machines had. Local video-cassettes weren't the same size as the ones in the home timeline. Except for that, nobody'd had to change a thing to start making the players again.

"I'm glad you like it," Paul said. "We want satisfied customers."

"Well, you've sure got one." Mouradian turned to his helper. "Come on, Dave. Let's head on back home."

"Okay," Dave said—the first word out of his mouth since he'd got there. They climbed into the truck. The windows rattled in their frames when they slammed the doors. Mouradian started the motor and put the truck in gear. It rolled away. The harsh diesel exhaust fumes made Paul cough. They didn't have hydrogen-burners and electrics in this alternate the way they did back home.

Dad was out front dealing with customers. That meant Paul got to lug the garlic down to the subbasement by himself. He could have done without the honor. By the time he got the last of it down there, he hoped he would never see another set of stairs as long as he lived. It all but surrounded the place where the transposition chamber would materialize. The operator would have to make several trips to get it all back to the home timeline. The biggest complication in buying produce here was making sure they didn't buy too much to fit in the basement.

Wearily, Paul went up and pushed the filing cabinet over the trapdoor again. Then he trudged all the way upstairs—not just to the back room, but up to the apartment over the shop where he and his father lived. He jumped in the shower. Till he did that, he wasn't fit to be around anybody. He made the water as hot as he could stand. It felt good on his back and shoulders and legs. He knew he'd still be sore in the morning. He didn't do that kind of hauling often enough to get hardened to it.

He laughed as he dried off his hair. His dad grumbled about aches and pains a lot more than he did. Paul didn't think it was because Dad enjoyed complaining, either. *He's past forty,* he thought. *No wonder he's wearing out.*

He'd never come out and said that to his father. They already argued about enough other things. Calling his old man an old man wouldn't help.

When he went downstairs and out into the shop, Dad was selling a clock radio to a fat woman with a mink stole draped over her shoulders. Paul's stomach lurched. In the home timeline, wearing furs wasn't illegal, but it was disgusting—sickening, even.

There, if not in more important things, he and his father agreed.

But no matter how sick Dad felt inside, he didn't show it at all. Part of growing up was learning to put up with stuff you wouldn't think you could stand. Paul, who'd never heard his dentist say *root canal,* didn't understand that as well as someone twice his age might have. But, at eighteen, he was starting to get the idea.

"You'll like that one, Mrs. Pastrano," Dad was saying. "It's got terrific sound, and it'll pull in stations from a long way away."

"Well, I sure liked the record player I bought from you," Mrs. Pastrano said. In the home timeline, records were even more outdated than videocassettes. If a few fanatics hadn't kept playing them and even making them, Crosstime Traffic would have had a lot harder time turning out players for alternates where people still used them. The local woman paused and sniffed. "I smell garlic."

I'll bet you do, Paul thought. His father only shrugged and said, "I've got a bit of a cold. I can't smell a thing."

"It's there," Mrs. Pastrano declared, and she wasn't wrong. She wrapped the stole around herself more tightly. The flying end almost hit Dad. Paul thought he would have lost his lunch if it had got him. Dad never turned a hair. Mrs. Pastrano said, "So how much do you want for this?"

The price tag was attached to the clock radio. The red numbers had to be five centimeters high. Again, Dad acted as if everything were ordinary. He said, "It's $199.95."

Mrs. Pastrano squawked, but she paid. If she could afford a mink stole, she could afford a fancy radio that cost eight truckloads' worth of garlic, too.

Four

Everybody talked about the midnight knock on the door. It was such a cliché—and held so much truth—the Imperial German censors had given up trying to stop that talk. It showed up in books, in movies, in radio plays, and even—for those who had the money—on TV.

The knock that woke Lucy Woo and her family didn't come at midnight. It came at ten after three, as she saw when she stared at the alarm clock on the nightstand. That was even worse. It meant she had a good fighting chance of losing the rest of the night's sleep. Of course, when people came knocking at midnight—or at ten after three—they weren't likely to care whether you lost sleep or not.

Yawning, more than a little punchy, she staggered out of bed. The pounding at the door went on and on. It would wake the neighbors, too. They wouldn't be happy about that. Lucy yawned again. She had bigger worries than the neighbors right now.

Her mother turned on a lamp in the living room. They both blinked at the sudden explosion of light. Then Mother did something Lucy admired forever. She went to the door and asked, "Who is it?"

That question had only one possible answer. But that Mother had had the nerve to ask it . . . ! The pounding stopped. A gruff male voice said, "The *Feldgendarmerie* of Imperial Germany. Open at once, in the name of the Kaiser!"

They would kick the door down, or maybe shoot through it, if Mother gave them any more trouble. She had to know that as well as Lucy did. She opened the door. But she couldn't help asking, "What's so important that it won't wait till morning?"

This time, she got an answer she didn't expect. The *Feldgendarmerie* men, all of them over six feet tall, shoved a much shorter man into the living room. "Father!" Lucy squealed.

"Hello, sweetheart," Charlie Woo said. He hugged Mother first, then Lucy, then her brother, who came running up in his pajamas. "I'm home."

"You would do well not to make the Kaiser's government suspect you," the big *Feldgendarmerie* man said. "Next time, you may not be so lucky."

"But I didn't *do* anything," Lucy's father said.

"If you had not done anything, we would not have arrested you." The German sounded as sure as if he'd said the sun would come up in the morning. "Just because we cannot prove it does not prove a thing." He also sounded sure he made sense. Lucy almost called him on it. But the weak didn't challenge the strong. America had been under the Kaiser's thumb for a long time. That was one lesson everybody in the country had learned, and learned well.

Without another word, the *Feldgendarmerie* men turned and strode off. Their jackboots thudded on the bare boards of the hallway. They slammed the door to the stairs behind them. Even so, Lucy could hear them clumping all the way down to the ground floor.

"Daddy! Daddy! Daddy!" Michael squealed. Her mother closed the door so his noise wouldn't bother the neighbors quite so much. Lucy didn't care if it bothered them. She joined right in. The Kaiser's secret police didn't let somebody go every day.

Paul kept his promise, she thought in surprise. She couldn't come up with any other reason the *Feldgendarmerie* would have released Father. *I owe him an apology. I ought to do something for him to keep things balanced, but I have no idea what I could do.*

Her mother's thoughts were running on different lines. "Let me get you something to eat," she said to Father. "What did they do to you while they had you?"

"Not as much as I was afraid they would." Father looked tired and he needed a shave, but Lucy didn't see any bruises or cuts on him. He stood there in the middle of the front room as if he couldn't believe he was free. As Lucy's mother disappeared into the kitchen, he went on, "They spent a lot of time yelling at me and asking questions, but that was all. They didn't try any strongarm stuff." He sounded as if he couldn't believe it, either. The *Feldgendarmerie* wasn't known for being kind and gentle.

"Here." Mother came out with a bowl of cold noodles and a steaming cup of tea she'd made in what seemed like nothing flat.

"Oh, my," Father said. By the way he dug into the noodles, the Germans hadn't fed him much while they held him. He ate standing up, as if he didn't want to waste time going over to the couch or a chair. When he finished, he made a small ceremony of handing the bowl back to Mother. "Thank you, dear. That was *wonderful.*" He sipped the tea and smiled. Just making the corners of his mouth go up took effort. Lucy could see that. But Father managed.

After Mother took the bowl into the kitchen, she came back and herded Michael into bed again. She didn't try to make Lucy go. That was a good thing, because Lucy didn't intend to. She knew she'd be even more tired than usual when she got home from work tonight, but so what? If this wasn't a special time, what was?

Besides, there were questions she wanted to ask Father. The first one was, "What *do* you know about Curious Notions?"

"Only what I told you before," he answered. "That's what I told the Germans, too. If I knew more, I would've sung like the Mormon

Tabernacle Choir. You'd better believe I would, sweetie. I don't owe those people at Curious Notions a thing. If they're in trouble with the Kaiser's men, it's their lookout."

"Um," Lucy said, and then, "Um," again, and finally, "I think maybe you do, Father."

"What do you mean?"

Lucy told him about her visits to the strange store and about her talks with the Gomeses, especially Paul. She finished, "He said he'd talk to officials who'd squeeze the Germans. The *Feldgendarmerie* doesn't turn people loose very often, so I guess maybe he did."

Charlie Woo scratched his head. He yawned. Lucy wondered how very tired he was. "I guess maybe he did, too," he said slowly. "That means he *knows* officials who can squeeze the Germans. He knows them well enough to get favors out of them. It's just an ordinary-looking little shop, though. How do the people who run it get that kind of pull?" By the way he sounded, he wished he had that kind of pull himself.

"The shop looks ordinary, but they don't sell ordinary things there," Lucy said. "You told me that, and I've seen it for myself, too."

"No, they don't," her father agreed. "They're . . . curious, the things those people sell—and the people, too, it sounds like." He yawned again, so wide that Lucy could see his tonsils. Then he finished his tea at a gulp. "I'm going to bed." He shook his head. "No. I'm going to take a bath, and then I'll go to bed."

That was just what he did, too. Lucy also went back to bed. She didn't go back to sleep, though. She hadn't thought she'd be able to. Yes, she'd be a zombie by the time she got home from work. "So what?" she said after tossing and turning for an hour. She got up again and got dressed. "So what? Father's home. Who cares about anything else?"

———

Paul's father said, "Well, I hope you're happy. They sprung that fellow from Chinatown." He didn't sound any too happy about it.

"Did they? That's great." Paul was plenty pleased for both of them. He had good reason to be pleased, too: "Nice to know people will come through for you once in a while."

"Maybe." Dad still seemed gloomy. "Trouble is, if you do pull strings like that, you get noticed. The locals will wonder why you did it. They'll wonder about this Charlie Woo—and they'll wonder about us. We don't want them wondering about us."

The shop had no customers in it, so they could talk freely. Paul hesitated when a man put his hand on the doorknob. But then the man got a look at the prices in the display window. He jerked his hand away as if the brass knob were red-hot.

Paul had seen that reaction before. He smiled as the almost-customer hurried off down the street. "If we don't want to draw *any* notice, we shouldn't sell most of the stuff we carry," he said. "We should stick to things just like the ones this alternate makes for itself."

They'd had this argument before. His father made the usual countermove: "But if we do that, we won't make so much money here. If we don't make money, how are we going to buy the produce? That's what we're really here for, that and making sure the locals don't start trying to go crosstime."

"How can we stop them if they do start making those experiments?" Paul asked.

"I don't know if we can," his father said, sending a sour look his way. "What we want to do, I guess, is make sure the idea never occurs to them in the first place."

"How?" Paul asked again.

"I already told you—one thing we need to do is keep them from noticing us," Dad said.

"Wait a minute. There's a hole in that," Paul said. "If we don't want them to notice us, we don't sell stuff that's any different from what they already make here. If they really get serious about finding out where what we've got comes from, isn't that a problem?"

"It hasn't been so far," his father said. "Curious Notions has been doing business here for years, and we haven't had much trouble." He made money-counting motions with his hands. Paul knew what that meant. If a local had got curious about the shop, Crosstime Traffic people had paid him enough to make him lose his curiosity. Why not? It wasn't as if it were real money from the home timeline.

That might have worked well in the past. No—that *had* worked well in the past. But could you count on it to keep working forever? Paul had his doubts. He said, "I wouldn't want to try bribing that Inspector Weidenreich. He looks like he's after any old excuse to bust us."

"There are ways around people like that," Dad said. He didn't say what those ways were, though. Maybe they were secret. Maybe he thought Paul already knew them. And maybe he was making it all up and didn't know them himself.

Paul wondered if asking that was worthwhile. Regretfully, he decided it wasn't. Either Dad would ignore him or he'd start a fight. And if he started a fight, it would be one Paul couldn't hope to win. He wouldn't convince his father. Making Dad change his mind was like wearing away Mount Everest with a feather. You could try, yeah, but you wouldn't get anywhere. Dad was that stubborn. (Paul's own stubbornness didn't even cross his mind.)

He wouldn't be able to persuade Crosstime Traffic that Dad was doing anything wrong, either. He already knew that. Dad wasn't going against Crosstime Traffic policies or guidelines. He was just following them in what Paul didn't think was the best possible way.

Nobody in the home timeline would listen to a kid complaining about his old man.

But Paul couldn't let it go without saying something. All he could think of was, "I sure hope you're right."

"I'm not worried," his father said. That didn't reassure Paul as much as Dad might have liked. His father hardly ever worried. He was always sure he was right. And he *was* right a lot of the time. Even Paul had to admit that. But he wasn't right as often as he thought he was.

A customer did come in. Paul and his father stopped sniping at each other. They sold the local a fancy tape deck. People in this alternate thought it was fancy, anyway. It was a long way behind the state of the art in the home timeline. Everything there was digital, and had been for most of a hundred years.

Inspector Weidenreich didn't show up at Curious Notions that day. Dad looked smug. Paul ignored him. Twenty minutes before they closed, he walked around the corner to buy a couple of hot dogs at Louie's, where he went a lot of the time. Everybody here called them franks or wieners, but they were hot dogs, all right. When he came back to the store, a skinny marmalade cat meowed at him. He tossed it a chunk of hot dog. It sniffed suspiciously at the meat, then gobbled it up.

"They're as bad as beggars on two legs," his father said when he went inside. "Now it'll expect a handout every time."

"Well, so what?" Paul answered. "Maybe I'll adopt it for as long as I'm here."

"Just so you don't try to bring it back to the home timeline," Dad said. "For all I know, it may be a boy. It'd make Crosstime Traffic have kittens either way, though." He gestured. "Take those upstairs, will you? We're supposed to look like we're a business. We can't do that if you're standing there feeding your face."

75

From what Paul had seen, at least half the shopkeepers in this alternate's San Francisco ate while they were open. If they didn't, they wouldn't be able to eat at all. Again, though, life was too short to argue. He started toward the stairway.

The bell over the front door rang before he'd taken more than three steps. He looked back over his shoulder, then stopped. There stood Lucy Woo, a large, closed basket in her hand. "Hello," Paul said.

She nodded shyly. "Hello. I wanted to thank you—I wanted to thank both of you—for helping to get my father away from the *Feldgendarmerie.*" She nodded again, this time to Paul's father. She plainly worked hard at being polite.

Dad nodded back, even though he hadn't had thing one to do with getting Lucy's father out of jail. "It was nothing," he said. Considering what he'd done—considering that he'd got her father into trouble in the first place—that was true enough for him.

"We were glad to do it," Paul said. He had been, anyway.

She hefted the basket. "I brought you something. I hope you enjoy it."

"You didn't have to do that!" Paul exclaimed. She'd told him where she worked. He had a pretty good idea of how much she'd make. If it was ten dollars a week, he would have been amazed. She couldn't afford much in the way of presents.

With dignity, she said, "I think I did. You did something special for my family and me. This is the least we can do to show we're grateful."

Paul realized he couldn't turn down the present, whatever it was. That would be a deadly insult. His father had figured out the same thing a couple of steps ahead of him. "Thank you very much, Miss Woo," Dad said. "This is really kind of you." He did everything but go over and kiss her hand. Dad could be charming when he wanted to, sure enough—charming to everybody but Paul.

Lucy came into the shop and set the basket on the counter. "Open it, please," she said.

Dad waved to Paul. He might have been saying, *This is your fault—you take care of it.* Had they been by themselves, Paul would have had some things to say about that. He couldn't say them with Lucy there. He flipped back the basket's hinged lid, hoping she hadn't had to buy the container with the present.

The biggest lobster he'd ever seen stared back at him. It had to weigh at least five pounds—maybe closer to ten. Rubber bands held its claws closed. It was still wiggling a little; it had come out of the sea very recently. "I got it at Fisherman's Wharf," Lucy said. "Throw it in a big pot of water and it will be wonderful."

How many benjamins would a lobster this size cost in the home timeline? Lots—Paul was sure of that. They thought in terms of dollars here. It had to cost two or three, maybe even five. Five dollars in the home timeline was a handful of little aluminum coins, worth next to nothing. Five dollars here . . . Five dollars here was a good part of a week's pay for Lucy.

Quietly, Paul said, "This is too much. You didn't need to."

"For helping my father?" Lucy shook her head. "It's not enough. I wish I could do more."

"Thank you very much," Dad said. "My son is right, I think—this wasn't anything you needed to do. But it was very kind of you anyhow. If you like, we will put it in the icebox today and cook it tomorrow. That way, you and your family can come over and share it with us."

Paul wished he'd come up with that. Yes, his father could be smooth when he wanted to, no doubt about it. He just didn't waste any smoothness on Paul.

But Lucy Woo drew herself up straight with pride. She still wasn't very tall, but she carried herself like a duchess. "No, thank you," she replied. "The lobster is for you. Taking any of it away wouldn't be right."

Arguing with her would have been a waste of breath. Even Paul could see that. She'd done what she thought she was supposed to do, and she wouldn't let anything or anybody change her mind. Paul's father managed to be gracious about it: "All right, then. Thanks again. But we'll think of you when we eat it."

"Think of my father, too, please." With a stiff little nod, Lucy turned and left Curious Notions. Neither Paul nor his father tried to take the last word from her.

The four and a half dollars Lucy had spent on the lobster for Paul Gomes and his father left a hole in the family budget. She didn't care, and neither did her mother or her father. Some debts were too important to stay unpaid. And, with Father back, the Woos would make up the money sooner or later.

Work went on. Work always went on. She couldn't get away from it. Hardly anyone in this whole downtrodden country could. Plenty of people put in more than her sixty hours a week, and made less money for their time. As these things went, her family had been pretty lucky till Father fell foul of the *Feldgendarmerie.*

Lucy wanted to walk past Curious Notions to find out if she could smell the cooking lobster. She made herself stay away. She'd given the gift. Paul and his father had accepted it. It was theirs now. What they did with it was their business.

Three days after she gave it to them, she was walking home from work when a Chinese man in his late twenties coming the other way bumped into her. "I'm very sorry," he said.

"It's all right—no harm done," Lucy told him.

"Please accept m apologies." He pulled a little leather case from the hip pocket of his jeans. "Here is my card. If I can do anything for you, you only need to ask. Sorry again to bother you." He tipped his wide-brimmed hat and hurried away.

STANLEY HSU, FINE JEWELRY, the card said. The address, on John Street, was only a couple of blocks from her father's shop. The card also had several Chinese characters Lucy couldn't read.

And it had a note, written in neat, small hand. *Please come tomorrow evening at eight o'clock. Very important!* Lucy stared at that. As far as she could see, it could mean only one thing. Stanley Hsu hadn't run into her by accident. He'd wanted it to look like an accident to anyone who happened to see it, but it wasn't. He'd done it just so he could give her this card.

"Why?" Lucy said out loud. Then she wanted to clap both hands over her mouth, but she didn't. She felt like a fool, ruining the secrecy he'd worked so hard to keep. But the question that had burst from her still needed answering. Why did Stanley Hsu want her to come to his shop, and why did he need to keep it a secret?

Lucy put the card in her handbag. She tried to forget it the rest of the way home. She didn't remember the note till after supper. (Supper was only rice and vegetables. The lobster would take its toll on the budget for weeks—but the gift needed giving.) Then she took the card out of the purse and showed it to her mother and father.

Her father scratched his head. "I've heard of Stanley Hsu, though I don't think I've ever said more than a couple of words to him. He has a good business. But why would he want to talk to you? Why would he give you the message that way?"

Her mother pointed to the Chinese characters on the card. "I think it has to do with the Triads," she said.

"The Triads?" Lucy and her father both stared. She asked, "Are they real?"

Back in the old days, the days before the Germans conquered the United States, the Triads had been very important in Chinese San Francisco. Outsiders usually called them Tongs. They were social clubs, but they were much more than social clubs, too. They helped poor members. They loaned money—often at poisonous interest rates, sometimes not, depending on who was getting it. They bought and sold things. Not everything they bought and sold was legal. Sometimes they fought among themselves. People still talked about the Tong Wars. And they'd had connections that reached all the way back to China.

After the Germans took over, they'd tried to put down the Triads. They'd made them illegal. The Americans had done that, too, but the *Feldgendarmerie* went after the Triads harder than American police ever had. They'd executed Triad leaders, or men they said were Triad leaders. Whatever the Triads did these days—if they did anything—they did quietly, in an underground way.

"They're real, all right," Lucy's mother said. Reluctantly, her father nodded. Her mother went on, "They're just . . . careful. They have to be."

"I never heard that Stanley Hsu was connected to them," her father said.

"If you heard things like that, the Kaiser's men would hear them, too," her mother answered. That made some sense, but only some. Such logic, if it was logic, could justify almost anything. Mother went on, "Besides, if it's not Triad business, what could it be?"

"But why would the Triads care about me?" Lucy asked.

Her mother hesitated. She had a hard time seeing an answer to that. So did Lucy—a very hard time. But her father snapped his fingers. "Curious Notions!" he said. "It has to be Curious Notions."

"Why?" Lucy said. "The people there aren't Chinese. They don't have anything to do with us—or they didn't, till the Germans arrested you."

"That's all true, honey," Charlie Woo said. "But something else is true, too—something I've talked about before. The people at Curious Notions sell things nobody else can match. Nobody. You think that doesn't make other people curious? It makes *me* curious, let me tell you. But I can't do anything about it. The Triads can."

"So you think I should go, then?" Lucy said.

"Oh, yes!" Her father and mother both spoke at the same time. Their voices both rose in a peculiar way.

They're frightened, Lucy realized. *They're scared of what might happen if I don't go.* How much did they know about the Triads? How much of what they knew had they kept to themselves? Quite a bit, it looked like.

"All right," she said. "I'll go." Her parents let out identical sighs of relief.

She wished Stanley Hsu hadn't picked a time after supper. To get to his shop by eight o'clock, she had to gulp down her noodles and vegetables and dash out the door. That left her mother stuck with the dishes. Mother didn't say a word. If that didn't prove how important she thought going was, nothing ever would.

Twilight deepened as Lucy walked over to John Street. She would have to come home in the dark. She didn't like that, either. The air was cool and moist. The streetlights that worked had halos around them. She thought the night would be foggy. Sometimes tourists came to San Francisco thinking that, since it was California, of course it would be dry and hot. They often got a nasty surprise.

Lucy almost went right past Stanley Hsu's shop. It was only half a storefront wide, and had his name on the door in the tiniest of letters. The door also held those Chinese characters. Did they really have something to do with the Triads? Lucy only shrugged. She couldn't tell, not to save her life. But she'd find out, or thought she would.

She opened the door. It had a bell set above it, just like the one in her father's shop—and the one in Curious Notions, come to that. The familiar clink made her a little less nervous. Stanley Hsu smiled at her from behind the counter. "Welcome," he said. "Look around a little, if you care to."

"Thank you," Lucy answered. His card said FINE JEWELRY, and it wasn't kidding. Strings of pearls gleamed, as if by moonlight. Carved jade and ivory stood on glass shelves. Gold shone everywhere. Diamonds glittered. Rubies and sapphires and emeralds glowed: tiny explosions of deep, rich color. There were hardly any price tags. If you needed to ask, you couldn't afford it. Even so . . . Wistfully, she said, "It's beautiful."

"You are too kind," the jeweler murmured with a smile that looked modest but was really full of pride.

"What do you want with me?" Lucy didn't feel like beating around the bush. "Why did you pick such a strange way of asking me to come here?"

"I have to be careful," he said, which didn't tell her anything. After a moment's pause, he added, "You never can tell who may be watching, or when."

"The *Feldgendarmerie*, you mean?" Lucy asked.

"Yes, the *Feldgendarmerie*." Stanley Hsu nodded. "And maybe others." He made a pagoda of his fingertips. "Would you be kind enough to tell me what you know of the people who run the business called Curious Notions?"

Lucy took a deep breath. It wasn't as if she hadn't expected the question. All the same, she needed a real effort to shake her head the way she'd planned. "I'm sorry, Mr. Hsu, but I don't think I want to do that."

"Oh?" Stanley Hsu didn't lose his smile or his manners. "Perhaps you would be good enough to explain why not?"

"They helped my family," Lucy said simply. "I'm not going to do anything that would get them in trouble. If that's why you asked me to come, I'd better leave."

"Please wait." If he'd made it sound like an order, she would have got out of there as fast as she could, but he didn't. She didn't *think* he would do anything nasty if she stayed, and so, warily, she did. He let out a long sigh. "It could be dangerous to me to reveal too many of my affairs to you. It could also be dangerous to you to hear too much."

"It's already dangerous for me," Lucy said. "For my father, too."

The jeweler dipped his head. It was almost a bow. "That is true. I cannot deny it. All right. I will tell you . . . something. I will not tell you everything, though."

"Well, of course not. You'd be crazy if you did," Lucy said.

Stanley Hsu took a deep breath of his own. "How would you like to see the United States a free country once more, out from under the Kaiser's thumb?"

Again, the question didn't startle Lucy all that much. But it was treason, nothing else but. Stanley Hsu had taken her into his confidence, sure enough. If she told the *Feldgendarmerie* he'd asked her that, he was a dead man. She said, "I don't know. Is it even possible? Wouldn't the Germans squash us flat if we tried? They've done it before. They have so many things we don't."

"They have a higher technology than we do," Stanley Hsu said, which was a fancier way of repeating Lucy's comment. He went on,

"They have the highest technology in the world, and they work hard to keep it that way. There are some places in . . . There are some places that are trying to catch up, but they haven't yet."

"Some places in China?" Lucy asked. "Some places with connections to San Francisco?" She didn't ask if he was one of those connections. That seemed plain enough as things were.

He gave her another smile, which did surprise her. "Since you've already figured that out on your own, you save me from a lot of troublesome explanation." She hadn't figured it out on her own—her mother had helped a lot. But she didn't have to say so to Stanley Hsu. Smiling still, he continued, "Yes, what you say is true. Because China is so far away from Germany, the Kaiser can't keep an eye on everything that goes on there. But now I have to come back to the people at Curious Notions. I am sorry, but I do."

"Why?" Lucy asked bluntly.

"Because, by what they sell, they can get hold of things made with a technology higher than Germany knows anything about," Stanley Hsu answered. "We want to know where. We want to know how."

Lucy found herself nodding. Her father had said pretty much the same thing. He hadn't put it the same way—Stanley Hsu talked like a man with a fancy education. But when you boiled it down, there wasn't much difference. Lucy nodded once more, this time to the jeweler. "I'm with you so far."

"Good." Again, Stanley Hsu sounded as if he meant it. That made Lucy want to like him, want to trust him. She knew neither might be a good idea, but she wanted to anyway. He said, "As far as we know, they sell only toys: radios and televisions and phonographs and portable music players. But those are all better—much better—than what comes out of Berlin. What sort of serious things do they have, if their toys are so fine?"

What did he mean by serious things? Calculating machines? Weapons? What else would matter to people trying to shake off the Germans? Lucy told the truth: "I don't know about any of that."

"I didn't think you did," Stanley Hsu replied. "But who would have a better chance of finding out than you do?"

Lucy turned and started for the door. Over her shoulder, she said, "I'm sorry you've wasted your time, Mr. Hsu. I'm not going to spy on them, and that's that."

"Don't you want your country to be free?" the jeweler demanded.

"If you're asking this kind of thing from me, would you make it free?" Lucy asked in turn. "Or would you just turn it into China's cat's-paw instead of Germany's?"

Stanley Hsu looked astonished. At first, Lucy thought that was because she'd had the nerve to ask him the question. Then she realized he'd never asked it of himself. People—she didn't know who—had told him things, and he'd believed them. Was he suddenly wondering whether he should have?

"You are a remarkable girl . . . uh, young woman," he said after a long, long pause.

"I don't know anything about that. I don't *care* anything about that," Lucy answered with a shrug. "I do know my father taught me never to buy a pig in a poke. Maybe somebody should have taught you the same thing, Mr. Hsu." She walked out of the shop, wondering if he'd chase after her. He didn't. Nobody bothered her all the way home.

When Paul Gomes stepped out of Curious Notions, he found that marmalade cat waiting for him. "Meow?" it said. He had no trouble translating from cat to English. *Where's my handout?* the beast wanted to know.

"Here you go." Paul tossed a dried anchovy on the sidewalk. They sold them in sacks at Fisherman's Wharf. Some people used them for bait. Paul supposed he wasn't the only one who used them for kitty treats.

The cat nosed this one, daintily bit it in half, and then ate each half in turn. Then it proved it was honest in its own fashion. It rubbed up against Paul's leg, purred like distant thunder, and let him scratch it behind the ears and under the chin. Some cats—a lot of cats, in fact—seemed to think they got handouts by divine right. This one knew better. If it didn't earn its treats, it did without.

Dad would have said it was just baiting the hook for Paul. Dad *had* said that, in fact, said it often enough to make a bore of himself. Maybe he was even right. Paul didn't much care. He was more inclined to keep on feeding the cat because his father had made a bore of himself than he would have been if Dad had just let it alone.

He tossed the marmalade tabby another dried anchovy. Its purr got even louder and deeper. He didn't do that every day. When he did, the cat made sure it showed it was grateful. Before too long, he planned on letting it into the shop. That would really give Dad something to complain about.

As it had before, the cat neatly bit the anchovy in half before starting on it. It made the tail end disappear. But then, instead of going on to the head end, it disappeared itself—it made a small, startled noise and ran around the corner.

"What the—?" Paul didn't think he'd scared the cat. He straightened up, turned around . . . and almost bumped into a short, stocky, neatly dressed Asian man standing behind him. "Excuse me," he said.

The man smiled and nodded. The nod was polite enough, but the smile never reached his eyes. They were as hard and dark and shiny as obsidian. "You're Paul, aren't you?" he said. "You work here." He nodded again, this time toward the front window of Curious Notions.

"That's right," Paul said. "Can I do something for you, Mr., uh . . . ?"

"You don't need to know my name," the man said. "You need to know we've got our eyes on you, and on your father, too. You can't go anywhere unless we know about it. You can't do anything unless we know about it. And if you want to tell the Kaiser's hounds about us, go ahead. We don't exist, you see."

What was that supposed to mean? It sounded like something out of a twentieth-century spy thriller. Carefully, Paul said, "If you won't tell me who you are, I don't think we want anything to do with you."

"It isn't your choice," the man said. "It's ours, and you need to understand that."

"You can't tell me what to do," Paul said. And he was right, right in a way no one who lived in this alternate could be. No matter what kind of problems he and his father had, the transposition chamber could take them away where nobody from here could follow. Knowing that made everything that went on here seem not so very important. It needed more than a two-bit punk to make Paul sit up and take notice.

Something in his voice must have told the Asian man as much. He sent Paul a perfectly filthy look—he expected people to take him seriously. "We can do all kinds of things," he growled. "You wouldn't want an accident to happen around here, would you? You wouldn't like it very much if it did."

Paul put his hand in the pocket of his jeans. All he had in there was a set of keys, but it was a big, lumpy set. Through the denim, who could be sure what it was? "We aren't the only ones who can have accidents," he said in his own best tough-guy voice. "You want

87

to remember that, you and your 'nameless' friends. You don't think I can find out who they are?"

That was pure bluff, too, but it rocked the older man. "I don't know what you can do with your lousy gadgets," he said. "But you'd better not mess with us, because you don't know what you're messing with. We've got connections you can't touch, no matter how smart you think you are."

"I don't care if your stinking connections go back all the way to China," Paul snapped. The Asian man's lips skinned back from his teeth in what was anything but a smile. Paul realized he'd landed another hit, even if he didn't quite know how. He'd just meant it as a figure of speech. He grinned a grin that said he knew more than he was letting on. He was—literally—lying through his teeth, but this fellow didn't have to know that.

"You'll be sorry, kid," the Asian man said. "You think you're smart and you think you're tough, but you don't know how much trouble you're in."

Paul took a step toward him. "I know how much trouble you're going to be in if you don't get lost."

"Oh, I'll go. But you haven't seen the last of me. You may wish you had." The man hurried down the street, turned the corner, and was gone.

Exit villain, sneering, Paul thought. But he didn't even know if the Asian man was a villain, or anything else about him. All he knew was that the fellow knew too much about Curious Notions.

He waited to see if either the man or the marmalade cat would come back. When neither did, he went back into the shop. He waited till a lull with no customers, then told his father what the Asian man had said. Dad, for a wonder, heard him out. When he finished, his father said, "That doesn't sound so good."

"I didn't think so, either," Paul said.

His father pointed a finger at him. "I bet it's got something to do with that Lucy What's-her-name. I told you that would end up causing trouble."

"You—" Paul stopped. He wanted to say his father didn't know what he was talking about. He wanted to, but found he couldn't. What Dad had said made altogether too much sense.

Five

Hank Simmons prowled through the shoe factory. He was looking for trouble. Lucy had seen him like this before. He would lash out at anybody who got out of line. If no one got out of line, he would lash out anyway. He was the foreman. What could the workers do to him? Nothing—and didn't he know it?

He peered at the basket by Lucy's sewing machine. His bald, shiny head gleamed under the fluorescent lights. The basket was nearly full. Even as the foreman watched, Lucy sewed on another instep strap and tossed in another shoe. Simmons only grunted. Even if he was looking for trouble, he couldn't find any here. Lucy went on working, doing her best to pretend he wasn't there.

Finally, muttering, he went on to Mildred's machine. She tried to ignore him, too. He picked a shoe out of her basket and held it about three inches in front of his nose. Then, angrily, he threw it back in. "You call that workmanship?" he demanded.

"Yes, Mr. Simmons." Mildred didn't get mad. No—she didn't show she got mad. There was a difference. "That's what I call it."

"Well, *I* don't," the foreman said loudly. "Those straps'll fall apart in nothing flat. Woo here can do it right. Why can't you? She didn't start that long ago, and you've been here since dirt."

Lucy knew Mildred was faster and neater on the sewing machine than she was herself. Mildred had to know it, too. But if she said what she was bound to be thinking, Hank Simmons would throw her out on her ear. All she did say was, "I'll try to do better, sir."

"'I'll try to do better, sir,'" the foreman echoed mockingly. "You'd better do better, or you're in big trouble. You hear me, sister? *Big* trouble."

Without even waiting for an answer, he stomped off to terrorize somebody else. Mildred muttered under her breath. Lucy couldn't make out everything she said. That was a shame, because what she could understand sounded highly educational. "If I was *his* sister, I'd break every mirror in the house," was some of the mildest of it. It got warmer from there.

Before long, Lucy was giggling helplessly. Mildred sent her a look that should have sliced through solid steel. Somehow, it only made her giggle harder.

"Yeah, go ahead," Mildred said in a low voice. "You can laugh. He didn't land on you like a sack of manure."

"Not this time," Lucy answered. "You think he hasn't, though?" She stopped, because steam was still coming out of the older woman's ears. Lucy made herself quit giggling. She said the only thing she could: "I'm sorry, Mildred."

Mildred tried to stay angry. Lucy could see that. However hard she tried, she started laughing a few seconds after Lucy stopped. "I don't know why I let him get to me," she said. "He *is* just a sack of manure. But when he's there telling lies right to my face, I want to take him and sew his lips shut, that's what I want to do."

Lucy had thought she was over the giggles. That started them all over again. She and Mildred both howled. So did several of the women around them who'd heard.

Naturally, the foreman came storming back. "What's this?" he shouted. "What's this? What's going on here?"

"Nothing, Mr. Simmons," Mildred said sweetly. It was a good

thing she answered, because Lucy couldn't talk right then. She kept imagining Hank Simmons under the sewing machine. Too bad it was only make-believe.

After lunch, Simmons called her away from her machine. Everybody stared at her. She wondered what she'd done. Simmons hardly ever let people stop working—she couldn't remember the last time, in fact. He'd found out somebody's mother was in an accident one morning, and he didn't tell the poor woman till lunch.

He took Lucy into the office and closed the door behind them. The walls were covered with pinup photos, big, small, and in-between. Simmons lit a cigarette. The smoke was especially nasty in the small, cramped space. He tapped ash into an ashtray on his desk that was already overflowing with butts.

From behind that smoke screen, he studied her as if she were a puzzle piece that didn't fit where he thought it should. *He's going to make me say something first,* Lucy realized. "What is it, Mr. Simmons?" she asked—the safest question she could think of.

"Fellow came in and wanted to talk about you earlier today," Simmons answered. "Not a big fellow, but important-looking. Important-sounding, too." He was impressed, no matter how he tried to hide it. "Fellow with connections," he added. "He made that real plain—*real* plain."

Till then, Lucy hadn't had any idea who this man might be. Now she did—or, if not who he was, what those connections were. She nodded back to the foreman. "I see," she said, as if she'd been sure all along.

"Why didn't you say you knew people with clout like that?" Hank Simmons stubbed out the cigarette and nervously lit another one. "Why didn't you tell me? You think I couldn't have fixed you up with a better job before this? I'm no dummy, Miss Woo. I know which side my bread's buttered on. You'd better believe I do."

Lucy blinked. He'd never called her *Miss* Woo before. She had to tell him something. "It was necessary," she said—let Simmons figure out what that meant.

He said, "Well, it sure isn't necessary now. This fellow made that real plain—*real* plain." He repeated the phrase again, this time with a kind of shudder. Then he asked, "You read and write, don't you?"

"Oh, yes," Lucy said, wondering why he cared.

He told her: "Okay, then. Starting tomorrow—no, starting right now—I'm taking you off your machine. You're a file clerk, as of today. Pay's fifteen dollars a week, and you get a half day off on Saturday. Go to the front office. Ask for Mrs. Cho. She knows you're coming. She'll show you what to do."

"Mrs. Cho," Lucy echoed in something not far from a daze. She got out of Hank Simmons' smelly office as fast as she could. *The Triads,* she thought dizzily. *It must be the Triads.* Had the "fellow with connections" said he'd murder Simmons if Lucy didn't get promoted? Or had he said he'd burn down the factory and everybody inside it? Whatever he'd said, it had done the trick.

Mrs. Cho was expecting Lucy. She showed her the paperwork that needed doing. It wasn't very hard. It was ridiculously easy, as a matter of fact. Lucy had dreamt of a job like this. She hadn't dreamt she could get one, though. And at almost twice the pay! *And* with a half-holiday on Saturday! It seemed too good to be true.

That brought her up short. Maybe it *was* too good to be true. The Triads hadn't got her this job because they were nice. They'd done it because they still wanted her help with Curious Notions. As soon as she thought it through, that seemed pretty plain.

And, as soon as she thought it through, it raised another question. What if she didn't help Stanley Hsu and his friends? They'd proved they could do things for her to get their way. What would they do *to* her if they didn't?

Paul's father often got on the telephone before he opened up Curious Notions. Farmers in the Central Valley had curious notions about when they were supposed to rise and shine. They were always up by the time Dad started calling them.

Usually, he talked about setting up deliveries or haggled over prices. This morning, he sounded angry at the world. "What do you mean you can't bring in those almonds, Mr. Triandos? We had a deal."

Chris Triandos had been selling almonds to people from the home timeline for years. Why shouldn't he? They paid better prices than anybody in this alternate would.

Dad paused to listen. The longer he listened, the madder he got. Paul could tell. His father didn't drum his fingers on the nightstand like that when he was in a good mood. At last, Mr. Triandos must have stopped talking. Dad burst out, "What do you mean, a little bird told you not to?"

Chris Triandos answered. Paul couldn't make out what he was saying, but he sounded excited. He always liked to talk. Paul had seen that whenever he brought almonds up to San Francisco.

"What are they going to do if you bring in the shipment anyway?" Dad asked when the farmer ran down. "Burn down your house and poison your dog?" He meant it for a joke—a sarcastic joke, but a joke just the same. Mr. Triandos said something else. Whatever it was, it was short and not very sweet. Dad flinched when he heard it. "Oh. They did?" The next sound from the other end of the line was a click. "Hello?" Dad said. "Hello?" Then he said something else, something that wasn't even close to hello. He hung up, too.

"Somebody doesn't like Mr. Triandos?" Paul said.

His father shook his head. "No. Somebody doesn't like us. They told him bad things would happen if he did any more business with us. They made him believe it, too." He scratched at his mustache. "I bet he's not going to be the only one, either."

"Who doesn't like us?" Paul asked. "Who *really* doesn't like us, I mean?"

"Could be the Kaiser's merry men—but I don't think it is," his father answered. "If the Germans wanted to put on the squeeze, they'd grab one of us and use him to make the other one talk. Or maybe they'd grab both of us and just start smashing. If you're in charge, you don't have to waste time getting cute. So what does that leave? The way it looks to me, it leaves lovely Lucy's little pals."

Paul wished he could tell his father he was nuts. After the unpleasant visit he'd had outside the store, he knew too well he couldn't. "What do we do now?" he asked in a small voice.

"Good question," Dad said. "What the people with Chinese connections don't seem to get is that we're here in this alternate for more than one reason. We're not going to dry up and blow away even if nobody sells us produce. We've got to keep an eye on the Kaiser's crew, too—make sure they don't get any bright ideas about alternates."

"Will Crosstime Traffic leave us here if we can't bring in the produce?" Paul asked.

"A lot of alternates, they wouldn't. They'd pull us out so fast, it'd make your head swim," his father answered. "Not this one, though. Like I say, they have other reasons to worry about this one."

"Maybe," Paul said. "But they won't be worrying about stuff like that here in San Francisco. They'll be worrying about it in Berlin, or wherever the Germans do their fancy research."

His father only shrugged. "We're here. Till they tell us to

leave, we're going to stay. And as long as we're gong to stay, we'd better not let the locals push us around so much that we can't do business."

Paul wasn't sure he liked the sound of that. "What have you got in mind?"

"Don't know yet." Dad shrugged again. "It'd be nice if we could get the Kaiser's men and the Tongs fighting each other, though. That way, they'd stop jumping up and down about us."

"Define 'nice,'" Paul said. "We're not far from Chinatown. If there is an uprising, or if the Germans go in there to clean house, we're still liable to get stuck in the middle."

One more shrug from Dad. "In that case, we go down to the subbasement and back to the home timeline. Then the locals can do whatever they want. After things calm down, we come back and start looking around again."

When he said *we,* he didn't necessarily mean Paul and himself. If the Germans—or the Chinese—were after them in particular, Crosstime Traffic could send in somebody else, somebody the locals wouldn't know. But whoever showed up in this alternate would make a living selling odd things. And whoever showed up would want to buy produce, too. If the Tongs—or the *Feldgendarmerie*—figured that out, they could make life harder for people from the home timeline.

The other side of the coin was, people from the home timeline often looked down their noses at locals. There were so many things crosstime traders couldn't tell people in the alternates they visited. There were good reasons why they couldn't tell them those things, too. Paul made a sour face. Dad had rammed that down his throat not so long ago. All the same, it seemed unfair a lot of the time.

Dad grunted when Paul told him as much. "You wouldn't say so if you didn't like that Lucy Woo."

He'd made that crack before, too. It wasn't true, or not the way he meant it. Paul didn't try to argue. Dad wouldn't have listened to him if he did. Dad was a lot better at talking than listening. If Paul had tried to argue, Dad would have said he was just doing it because of Crosstime Traffic rules. They banned what they called fraternizing, which meant getting too friendly with the locals.

Crosstime Traffic had its reasons, too. In spite of the rules, people from the home timeline did fall in love with locals every once in a while. Those romances hardly ever had happy endings. They were often a bigger danger to the secret of crosstime travel than the *Feldgendarmerie* and the Tongs put together.

Paul wasn't in love with Lucy. The more he tried telling his father so, though, the less Dad would believe him. He could see that coming like a rash. He just gave back a shrug of his own and went outside.

"Mrowr?" the marmalade cat said. It rolled on its back on the sidewalk and stuck its feet in the air and glanced at him with its head cocked at a silly angle and generally looked ridiculous. He laughed. He couldn't help it. He bent down and rubbed the cat's belly and scratched the velvety skin just above its nose. An angry breath escaped him. Dad hadn't even wanted him making friends with a cat here.

How could you not want to make friends with a cat like this, though? It purred like far-off thunder, and then even louder, like thunder that wasn't so far off. It scrambled to its feet and stropped itself against his leg. It shoved its face into his hand and purred louder still. He petted it some more. He didn't even have any goodies to give it right now. It was just being friendly. When he got to his feet and walked down the street, it followed him like a German shepherd.

He wished he hadn't thought of that particular breed of dog. It made him think of Germans, of *Feldgendarmerie* men. (The *Feldgendarmerie* didn't use German shepherds, though. They used Alsatians, which were bigger and meaner.) He looked down at the cat. It kept trotting along, half a pace to his left and half a pace behind him.

Finally, when it spotted a squirrel that might have strayed too far from a tree, it peeled off. Even then, though, it looked back over its shoulder once before starting to stalk. It might have been saying, *Sorry, friend, but this is business.*

Or maybe I'm really starting to imagine things, Paul thought. He didn't stay around to see whether the cat caught the squirrel. He wished it luck. As far as he was concerned, squirrels were nothing but rats with fluffy tails. But what he most wanted to do just then was get as far away from Curious Notions and his father as he could. He kept on walking.

Five minutes later, he stopped in the middle of the sidewalk, wondering if he'd made a mistake. The cat was the only thing he'd find in this alternate that he could like without worrying whether he'd get in trouble or it would get him in trouble.

Clerks in the front office at the shoe factory complained about their hours. They grumbled about how hard they had to work. Listening to them, Lucy didn't know whether to laugh or to cry. They had no idea how well off they were. If they went back to the machines, they'd find out in a hurry.

She wondered if they would give her trouble because she'd escaped from the factory floor. People were often mean like that. The clerks here didn't seem to be, though. Oh, she got some of the jobs nobody else much wanted, and she did all the coffeemaking the first couple of weeks she was there. But that sort of thing happened to anybody who was new anywhere. Lucy didn't let it worry her.

Maybe because she didn't, she got on pretty well with the other girls and women. As they got to know her, they treated her like one of themselves. They gossiped with her, they borrowed dimes from her, they didn't mind when she borrowed pens from them. She was . . . part of the gang.

This is too easy, she kept saying to herself. *Something will go wrong.* And something did, though it had nothing to do with the other clerks—or she didn't think it did, anyhow.

While she was eating lunch one day, somebody left an envelope on her desk. She didn't think much of it when she came back. People here left one another notes all the time. But when she opened the envelope, it didn't hold a note. One of Stanley Hsu's business cards fell on her desk. When she turned it over, she found he'd written, *Please come to my shop tomorrow at eight. We have a lot to talk about, don't we?*

"No," Lucy whispered. "I don't think we have anything to talk about." She tore the card into tiny pieces and dropped them in her wastebasket.

That didn't make her forget, however much she wished it could. It didn't mean she didn't go see the jeweler, either. Had she been alone in the world, she might have tried ignoring him. But she wasn't. Whatever he and her friends did, they wouldn't do just to her. The rest of her family made such lovely, tempting targets.

When she told her mother and father she'd got the note, they only nodded. It didn't surprise them. To her relief, they didn't tell her to do whatever Stanley Hsu wanted. She didn't think she could have stood it if they'd said that.

Her mother did say, "Be careful. These people mean business."

Lucy nodded. "I know that. I knew it as soon as they got me the promotion. Mr. Simmons is a tough man. Nobody can stand him, but he's tough. And he looked scared to death while he was talking to me."

"Better him than us," her father said. But he didn't say, *Better the people at Curious Notions than us*. He might have been thinking it—he probably was thinking it—but he didn't say it. Lucy was grateful for that.

Even coming back to it a second time, Lucy almost walked right past the jewelry shop. Fog rolled in as light faded from the sky. She hoped it wouldn't be too thick when she came out. She couldn't do anything about it, though. She couldn't do anything about going inside, either. In she went.

As it had before, the jewelry dazzled her. This time, she made herself look at what price tags there were. A lot of the pieces cost more than she made in a year, even with her new job and new salary. And the ones without the price tags? Well, they had to go up from there.

Stanley Hsu waited politely while she looked around. He was polite almost to a fault. He used good manners as a shield, so nothing would stick to him and so he wouldn't reveal his true self. If he'd shown more temper, Lucy would have had a better idea where she stood.

At last, he said, "I hope everything is going well for you?"

"You would know about that, wouldn't you? Lucy said.

He didn't tell her yes or no, not straight out. He just smiled, showing off very white teeth. "I was delighted to hear you had a new position."

"What did your friends tell Mr. Simmons to get him to do that?" Lucy asked.

"Nothing much." With a graceful flick of the hand, Stanley Hsu brushed the question aside. "He turned out to be a sensible man. He did the sensible thing."

What would have happened to him if he hadn't been . . . sensible? Would he have lost a finger? An eye? A leg? Both eyes? Would his mother have had a sad accident? Would his wife? His son?

What will happen to me if I'm not . . . sensible? The thought was snowstorms and icicles inside Lucy. She said, "You're going to tell me what you want from me now, aren't you?"

"I understand you do not care to do anything that might cause problems for the people at Curious Notions. I even understand why, I think." Stanley Hsu's nod was sober, considered, calculating. "Your reasons do you credit."

"That doesn't mean you care about them, does it?" Lucy asked. The jeweler didn't brush that aside, but he also didn't answer. Not answering, here, was the same as answering. Harshly, Lucy said it again: "Tell me what you want from me."

"One simple question will do," Stanley Hsu replied.

"What is it?" she asked suspiciously. Stanley Hsu told her. She tried not to show how surprised she was. That wasn't what she'd expected at all. She said, "That's it?"

The jeweler nodded. "That's it." He held up his right hand, as if taking an oath. "So help me, that's it. And that's all. Tell me exactly what Paul Gomes or his father says when you ask it. I want to know just the words they use. Do that, and you will meet your half of our bargain."

Lucy hadn't made the bargain. Stanley Hsu and the Triads had forced it on her. But if this would satisfy them . . . "You're sure?" she asked, suspicious still.

He held up his hand again. "So help me, I'm sure."

"What will you do if you don't like the answer?"

"Whatever seems necessary," he replied with a shrug. "But it won't have anything to do with you, whatever it is."

Things weren't that simple. Lucy could see as much. She could also see that Stanley Hsu's friends would do whatever they were going to do if she didn't get them their answer. That helped clear her conscience. "All right," she said. "I'll ask it."

"Yes, ma'am." Paul tried to sound enthusiastic about a stereo system that would have been a hopeless antique in the home timeline. "This one will make your records sound better than they ever have before." Even talking about records made him feel as if he'd fallen back into the dim, dark days of the twentieth century.

"That's nice," said the woman who was admiring the stereo. "And it will also be something most of my neighbors don't have, won't it?"

"Oh, yes." Paul tried to exude sincerity. "This is our very latest model."

She smiled at him. Her teeth had braces on them. That was much much less common and more expensive here than in the home timeline. Her dress was of a turquoise silk that glowed under the lights in the shop. She wore a wedding ring with a fat diamond in it, too. She was old—about his father's age—and kind of dumpy, but she had money. Maybe she was a nob of Nob Hill. Paul had always liked the sound of that.

"I'll take it," she said. Only after she decided that did she bother to ask, "How much does it cost?"

"Like I told you, this is our very top-of-the-line model," Paul answered. "It's $499.95." *Not even five benjamins,* he thought. But it wasn't the same thing. Five benjamins, in the home timeline, meant a burger and fries and a soda at Burger King. Some people here didn't make five hundred dollars a year.

She reached into her purse. She reached into her wallet. Out came five hundred-dollar bills. She was as casual with them as if they were benjamins back home. "Here you are," she said grandly. "Let me get my chauffeur. He'll carry it to the Mercedes."

She threw that right in Paul's face. It was supposed to hit him even harder than the cash. Hardly any Americans in this alternate could afford a fancy German car. She wasn't just rich, then. She was *very* rich. And she had connections, too, or she would have had to get along with a Cadillac or an Imperial.

The chauffeur was a big, beefy man. Paul held the door open for him. He lugged the stereo system down the street to the car. The Mercedes was a big one. Somehow, Paul wasn't surprised. The trunk swallowed the system. The chauffeur closed it with a thud. He opened the rear door for his boss, then got in himself and drove away.

Paul was glad to put the money in the register. He wanted to rub his hands on his jeans even after he got rid of it. It didn't feel clean to him. What had that woman or her husband done to earn it? Did he really want to know?

He made a sour face when the bell chimed again a minute later. Someone else who had more money than he or she knew what to do with and wanted a new toy to impress the neighbors? But then Paul found himself smiling. "Hello, Lucy," he said. "How are you?"

"I'm doing pretty well, thank you." She strolled up and down the aisles. "So many wonderful things here."

She didn't sound as if she wished she could afford them, though Paul knew she couldn't. He remembered that her father worked with this alternate's electronics. Maybe that helped her see how much better this stuff was, even if it would have been junk in the home timeline.

"We try to stock the best," Paul said—which was true, if you compared it to the state of the art here.

Lucy Woo nodded. "And you do." Now she smiled at him. "Did I tell you I got a promotion? Now I'm a clerk—they took me off my sewing machine."

"That's terrific! Congratulations!" Paul said. "Did you get a raise, too, I hope?"

"Oh, yes. A nice one," she said. "And I only have to work half a day on Saturday."

"Wonderful!" Paul worked hard to sound happy for her. The hours people here put in would have been illegal back home. Working half a day on Saturday on top of long hours Monday through Friday was no bargain, not to him. But it was better than what she'd had before. Paul tried to change the subject: "I hope your father is doing all right?"

"Yes, he's fine now. The Germans haven't been back." Lucy seemed to intend those two sentences as two halves of the same thought. She waved again. "He does wonder where you come by some of these things."

"We make them ourselves, in the basement." Paul laughed. Of course Lucy's dad would wonder where Curious Notions got the gadgets from the home timeline. Paul couldn't very well tell Lucy or her father or anyone else from this alternate.

Lucy smiled a little—just enough to show she knew he was joking. She walked up to the counter, leaned one elbow on it, and said, "Tell me something, would you please?" She studied him like a birdwatcher eyeing a brand-new warbler.

"What is it?" Paul asked cautiously.

"Where are you really from?"

"Right here. San Francisco." That was the answer he had to give. It was not true and true at the same time. The lively city he lived in wasn't much like this sad, sorry place. But then he had a question of his own: "Why do you want to know?" That was an urgent question, an important question. Did she think he was from somewhere else in these conquered United States? Or did she think he was from somewhere else altogether? She wasn't supposed to think that, not even when it was so. Especially not when it was so.

She said, "It's not just me. There are . . . people who want to know about you. If you don't tell me, they might find someone else to ask you. Whoever that is, he won't be so friendly."

"I think I've already met somebody like that," Paul said. As a matter of fact, he was sure he had. And making sure growers in the Central Valley didn't sell to Curious Notions hadn't been friendly, not even a little bit.

"I'm not surprised," Lucy said. "You've made people notice you. What you've got here makes people notice you. If you're not . . . big enough, getting noticed like that can be awfully dangerous."

By themselves, Paul and his father weren't anything much. When you added in what they could call on from the home time-line, it was a different story. But the home timeline had only limited access here. This was the Kaiser's home ground—and also that of the Chinese who'd grown curious about Curious Notions. That made things a lot harder.

Even so, Paul said, "We can take care of ourselves." *And if we can't,* he thought, *we can scoot back to the home timeline. Let's see anybody bother us there.*

"I hope so." Lucy's tone of voice couldn't mean anything but, *You've got to be kidding.*

"We can." Paul knew getting angry was silly, but he couldn't help it.

"I hope so." Now Lucy did sound as if she meant it, which surprised him. She went on, "I don't think you're really from here. I've never met anybody from here who's anything like you. You don't even talk quite the way I do."

What was she reacting to? That he didn't come from an occupied country and did act like a free man? That was probably part of it. People in these United States had been downtrodden for 140 years. They were cowed. The Germans made sure they were cowed. Paul wasn't. His United States was free, and the strongest country in the world. He didn't need to worry about any opinion but his own. It had to show.

As for the way he talked . . . English here wasn't much different from the way it was in the home timeline. San Francisco didn't have any special accent, the way Boston or New York City or New Orleans did. Maybe it was a matter of style, not one of word choice or vowel sounds at all.

"I grew up on Thirty-third Avenue, south of Golden Gate Park," he said after a pause only a little longer than it should have been. And that was also both true and untrue. Thirty-third Avenue, yes, but not in this alternate.

Lucy shook her head. "I don't believe it. That's a tough part of town. You'd be different if you came from there."

Paul muttered something under his breath. It wasn't a tough part of town in the home timeline. It had been, back in the early days of the twenty-first century, but the neighborhood had changed the other way as time went by.

"Well, I did," he said out loud. "Believe it or not. I don't care."

"One of these days, maybe you'll tell me the truth," Lucy said. "Till then . . ." She nodded to him, turned around, and walked out of the store.

How bad did I mess that up? Paul wondered. He did some

more muttering. By the way things looked, by the way they felt, he couldn't have messed it up worse if he'd tried for a week.

Lucy didn't want to go back to Stanley Hsu's shop. She didn't know what to make of the answer Paul had given her. She was afraid the jeweler *would* know. If he did, what kind of advantage would that give him over the people who ran Curious Notions?

She thought about making up a story. But what could she say? She didn't know what kind of lie the jeweler might believe. Besides, she'd made a deal with him. Once she told him what Paul had said, he'd leave her alone.

"Hello, Miss Woo," he said when she walked into his shop. She might have been a German countess by the way he treated her. "I was hoping I might see you soon."

Everything he said had a hidden meaning. Was he just telling her he was glad she'd dropped by? Or was he saying he'd had her followed and knew she'd gone to Curious Notions? She couldn't be sure. She couldn't be sure of anything with him.

He smiled, and went right on smiling. For all that smile had to do with what he felt, it might have been a Halloween mask. But she couldn't see past it. It hid whatever was really there.

"What have you got to tell me?" he asked.

"I went to Curious Notions and asked Paul Gomes the question you told me to," she said.

"Good. Very good." Stanley Hsu leaned forward across the counter. He might have been a hunting dog taking a scent. "And what did he say?"

"He said he was from right here in San Francisco. He said he was raised on Thirty-third Avenue south of Golden Gate Park," Lucy answered.

"Did he?" Whatever the jeweler thought of that, he kept to himself. Yes, he used his smile as a mask, but it was a good one. "Do you believe him?"

"I don't know," Lucy answered slowly. "He didn't sound like he was lying, but everybody knows what the Sunset District is like. He doesn't act like somebody who comes from there. He acts like somebody rich, somebody who doesn't have to worry about anything. He almost acts like a German—like he can do whatever he wants, whenever he wants to do it."

"Interesting." Stanley Hsu nodded. "We didn't make a mistake when we got that clerk's job for you, did we? You're plenty clever enough to do it. If you had a better education, you could do much more than that. I'm sure of it."

Lucy didn't say anything. She was lucky to have got as much schooling as she had. Most of her childhood friends had gone to work even before she did. If your family needed money, what were you going to do? Whatever you had to.

"Why did you want to know what he'd say to that question?" she asked.

"Because I was curious." But that was no answer, and Stanley Hsu seemed to realize it wasn't. He tried again: "Because I think you're right, and he doesn't belong to San Francisco. The things he sells don't belong to San Francisco, either. They hardly seem to belong to this world at all."

What was that supposed to mean? "They don't come from Mars," Lucy said. The Germans had sent unmanned probes to Mars. It was cold and almost airless and good for nothing—certainly not worth having people go there.

"No, they don't," Stanley Hsu agreed. "But they don't come from any country on Earth, either—not even from Germany. The

Feldgendarmerie wouldn't be so interested in Curious Notions if it just smuggled German goods. They don't know where those people are getting them, either."

"Paul said he and his father make them in the basement," Lucy said.

"Heh." Stanley Hsu made a noise that sounded like a laugh but wasn't. For the first time, he looked angry. "He was playing with you. He plays with us. He plays with the *Feldgendarmerie*, too. What will it take before he sees that this is not a game?"

"I don't understand," Lucy said.

"Maybe a man will laugh at the Triads if he does not know them well," the jeweler said. "I can see that, especially if the man is not Chinese. But who in his right mind laughs at the *Feldgendarmerie*? No one. The Kaiser's secret police are no laughing matter. The whole world knows it. *I* take the *Feldgendarmerie* seriously, and I have strong friends on my side. Do the people from Curious Notions? It doesn't seem so, not to me."

It didn't seem so to Lucy, either. She said, "Maybe that's why I had trouble believing Paul when he said he came from San Francisco. If he did, he'd be more like everybody else."

"Just so," Stanley Hsu said. "He would be more like everybody else, and the things Curious Notions sells would be more like what you could buy from everybody else. Since they are not . . ." He didn't go on.

"Well, what, in that case?" Lucy asked.

For a moment, Stanley Hsu looked just as confused as she felt. "I don't know," he admitted. "But you have to understand that while I am a captain, I am not a general. Other people will hear what you've said, and they will decide what to do next. Once they decide, they will tell me what to do, and I will do it."

He took Lucy by surprise. He gave her orders as if he had every right to do it. So there were people who gave him orders the same way? She hadn't imagined that. He'd seemed a very big fish to her. But she was getting the idea that this new ocean in which she found herself was a much larger and much more dangerous place than she'd ever even dreamt of.

Six

As a customer closed the door behind him, Paul suddenly said, "Hey, Dad, let's take the afternoon off."

"What?" His father frowned. "Close on Sunday afternoon? You know how much money you want to throw away?"

"For once, I don't care," Paul answered. "Let's go somewhere. When I'm here these days, I've always got the feeling somebody's watching me."

"I think you're worrying too much," Dad said.

"I don't," Paul said. "All the growers who don't want to sell to us, those questions Lucy Woo was asking, and Inspector Weidenreich, too . . . It's too much, Dad. I feel like I'm in the crosshairs all the time."

"No need to start getting nervous till they start planting microphones," Dad said with the sort of calm that annoyed Paul instead of making him feel better. His father went on, "They haven't done that yet. Our bug sniffers would have picked it up if they had. Will you tell me I'm wrong?"

"No." Paul shook his head. He couldn't, and he knew it. "I still want to get out of here, though. There's a big soccer game at Kezar Stadium. Can we go?"

Dad yawned. Paul understood that. In the home timeline, soccer was still a minor sport in the United States. People noticed it at

World Cup time, then forgot about it for another four years. Things were different here. Whether you backed the Seals or the Missions said a lot about where you lived, how much money you made, and what you did for a living. When the two teams met, it was almost like a civil war in the city.

But then Dad said, "Well, why not? A lot of people who might be customers will go the the game instead."

"Yeah," Paul said, and no more. Better to let his father talk himself into going.

Kezar Stadium was in Golden Gate Park. It was a shabby old oval. It had been built back before Germany beat the USA. Nobody'd spent a whole lot of money on it since. But as long as it didn't fall down, they'd keep playing games in it.

Seals backers wore orange and black. They carried trumpets to make noise for their heroes. Missions fans wore brown or tan. They brought drums, all kinds of drums, into the stadium. Both sets of fanatics sneered at ordinary people like Paul and his father who didn't dress up.

The stadium crawled with cops, on foot and on horseback. About every other year, a Seals-Missions match caused a riot, cops or no cops. Oddly, though, Paul felt safer here than he did at Curious Notions. The police here weren't worried about *him*. All they cared about were rowdies. If police back near Curious Notions noticed him, they were liable to run him in for questioning about the business. He didn't want to have to worry about that for a while.

The trumpets roared and brayed when the Seals—also in orange and black—ran out onto the soccer pitch. Paul's father clapped for the Seals. The people who rooted for them were mostly the ones who were better off. Paul cheered for the Missions. Drums thundered when they came out. More people backed them, but the ones who pulled for the Seals could have bought and sold the Missions fans.

Back and forth across the pitch the two teams ran. They didn't like each other any better than their backers did. The play was often rough. The referee did what he could to keep things on the up and up, but he couldn't be everywhere at once. And players on both sides hammered it up for all they were worth whenever there was anything close to a foul. That didn't make the ref's job any easier.

When the Missions scored first, the drums made the stadium shake. People in brown danced in the aisles. The Seals fans sat there in glum silence. Paul thought the Missions got another goal a few minutes later. The referee waved it off, saying they were offside. Boos rained down on him. Only a few bottles came flying out of the stands, though.

Just before halftime, the Seals tied the match. The bicycle kick their forward scored with was so pretty, even the Missions fans couldn't boo. The trumpets wailed. Most of the people who blew them could only make noise with them—they couldn't really play. They made a *lot* of noise. Paul's head began to throb.

In the second half, the Seals scored again. Their rooters looked smug, as if they'd expected nothing less. They were the sort of people who would have been Yankee fans in the home timeline. It was like rooting for Microsoft.

Minutes leaked off the clock. The Missions fans pounded on their drums. They shouted at their team to do something—to do *anything*. They lost more often than they won, on the soccer pitch as well as in life. With about ten minutes left in the match, though, the Missions banged home another goal.

It ended in a 2–2 tie. Soccer here saved overtime for championship games. This one wasn't. The draw sent everyone home . . . not too unhappy. Drums thumped and trumpets wailed as people filed out of the stadium.

"That wasn't bad," Paul said.

"Not too," his father agreed. The lines for eastbound buses were long. People filled up one bus at a time. The ones who couldn't get on waited for the next bus to pull up. They were more patient about waiting in line here than they were in the home timeline. They needed to be, too—they had to do it far more often.

At last, Paul and his father dropped their nickels into the fare box. All the seats were already taken. They stood in the aisle and hung on to the rail when the bus lurched into motion.

It didn't stay very crowded for long. After it left Kezar Stadium, more people got off than got on. Paul and his father got to sit down about three stops before the one where they would leave. Paul thought that was pretty funny.

Curious Notions was a block and a half from the bus stop. Somebody in an upstairs apartment was singing the Missions' fight song. Paul winced. Whoever the singer was, his enthusiasm couldn't make up for lack of talent. Dad put his hands over his ears for a minute.

When they got to the shop, the door stood open a crack. They looked at each other. Each of them said, "You forgot to lock it." They both shook their heads. "Uh-oh," Paul said. Dad's hand dove into his pocket. Owning a gun was a serious crime in this world. That didn't stop anybody from doing it. It did give the Germans an excuse for making sentences longer when they decided they needed to.

Dad went in first. Paul stayed close behind him. His eyes went up and down the aisles. He knew the stock well. Nothing seemed to be missing. When he said so, though, his father looked through him and asked, "How do you know what people were looking for?"

Nobody was in the back room. Nothing there had been stolen, either. Paul began to breathe a little easier. And whoever the burglar was, he hadn't found the secret stairway down to the subbasement. That had its own alarm.

"Not too bad," Paul said.

"Not yet," his father answered. "We haven't been up to the apartment."

"Why would anybody want to take stuff out of there with all the goodies down below?"

"To find out who we are," Dad said. "I told you—we didn't know why we had a break-in. I think we've found out it wasn't ordinary thieves."

"Oh." Paul shut up, feeling foolish.

His father had the pistol out as they went up the stairs. Nobody was in the apartment, either. But that was where the thief had been snooping, all right. It looked as if a tornado had gone through it. All the drawers were spilled on the floor. So were the clothes from the closets. So were the medicine cabinets in the bathroom. Even the pillows had been slit open.

Paul called the burglars the nastiest name he could think of. His father nodded. "Yes, but which set?" he asked. "The Kaiser's chums, or your Lucy's friends?"

"She's not my Lucy, and I don't think they're her friends," Paul said.

"No? Would they be bothering us if you hadn't got friendly with her?"

"They might," Paul answered. "You were the one who gave her father's name to the Germans, after all."

Dad waved that away. Paul might have known he would. His father was good at ignoring things he didn't want to hear. He said, "They must have noticed us before that." He'd just shot his own argument about Lucy in the foot, but he ignored that, too. He might well have been right about people noticing them before. Paul remembered that Lucy had said her father wondered where Curious Notions got its goods. But was it certain, the way Dad said? Paul didn't think so.

He asked, "Did they get anything that proves we're not from here?"

"We'd better find out, hadn't we?" His father didn't sound happy at all. The rules said you weren't supposed to leave the locals any clues you came from a different timeline. But when you got comfortable somewhere, did you always pay attention to the rules? Curious Notions' merchandise bent them as far as they would go. And Paul was pretty sure he'd been careless. He would have bet his father had, too. Dad always thought he had the answers. Sometimes he did. Sometimes . . .

They cleaned up the mess the burglars had left. Not much was missing. They both saw that right away. It too said the thieves had been after information, not money or other valuables. And no ordinary burglar would have knocked everything out of the medicine chest in the bathroom. Paul and his father were all right there. All their razors and soap and toothbrushes and toothpaste and such came from this alternate.

"I *think* we're okay," Dad said at last. He started to laugh.

"What's so funny?" Paul asked.

"It's not like we're going to call the cops," his father answered. "That'd just give them the excuse to tear this place to pieces, too."

"Oh," Paul said, and then, "Yeah." And then he started laughing, too. He didn't like that very much, but it *was* pretty funny.

Lucy's new boss, Mrs. Cho, was a lot nicer than Hank Simmons had ever been. She never complained about the work Lucy did—Lucy made sure she never had reason to complain. But she did start to ask questions like, "Are you sure you're happy here, dear?"

"I'm just fine," Lucy answered the first time she heard that.

When Mrs. Cho began asking it three or four times a day,

though, Lucy began to suspect a trend. The second she did something to give her supervisor an excuse, she'd be back at her sewing machine. Either that, or Mrs. Cho would just up and fire her.

It wasn't fair. She'd made a bargain with Stanley Hsu, and she'd kept her end of it. He and his friends were supposed to do the same thing. One evening after work, she stopped at his jewelry store on the way home. He was speaking Chinese with another man in an expensive suit when she walked in. They both fell silent. Lucy got the idea they hadn't been talking about diamonds or jade.

"Hello, Miss Woo," the jeweler said, very little warmth in his voice. "I didn't expect to see you here today."

"I did what you wanted," Lucy said. "I did just what you told me to do. Now it looks like I'm liable to lose my job. That wasn't part of the deal we made."

The stranger in the fancy suit gave her the nastiest smile she'd ever seen. "And what are you going to do about it?" By the way he talked, she might have been a spoiled mushroom he'd found in his salad.

Later, she realized he was trying to scare her. At the moment, all he did was make her mad. "What will I do?" she echoed. "I'll tell you what. I'll tell all my friends and neighbors that you can't trust the Triads, that's what. They make deals and then they go back on them."

"I don't think you want to do that," the man said.

"I don't think you want to make me do that," Lucy retorted. "If you break your word, how are you any better than the Germans?"

He stared at her. How big a big shot was he? When was the last time anybody had stood up to him? Unless Lucy missed her guess, it was a long, long time ago.

Stanley Hsu said something in Chinese. The man in the expensive suit answered in the same language. The harsh rattle of syllables meant nothing to Lucy. Her parents didn't speak Chinese, either. Her mother said *her* mother's mother and father had sometimes used it when they didn't want Granny to know what was going on. For most people in San Francisco's Chinatown these days, it was a closed book. But not for these two, obviously.

After a little back-and-forth in the old language, Stanley Hsu switched to English: "She's right, and you know it."

His—friend?—gave Lucy another *Waiter! Look what I found in my salad!* look. "She ought to get what she deserves for talking to me like that," he snapped, also in English.

"She ought to get what she deserves for meeting her end of the bargain," the jeweler said.

"She didn't tell us anything we didn't know already," the well-dressed man snorted.

"She asked the question we told her to ask. If she didn't get the answers we thought she might . . . well, that's information, too," Stanley Hsu said.

The other man said something in Chinese. Lucy had no idea what it meant. She thought she could make a pretty good guess, though. He glared at her again. "You're nothing but a nuisance. You know that?"

"Easy enough for you to say so. You're not worried about your job. You're not worried about going hungry." Lucy saw he had on a wedding ring. "Does your wife wear shoes I helped to make? How many pairs of them has she got? You make me want to throw something at you. You've got all that money, and you look down your nose at me because I don't." Her nose stung and her eyes watered, but she would have jumped off a cliff before she gave him the satisfaction of seeing her cry.

He stared at her once more, this time as if he hadn't seen her before. Maybe he hadn't, not really. Slowly, he said, "You've got more nerve than you know what to do with."

Lucy only shrugged. What she wanted to do was find something large and hard and hit him over the head with it. Stanley Hsu spoke to him: "You go on and on about accounting. Keeping this bargain will be a lot cheaper than breaking it."

Fury filled Lucy. The man with the fancy suit had wanted to break a promise because breaking it saved money? He *deserved* getting clobbered, in that case. Then she realized Stanley Hsu was on her side. He thought it was funny that she was giving the other man a hard time.

"I—" The man in the expensive clothes stopped short. He'd just figured out the same thing Lucy had. It took him a little longer, but not much. "All right. *All right.*" By the way he said it, it wasn't even close to all right, but he couldn't do anything about it. "We'll leave that alone then. You think you're so smart." He added something else in Chinese that sounded hot, then stormed out of the shop.

Stanley Hsu eyed Lucy. "Do you have any idea who that was?"

She shrugged. "Not really. He's somebody who can afford a nice suit." As far as she was concerned, that was a point against the man who'd just left, not a point for him.

"He's—" The jeweler shook his head. "You don't need to know his name. What you don't know, you can't tell. But he's important—he's very important—in the Triads. I would never have the nerve to talk to him like that." Lucy thought he was done, but after a moment he went on, "And you're right—he can afford a nice suit. He can buy and sell me, I'll tell you that."

Lucy had looked at the prices in the shop. She'd looked at the pieces that didn't have prices, too, the really expensive ones. Stanley Hsu had more money than she'd ever dreamt of. To imagine someone could buy and sell him the way he could buy and sell the Woo family . . .

"That may be the scariest thing I ever heard," Lucy said.

"There's nothing wrong with having money," Stanley Hsu told her. "There may be something wrong with what you do with it. If you have a lot of money, you can do a lot of good." He quickly held up a hand. "And yes, you can do a lot of harm, too. I know that. The . . . gentleman you met also knows it."

"That's nice." Lucy sighed. "I wish I had the chance to find out what I could do with a lot of money," she said wistfully. There were times when she wished she had the chance to find out what she could do with even a little money. She kept quiet about that. She was afraid she would sound sorry for herself.

By the way Stanley Hsu smiled, he guessed some of what she wasn't saying. He said, "Don't worry. Mr. Lee will keep his promise." He made a face. The name had slipped out. Lucy didn't see the trouble—it was a common one in Chinatown. Stanley Hsu went on, "Your job is safe as long as you do it well. If you don't, no one can help you. But I don't think that will be a problem, will it?"

"I can do what they've given me to do. It isn't very hard," Lucy said. That covered what the jeweler had said, or at least what she'd heard in what he said. If she hadn't heard quite everything . . . well, maybe he hadn't intended her to hear quite everything. She said her good-byes and hurried home.

Her father had got there ahead of her. He didn't usually do that. He and her mother were both worried about her. "It's all right," she said. "I was just checking on something with Mr. Hsu."

"Oh?" Both her parents said it at the same time and in the same tone of voice. They knew she'd had some trouble at the factory. Still sounding worried, her mother asked, "And how did it go?"

"Fine, I think," Lucy said. "Another man was there, someone

Mr. Hsu listens to." That got her mother and father's attention. Anyone the jeweler paid attention to had to be a big shot. She went on, "He promised Mrs. Cho wouldn't bother me any more."

"Good. That's very good," Mother said. She and Father were suddenly all smiles.

Lucy didn't say anything about the way she'd had to prod Mr. Lee to get what was right. She'd got it. How she'd got it would only worry her parents. Thinking back on how she'd got it, though, made her smile, too.

Paul scratched the marmalade cat under the chin and by the side of its jaw. Purring, it closed its eyes and gave him a kitty smile. "You like that, don't you?" he said. "I thought so. You're not the only cat I know that does."

The cat pushed its face into his hand. It purred louder than ever. He wondered how such a friendly beast had turned into a stray. Then he laughed. It was hardly a stray any more. It was his cat, the Curious Notions cat.

He straightened. The cat twined itself between his legs. Whenever he looked around in this San Francisco, the skyline jolted him. The biggest reason for the jolt was that there wasn't much of a skyline. No high-rise hotels and office towers, no Transamerica Tower looking like an SST sticking up from the ground, not much of anything. In the home timeline, they built tall and did everything they could to quakeproof what they built. They could do a lot, too. Here . . .

Here, they couldn't do nearly so much. They couldn't afford nearly so much, either. And so they'd kept the laws the San Francisco and Los Angeles of the home timeline had given up, the laws that said a building couldn't be taller than so many stories. It made for a much duller-looking city. It also made for a city that couldn't hold as much or accomplish as much as the one he'd grown up in.

If San Francisco were a German city . . . The Kaiser's architects and engineers knew plenty about building skyscrapers. Berlin and Munich and Hamburg and Breslau soared up to the heavens. But the Germans weren't interested in building in the United States. They weren't interested in having American builders learn their tricks, either. They took secrecy seriously, and they were good at it.

After Paul shook his head at the sorry skyline, his gaze dropped to the sidewalk again. He wondered who was watching him. Who was watching the shop? He couldn't pick out anybody on the street. He wished he could. He suspected both the Germans and the Tongs were keeping an eye on everything he and his father did. He wanted to be able to watch the watchers, too. That might help keep him safe.

No matter what he wanted, he wasn't going to get it. The only familiar faces were those of other shopkeepers and neighbors. If the *Feldgendarmerie* or the Chinese had hired some of them to spy, he'd never know till too late. If they hadn't, if they used other people, they moved them in and out too often to let him spot them.

But the spies were there, whether he saw them or not. He was sure of it. That wasn't a logical feeling, though logic also said they'd be around. He felt it with the pit of his stomach, with the hair at the back of his neck. It was the feeling you got when somebody stared at you from behind. Your body could tell, even if your head couldn't.

Shaking his head again, he went inside. The cat scooted in, too. It was doing that more and more often. It knew which side its bread was buttered on. Paul's father saw it. He said, "You're the one who cleans up after that fuzzy freeloader."

"I know," Paul said patiently. After a few seconds, he added, "I think we should get out of here—just disappear."

"Crosstime Traffic wouldn't like it," his father said.

"Would they like somebody grabbing us and squeezing us?" Paul asked. "That's what's going to happen. Don't you feel it, too, Dad? If Elliott couldn't, he really was blind."

"If I started worrying whenever I felt something, I'd be looking over my shoulder every minute of every day. That's no way to live," his father said. "Besides, we need to be in place to keep an eye on things here."

"There are others in this alternate to do that," Paul said. "They aren't being watched like we are, either."

"There aren't that many others in this alternate. There aren't that many in any one alternate. The home timeline is spread too thin," Dad said. Paul wished he could argue about that. But he knew how true it was. His father went on, "Besides, how do you know they aren't being watched, too?"

Paul grunted. He didn't know that. Crosstime Traffic people traded. They had to—Crosstime Traffic wasn't in business for its health. And when you traded, you drew notice. Maybe the *Feldgendarmerie* was keeping an eye on other people in this alternate who sold odd and interesting goods. How could you know till they dropped on you—if they did? You couldn't.

Dad added, "Besides, if we pull out and it turns out we didn't need to, we get a black mark on our records."

There it was. Paul knew the real reason as soon as he heard it. Dad wasn't just worrying about this alternate. He was worrying about the home timeline, too. That was all very well, within limits. But . . . "What happens if we need to pull out and we don't?" Paul asked, and answered his own question: "You know what happens." He made a horrible noise, the kind of noise a man getting strangled might make.

His father waved that away. "You're seeing shadows where

there aren't any. Everything's going to be fine. I've even got some new produce suppliers lined up."

"Terrific," Paul said. "How long before *they* get scared off?"

His father turned away. He didn't want to listen. He hardly ever did. Maybe he was right. He often was. Paul hoped so. He'd never wished so strongly that he himself were wrong.

When the Triads spoke, the people at the shoe factory listened. Lucy's supervisor stopped asking her if she was happy. Instead, Mrs. Cho praised her whenever she did anything well. Before long, Mrs. Cho was praising her even when she didn't do things especially well. That only annoyed Lucy. She didn't want praise she hadn't earned. But she couldn't see any way to tell the supervisor that.

She supposed praise she hadn't earned was better than blame she hadn't. At least it couldn't land her in trouble. Even so, she would sooner have done without it.

What she liked most about the new job wasn't the work itself. She hadn't minded the sewing machine that much. Putting up with Hank Simmons had been a pain, but you could have a bad boss wherever you worked. No, the nice part of the clerk's job was the Saturday half-holiday.

Lucy had got used to working six days a week. The first couple of weeks after she got her new job, she hardly knew what to do with the extra time off. Before long, though, she started spending her Saturday afternoons at the zoo. She met Peggy Ma there when her friend could get free, too. Otherwise, she headed over by herself.

The zoo was way on the west side of the city, jammed in between the Pacific and Lake Merced. She rode the bus to get there. It went through the Sunset District, where Paul Gomes had said he was from. Most of the people who got on in that part of town were either drunks or crooks or plainly tough in a way Paul wasn't. Lucy couldn't believe he'd grown up on Thirty-third Avenue. The way he'd said it, though, she couldn't believe he was lying, either.

She didn't know what to think.

Like so much of San Francisco, the zoo had seen better days, better years, a better century. It was built in the dim and vanished 1930s. The time seemed as distant to Lucy as the days of ancient Egypt. Nobody had been able to tell the United States what to do back then. When the economy fell off a cliff, the President said, *Well, build things!* And people did.

Maybe it helped. It didn't help enough, though. When the USA and Germany fought twenty years later, the Kaiser's side wiped the floor with Uncle Sam. Nobody'd spent much money on the zoo since. The concrete animal enclosures were crumbling. Some of them were empty. But the zoo still had lions and tigers and bears. It had camels and zebras and hippos and elephants. It had monkeys doing gymnastics and acting like clowns. It had a reptile house full of iguanas and turtles and cold-eyed snakes and mean-looking crocodiles.

Lucy loved watching the animals. She always had, ever since she was little. Some of them didn't look as if they ought to live on Earth at all. If a hippo wasn't the most ridiculous thing in the world, what was? Everyone once in a while, Lucy wondered about that a little. When a hippo yawned, its tusks didn't look ridiculous at all. They looked ready for trouble.

Ivy and other plants crawled all over the enclosures and up the slopes behind them. Ivy was a perfect plant for San Francisco. Winters hardly ever got below freezing, so the stuff never died back. It just grew and grew and grew.

Gulls wheeled overhead. Other birds hopped and flew in and out of the ivy: little brown sparrows, screeching jays with heads of blue so dark it was almost black, hummingbirds whose backs were rusty and green. The hummingbirds mostly ignored the others— except the jays, which they didn't like. But they went after one another like fighter planes. They zoomed and darted and made angry buzzing noises. Once Lucy saw two of them collide in midair with a sound like a fist smacking into an open hand. She'd had to pay a quarter to get in, but they put on their show for free.

She wondered why they quarreled so much. What did hummingbirds have to fight about? Bugs? Nectar? Lady hummingbirds? Whatever it was, it didn't seem like enough. They should have just been pretty and peaceful.

She laughed. To a hummingbird, the things she worried about would have seemed silly, too. Money? The Triads? Curious Notions? No, none of them would have made any sense to a bad-tempered little bird.

Sometimes she wished they didn't make any sense to her, either. Some of them didn't, in fact. And those were the ones she wished she knew more about! A hummingbird wouldn't have understood that at all. Lucy didn't fully herself.

One sunny afternoon, she splurged on a wiener. Her mother would click her tongue between her teeth at the dime gone forever. Lucy sniffed. Didn't her raise entitle her to a little fun? She knew what Mother would say. She'd say Father's time in jail had cost so much, they still had to watch every penny—to say nothing of dimes.

Lucy found herself telling Peggy a little about Paul Gomes. "I like him," she said, "but he's so strange."

"Boys can be like that," Peggy said, which wasn't the kind of sympathy Lucy wanted. Peggy had a boyfriend, and thought Lucy needed one, too. Lucy wasn't so sure. Didn't she have troubles enough? She didn't think she liked Paul *that* way, anyhow . . . and she decided she'd probably made a mistake saying anything at all to Peggy.

While her friend gave her advice she didn't much want, she finished the wiener. That, she enjoyed. If you couldn't even have a wiener once in a while, what kind of a life was that? But she knew what kind of life that was. It was the kind people only a little unluckier than she was had to live. It was the kind she would have had to live, too, if the *Feldgendarmerie* hadn't let Father out of jail.

That they had still amazed her. What kind of connections did Paul and his father have? Lucy would have tried to learn that for the Triads in a minute. He'd mentioned Fatty Horvath and that city lawyer. Who else? Could Stanley Hsu and his friends have got Father out? Maybe. Some of them were important people. But would they have bothered? She doubted it—not from what she'd seen of Mr. Lee.

"Thirty-third Avenue," Lucy muttered.

"What?" Peggy said.

"Nothing." Lucy couldn't, wouldn't, believe Paul had grown up in the heart of the Sunset District. He would have been a different person. He would have been a different kind of person. If he'd grown up in the Sunset District, it was a different Sunset District from the one she'd always known.

She laughed at herself. That was absurd, and she knew it. How could there be more than one Sunset District? It was like imagining more than one San Francisco. Lucy laughed again. If she could imagine any San Francisco at all, what would it be like? It would be a place where people could make more than eight dollars a week—more than fifteen dollars a week, too. It would be a place where *Feldgendarmerie* men with Alsatians couldn't poke their noses in wherever and whenever they wanted to. It would be a place where the gadgets Curious Notions sold weren't anything special. It would be a place where anybody—everybody—could afford gadgets like that.

What kind of Sunset District would a San Francisco like that have? One nicer than the tough, grimy horror that held Thirty-third Avenue here? One that was nice enough to have turned out somebody like Paul Gomes?

Lucy laughed one more time. *You're crazy,* she said to herself. A sparrow hopping around by her feet looked up at her. It didn't think she was crazy. It just wanted a piece of her bun. She tossed down a few crumbs. The little bird got one. More sparrows and pigeons nabbed the rest.

But even though Lucy kept laughing, she kept thinking hard, too. *Another* San Francisco made more sense the longer she looked at the idea. It would explain how she'd felt Paul was telling the truth and lying at the same time when he said he'd grown up here. It would also explain how Curious Notions got curious things. Simple—they just came from that *other* San Francisco.

The golden city on lots of hills, she thought. Had the Triads had the same idea? Was that why Stanley Hsu had told her to ask Paul where he was from? The notion would explain everything except how Paul and his father and everything in Curious Notions got to *this* San Francisco, to everyday, ordinary San Francisco. *Magic. It would have to be magic.* She didn't exactly disbelieve in magic. Plenty of magicians and fortune-tellers in Chinatown said they could make you healthy, happy, wealthy, and wise—for a price, of course. Of course.

But if magic really worked the way people said it did, how come everybody wasn't healthy, happy, wealthy, and wise? How come so many magicians and fortunetellers weren't healthy, happy, wealthy, and wise?

See? You're being silly, Lucy told herself. But was she really?

Sure as sure, the Triads couldn't believe anything connected with Curious Notions really belonged to this world, either.

If not by magic, though, how had Paul Gomes got here? Lucy imagined an airplane flying from that other San Francisco, wherever it was, to this one. That did it. Shaking her head, she turned to Peggy. "Let's go home," she said. When she got ideas that silly, it was time to call it a day.

Heading for the produce market with two hundred dollars in his pockets, Paul felt rich. That was pretty funny, when you got right down to it. In the home timeline, two benjamins would buy him a burger, but not the fries and the soda to go with it. Here, he could live for months on two hundred dollars—not that he'd call it living.

So many things even the richest man in this alternate couldn't have. Nobody here had ever heard of neobiotics, let alone subflexive fasartas. *Poor devils*, he thought with mild sympathy.

Paul wasn't someone who liked making noise for the sake of making noise. He had to be noisy at the produce market. If he'd kept quiet, nobody would have noticed him. Farmers and customers shouted at one another. Their fingers flashed in price signals—and other gestures. Half of what they yelled singed Paul's ears.

Sellers liked him because he was willing to go high. Buyers swore at him for bumping up prices. But he didn't get the deals he thought he'd clinched. The Tongs must have got there ahead of him. As soon as sellers found out who he was, they didn't want to deal with him any more.

"Beat it, kid," one of them said, not unkindly. "I'm gonna have to unload my scallions on somebody else."

"Why?" Paul demanded. "You won't come close to getting my price, and you know it."

"Maybe not." The farmer shrugged. He lit a cigarette, which disgusted Paul almost as much as wearing furs. "I'll tell you this, though—whatever price I do get for 'em, I'll be in one piece to spend it." He blew three smoke rings, one right after another. That fascinated Paul and grossed him out at the same time.

He said the only thing he thought might help: "How would they know?"

"Kid, they'd know." The fellow with the scallions had no doubts at all. He was probably right, too, even if Paul didn't want to admit it.

Paul left the produce market much less cheerful than he'd gone there. What good was his money if he couldn't use it? No good at all. He might as well have been trying to pass benjamins in this alternate.

What would his father say when he came back with all the money and without any deals for produce? Dad wouldn't be very happy. That was putting it mildly. Paul shrugged. If Dad thought *he* could buy, he was welcome to try it himself. Paul didn't think he'd have any better luck. The farmers didn't want to deal with the people from Curious Notions. Paul shook his head. No, that wasn't it. The farmers were scared to deal with the people from Curious Notions. There was a difference, a big difference.

How far did the Tongs reach here? Down into the Central Valley, certainly. Across the sea to China, probably. How much could they do against the power of the Kaiser? Not enough to overthrow it, plainly. But enough to give it a hard time in and near San Francisco? It sure looked that way.

Around the last corner. Heading for home, or the closest thing Paul had to a home in this alternate. The marmalade cat came out of Curious Notions and trotted over to rub up against him. He was bending down to pet it before he realized the front door shouldn't have been open like that. He straightened and started to run towards it.

Somebody shouted, "Get out of here, fool, before they grab you, too!"

That was bound to be good advice. Paul hurried into Curious Notions anyhow. The shelves were bare. Whoever *they* were, they'd carted off all the merchandise.

"Dad?" Paul called, hoping against hope.

No reply. Only silence. He went up the stairs two at a time. He knew he could be walking into a trap, but he did it anyhow. His father wasn't up there. Luckily for him, neither was anyone else. *They* had torn the apartment over the shop to pieces again. Paul's stomach felt as if it had jumped out a fifth-story window. What was he going to do now?

The answer formed on the heels of the question. He was going to get out before they came back and grabbed him, too. First, escape. Everything else could come later—if there was a later.

Seven

"I have news," Lucy Woo's father said over dinner, and then, "Pass the mushrooms and broccoli, please."

The bowl sat in front of Lucy. She sent it down the table. When Father served himself and didn't say anything more, she asked, "What is the news?"

He looked at her for a moment before answering. Then, his voice oddly flat, he said, "They've closed Curious Notions."

"What? Paul Gomes and his father?" Lucy couldn't believe it. "Why would they do that? They had to be making money hand over fist."

Father shook his head. "I don't think the people who ran it closed it. I think they had it closed for them." He sat very straight in his chair and looked stern and serious. When people in the United States did something like that, they always meant the Germans. "Everything was gone. You could look in the window and see that. And the neighbors say the wagons were there the other day."

"How terrible!" Lucy said. "Can we do anything for them?"

Normally, that would have been a dumb question. If the *Feldgendarmerie* took you away, odds were you were gone for good. But not always. Father was here mixing vegetables and rice to prove that. Mother said, "Maybe *you* can do something, Lucy. You're the one who knows the Triad people."

"Lucy thinks that Paul fellow is cute," Michael said.

Lucy was reminded—not for the first time—what horrible, poisonous creatures little brothers were. She sent Michael a glare that should have knocked him flat. He was tough as a weed, though. As far as she was concerned, the resemblance didn't end there. "Why don't you talk about things you know about—if you know anything?" she hissed.

Michael stuck out his tongue at her. "You do, too!" he jeered. "Nyah, nyah!"

"That will be enough of that," Mother said. "That will be enough of that from both of you, in fact." She pointed a finger at Lucy. Lucy didn't think that was fair. Her brother had started it. She hadn't given him half the trouble he'd given her.

Besides, he was wrong . . . wasn't he? Lucy liked Paul pretty well. He was interesting—a lot more interesting than anybody at the shoe factory, not that that said much. She liked him, yes. But did she *like* him? She hadn't even thought about it. She wondered why not.

He's strange. The answer formed in her mind as soon as the question did. She'd said as much to Peggy. He was very strange—nice, but strange. Thirty-third Avenue? Not likely! Maybe that silly idea she'd had about different worlds wasn't so silly after all. If anything could make her wonder, it was how strange Paul Gomes was.

Then she shook her head. No, it wasn't just Paul. The things Curious Notions sold—*had* sold—didn't come from any place she knew, either. Her father would have agreed with that. Where did they come from, then?

The same place as Paul, obviously. But where was that?

"Do you think the Triads *would* do anything?" her father asked.

"I don't know," Lucy answered. "They might. They were sure interested in anything that had to do with Curious Notions."

Her father drummed his fingers on the desktop. "I was in the Germans' jail. I don't like to think about anybody going in there. If you can get them out, you should."

"I'll try," Lucy said. "I don't know if the Triads will listen to me. Even if they do, I don't know what kind of price they'll ask."

"There usually is a price," Father agreed.

"Always," Mother said softly.

Lucy had already seen that. Stanley Hsu took the idea for granted. To him, it was just the way the world worked. The jeweler had helped her—for the price of a question. Getting people away from the *Feldgendarmerie* was bound to cost more. How much more? And in what coin? Lucy could only go and find out. If it wasn't the sort of price she thought she ought to pay . . . then the German secret police would hang on to Paul and his father.

"I'll do what I think I can, that's all," Lucy said. Her mother and father both nodded. If Michael made small, disgusted noises . . . Well, she didn't have to pay any attention to him. She didn't have to, and she didn't.

Paul wished he'd fled back to the home timeline when he had the chance. Maybe the two hundred dollars in his pocket had kept him from going down to the subbasement and calling for a transposition chamber. Maybe—he hoped more likely—his first thought had been rescuing Dad all by himself.

If so, it only went to show that thinking twice was a good idea. When he first came back to the building that housed Curious Notions, there weren't any *Feldgendarmerie* men or American police or men from the Tongs inside. (Perhaps the people who'd taken his father thought a kid wasn't worth bothering with. In that case, their first thoughts weren't so hot, either.)

They thought twice before Paul did. Curious Notions was shut up tight now. He couldn't get to the subbasement even if he wanted to. There'd be traps inside, just in case he was dumb enough to try.

He'd taken a room in a grimy old hotel in the Tenderloin District: a dollar a night or five dollars a week. The brick building was so rundown, he wondered if it dated from before the 1906 earthquake. But it wasn't quite that ancient. One of the bricks above the front door had a date carved into it: 1927. It was so very dirty and worn, he needed several days to notice it.

The room itself had seen endless coats of paint. The last one, a sad beige, had been a long time before. It was faded and peeling and filthy. The room had a sink and toilet and tub, a tiny table with two chairs, and a hot plate for cooking. The smell of cheap grease had soaked into the paint. A lot of people on the way down who hadn't quite hit bottom yet had lived here. That fit Paul to a T right now.

There was no thermostat on the wall. Heat came from a cast-iron steam radiator in a corner. It bubbled and clunked and, every once in a while, dripped a little rusty water on the cheap green carpet. The size of the rust stain there said it had been doing that for a long time.

Several locks and dead bolts did their best to make sure the door stayed closed and intruders stayed out. When the desk clerk handed Paul half a dozen keys, he'd eyed them in dismay. What dismayed him even more was that they might not be enough. You didn't use hardware like that where it wasn't needed.

After he got a good look at some of the people who lived in the hotel, he wished the door had twice as many locks on it. If they weren't the people his parents had warned him about, he'd never seen anybody who was. He didn't want to think about what they did for a living. More than a few of them didn't do anything visible for a living. They seemed proud of doing nothing, too.

And they figured Paul was in the same boat they were. He didn't do anything visible, either. If anything, that won him respect in the Tenderloin. A ferret-faced little man with a scar on one cheek grinned as they passed each other on the stairs in the middle of the morning. "Beats working, don't it?" he said.

"Uh-huh," Paul answered with a silly nod. He knew he should have said, *Yeah,* out of the side of his mouth. But the man with the scar just nodded back and kept going up the stairs.

In this alternate, German college students still dueled with sabers. They got scars like that. Students at a few American colleges imitated the Germans. Paul would have bet a thousand benjamins against a dollar that this fellow hadn't been anywhere close to a college, except maybe to break into a dorm. He'd probably got his scar in a real knife fight. Paul wondered what had happened to the man he'd been fighting. Better not to know, maybe.

Getting away from the hotel and back to his neighborhood was a relief. Curious Notions wasn't in the best part of town, either. Compared to where he was staying now, though, it looked like paradise.

He ducked into Louie's, the hamburger and frankfurter place where he'd bought a lot of lunches. There was no McDonald's or Burger King or Jack in the Box in this alternate. All the hamburger joints and frankfurter stands and pizza parlors here were mom-and-pops. Behind the counter at Louie's stood . . . Louie. He was a Greek with slicked-back hair under a white cap that looked like the one Boy Scouts wore in the home timeline.

He did a double take when Paul walked in. Nobody else was in the little restaurant. It got busy at lunch and dinner. In between times, no. "What are you doin' here, kid?" Louie rasped in a voice rough from too many cigarettes. "You outa your mind or somethin'?"

"I'm trying to find out about Dad," Paul said.

"You'll find out, all right," the cook said. "You'll keep him company in the calaboose, that's how you'll find out. *Feldgendarmerie* wants you bad, sonny. You're hotter'n a two-dollar pistol on Saturday night." He swiped a wet rag across the counter.

"It *was* the Germans who got him, then?" Paul asked.

"Who did you expect? Santa Claus and the elves?" Louie lit another Camel. Paul tried not to flinch. Smoking in restaurants had been illegal for a hundred years in the home timeline. Smoking itself wasn't illegal there, but people who smoked did it in the privacy of their own homes. Smoking in public was as nasty as picking your nose in public. Paul had never seen Louie do that. But he smoked like a chimney.

Paul said, "I don't know. I wondered if the Chinese had anything to do with it."

"Oh. On account of the competition, you mean?" Louie probably had a grade-school education at best, but he was no dope. He shook his head. "Nah, wasn't them. This was *official*. Besides, they don't like the Kaiser more than they don't like your old man, you know what I mean?"

"Yeah." Paul nodded.

"But you gotta get lost," Louie said. "There's a reward out for you—two hundred and fifty bucks." That was a lot of money in this alternate. Louie went on, "Some of the clowns around here, they'd turn in their mother for a buck ninety-five."

He was probably right. Paul knew that, no matter how much he wished it weren't so. Trying to sound tough, he said, "I'll be okay."

"Yeah, sure you will. And pigs have wings." Louie waggled his eyebrows and rolled his eyes. "Go on. Get lost. No, hang on." He held up a hand, like a cop stopping traffic. This, that, and the other thing went into a paper bag. When it was bulging, he thrust it at

137

Paul. "*Now* get lost—and if the cops come around, I never seen you."

The bag held burgers, fries, and some of the honey-soaked baklava that was a labor of love at Louie's. "You're a lifesaver," Paul exclaimed. "Here, wait, though. I can pay you for this stuff."

Louie turned his back. "Like I said, I don't see you. I don't hear you, neither. And I'll tell the . . . *Feldgendarmerie* the same." Paul didn't know what the Greek word in front of *Feldgendarmerie* meant. It wasn't a compliment, though. He was sure of that.

"Thanks," he said. "I won't forget this."

"Ghosts. Who'd figure a lousy Frisco burger joint had ghosts in it?" Louie wouldn't turn around.

Paul gave up. He hurried out of Louie's place and out of the neighborhood. Nobody came after him. No policeman's whistle screeched. The bag was heavy with food. He went over to Union Square, not far away. The Victory Monument stood here, as it did in the home timeline. The breakpoint between the two worlds came after the Spanish-American War. In this alternate, that was almost the last glory the USA had won. Pigeons perched on the bronze figure representing naval power atop the tall column in the center of the square. Considering what the birds did to that figure, maybe they stood for air power.

Like so much of this San Francisco, the square looked sad and run down. The grass needed watering and mowing. The wind swirled dust and wastepaper around the base of the Victory Monument. Nobody'd painted the park benches in a long, long time. When Paul sat down on one of them, the planks creaked and shifted. He wondered if it would hold his weight, and got ready to jump in a hurry.

He gulped down one of the big, juicy hamburgers—heavy on the onions—and some fries and a chunk of baklava. By the time he got done, he felt as if he'd swallowed a bowling ball. The bag still had a lot of food in it. When Louie gave, he gave with both hands. Paul knew what he'd do for supper tonight.

He wished he knew what to do *after* supper. The closest people from the home timeline he knew of were in Germany. Getting hold of them would have been easy . . . if he could have gone into Curious Notions.

Dumb, Paul. You were really dumb. He made a fist and slammed it down on the bench. That was true, but did him no good. *How do I fix things?*

"Don't be dumb," he said. Saying it was easy. Doing it? Doing it looked anything but.

Every so often, Lucy walked by Curious Notions on the way home from work. She didn't know why. The place stayed closed. But she did think walking by was safe enough. She was just one face on the street, and she never stopped. She didn't even turn her head as she walked past. She just flicked her eyes to the right and kept on going. Plenty of people in the United States had learned that look-without-seeming-to glance. *Not* showing what you had in mind was often a good idea.

Once she happened to see somebody coming out of the place. It was neither Paul Gomes nor his father. They weren't the only ones who'd run the shop, though. Lucy paused. She pretended to think about buying a *Chronicle*. In fact, she gave the stranger a quick once-over.

She needed about three seconds to decide he was a German. *Probably a* Feldgendarmerie *man,* she thought. His denim and big belt buckle and broad-brimmed hat were what an American would have worn. The way he walked wasn't even close to American, though. He didn't slouch along the way most men did. He marched.

Lucy could almost hear the trumpets and tubas and drums behind him.

And the way he looked around . . . Americans had known for well over a hundred years that they weren't masters in their own homeland. They acted like it. They had to act like it—the ones who didn't ended up in trouble or dead. A few of those lessons went a long way, especially when the Germans weren't shy about dishing them out. This fellow looked at the world as if he owned it. For all practical purposes, he did. People on the street scrambled to get out of his way. Lucy wasn't the only one who could figure out what he was.

His cold, self-satisfied gaze fell on her. He had a face that ached for a slap, but who could deliver it? By the time he looked away, she was staring hard at the newspaper. He didn't notice that she'd been eyeing him. On down the street past her he went. That invisible, inaudible oompah band still seemed to hover behind him.

Lucy sighed. With people like that coming out of Curious Notions, Paul and his father had to be in a *Feldgendarmerie* jail. *And I do have to see Stanley Hsu.* She sighed again. She'd put if off as long as she could, and even a little longer than that. She didn't want to have anything to do with the Triads. But fair was fair. She knew what she needed to do if she wanted to be able to go on looking at herself in the mirror.

Maybe the jeweler would laugh at her. Maybe he'd ask an impossible price—she knew what she wanted wouldn't come cheap. Maybe the Triads would do their best and fail. They weren't top dogs—the Kaiser's men were. Lucy wouldn't feel ashamed if the Triads failed. They were her best hope. Trying her hardest to help the people who'd helped her was what counted.

She started up the street toward Stanley Hsu's shop. It was only a few blocks—but it felt like a long, long way. She didn't want to make a fool of herself. She shrugged. *If I do, I do, that's all*, she thought. It wouldn't be the first time. It wouldn't be the last. Everybody was a fool now and again. Acting the fool was part of living. The trick—or one trick, anyhow—was trying not to make a fool of yourself the same way twice.

"Lucy! Is that you?"

The voice came from in back of her. She whirled. "Hello!" she said. "What are you doing here? I thought you were . . . somewhere else." Blurting out his name or that she'd thought he was in jail wouldn't do. That might be the quickest way to land him there.

His face twisted. "Just dumb luck that I'm not . . . somewhere else." He understood what she meant, all right. He went on, "Happened I wasn't home when we had, uh, visitors." He came up to her. "It's good to see you. It's good to see anybody with a friendly face."

"I'm glad to see you, too," Lucy answered. "I didn't know if I would."

"Luck, like I told you," Paul said. "Ah, you ought to know that there's a price on my head. I look like a desperate criminal, don't I?"

He looked tired and worried and on edge. Lucy would have felt the same way. She asked, "What are you going to do now?"

"Try to stay out of trouble myself. Try to get Dad out," he answered. "I don't know what else I can do right now. Things at Curious Notions didn't exactly work out the way I wish they would have." He hesitated. "I was thinking about asking the Tongs for help, but I'm not sure how to go about it."

"I was going to ask them for help for you—and for your father," Lucy added hastily. "Do you want to come with me? I can put you in touch with someone who's able to say yes or no, anyhow." What else Stanley Hsu might say was an interesting question.

Paul nodded. "Would you do that? Thank you very much."

Another pause. "You don't suppose he'll turn me in for the reward, do you?"

"He doesn't need the money," Lucy said, remembering the jeweler's sharp clothes and the fancy gems he sold. Then she realized that wasn't all Paul was worrying about. Might Stanley Hsu have his own reasons for making some sort of deal with the Kaiser's men? Of course he might, and Lucy knew it.

The same knowledge showed on Paul's face. One corner of his mouth twisted up in what wasn't quite a smile. "Beggars can't be choosers, and I'm a beggar right now," he said. "Let's go."

"Are you sure?" Lucy asked. He nodded again. She liked the way he made up his mind without a lot of fuss. He didn't like what he was about to do, but he aimed to go ahead and do it.

He grunted when she opened the door to Stanley Hsu's shop. It didn't look like much on the outside. He grunted again, on a different note, when he saw the kinds of things the jeweler had on his shelves. *That's more like it,* he might have said without words.

Stanley Hsu was standing behind the counter writing something when Lucy and Paul came in. "Hello, Miss Woo," he said, polite as always. "Who is your . . . friend?" He too spoke without words, asking, *Who is this stranger you've brought here?*

"I'm Paul Gomes." Paul spoke for himself. He waited to see if his name meant anything to the jeweler.

For a moment, it didn't. Then Stanley Hsu's dark, clever eyes narrowed. "Are you?" he murmured. "How interesting. I am very pleased to meet you, sir."

"I'm not nearly sure I'm pleased to meet you," Paul said. "I suppose you know why I'm here."

Lucy shot him a warning glance. You had to be watch what you said if you wanted something from the Triads. But Stanley Hsu didn't seem offended. Maybe he made allowances because Paul wasn't Chinese. "I think I may," he answered, his voice smooth as silk. "I suppose you know everything has its price."

"Oh, yes," Paul said. "Well, my price is getting Dad out of the Germans' jail. Do that, and we may have some more things to talk about."

Stanley Hsu's nostrils flared. He'd been about to set the Triads' price for helping Paul. Plainly, he didn't like getting beaten to the punch. "You are not without gall, are you?" he said in a low voice.

Shrugging, Paul answered, "I'm doing what I have to do. If you want to talk with me later, you'll play along."

"I have other choices, you know," the jeweler remarked. "The easiest would be to let the *Feldgendarmerie* have you along with your father."

"No!" Lucy said, though she'd thought of that, too.

Paul amazed her by tipping her a wink. "Go ahead," he told Stanley Hsu. "Yeah, go right ahead. Then when the Germans pump both of us, they'll get whatever we know, and you'll be sitting out in the cold. Enjoy it."

Just for a moment, the jeweler looked as if he'd bitten down hard on a lemon. Then all expression vanished from his face. "You *do* have gall," he murmured. "We could also squeeze you ourselves, you know."

Lucy started to say *No!* again. Before the word could come out, Paul held up a hand to stop her. He smiled at Stanley Hsu. "Yes, you could," he agreed. He sounded . . . friendly. Lucy couldn't imagine how he made himself sound that way, but he did. Smiling still, he went on, "You can squeeze as hard as you want, Mr. Hsu. Squeeze hard enough, and I'll tell you all sorts of things. I'm sure of it. But how will you know which ones to believe? Simple—you won't."

"I should not care to meet you when you are as old as I am

now," Stanley Hsu said after half a minute's silence. "You would be very difficult."

Proudly, Lucy said, "He's already very difficult, and you know it."

That made the jeweler laugh out loud. "Well, what if he is? You don't want me to give him a swelled head by admitting it, do you?" He nodded to Paul with what looked like real admiration. "You certainly have an interesting way to bargain. I can think of one thing that might bring you into line."

"Oh?" Paul said. "What's that?"

"I might squeeze Miss Woo. I think you would give true answers to make sure I didn't." Stanley Hsu played the game for its own sake. Anyone who got in his way was just an obstacle. He would go on through no matter what.

He horrified Lucy. If he horrified Paul, the young man from Curious Notions didn't show it. "Come on, Lucy," he said. "This wasn't a good idea. But that's okay." He patted a pocket. "I've got a recording of Mr. Hsu saying that. Playing it in the right places ought to do us some good."

"Wait!" Stanley Hsu said. A pistol appeared in his hand as if by magic. "When I say wait, I mean it."

"No, you don't," Paul said. "Think it through. If you shoot me, you don't get any of the answers you want. If you shoot Lucy, you kill the only chance you've got of making me want to play along with you."

"You trust logic too far," Stanley Hsu said. Even so, the pistol disappeared as fast as it had appeared. The jeweler added, "You tempt me to shoot you for no better reason than to show you that you don't know it all."

"If I knew it all, I wouldn't be in this mess, and neither would my father," Paul said. "But I know enough to be worth something to you, and you can do some things I can't. If you spring Dad, we can talk. If you don't . . . well, I can talk to the Germans if I have to. I don't want to, but that's not what this is about."

Stanley Hsu gave Lucy a little bow. "You were right, Miss Woo. He is already very difficult."

"I told you so," she said. Yes, she *was* proud of her strange friend from—and maybe not from—Thirty-third Avenue.

The jeweler gave Paul Gomes a bow just like the one he'd sent Lucy's way. "I believe we have a bargain. My . . . friends will do what they can for your father. If and when they get him away from the *Feldgendarmerie*, you will speak freely about some things that interest us."

"Yes. I agree." Paul didn't look happy about the deal. What did he know that he didn't want to tell? Lucy knew she couldn't ask him. Some of the things he knew, he didn't want to tell her, either. She turned to go. Paul started to follow her.

They both stopped when Stanley Hsu coughed. "Excuse me," he said. "I do not wish to be annoying, but there is that recording you made, Mr. Gomes. I would like to have it, or to see it destroyed. Some people might, ah, misunderstand if you made it public."

"Might understand, you mean," Lucy said. Stanley Hsu's shrug was a small masterpiece.

Lucy and the jeweler both stared at Paul when he laughed. "Excuse me," Stanley Hsu said again, "but I do not see the joke." Ice could have formed on his words.

"Well, then, I'd better explain it," Paul said. "The joke is, there never was any recording. I've got the clothes on my back, and that's about it."

Stanley Hsu didn't say anything for more than a minute. He looked at Paul the way he had to look at a stone in a setting when he was trying to decide if it was a diamond or a fake. At long last, he nodded. "All right," he said. "I believe you. I don't think any-one your age has ever bluffed me before. I don't think you had bet-ter try it again, either." He sounded quietly furious—at himself, at Paul, or maybe at both of them at once.

Paul looked ready to say something snotty right back. Lucy sensed this wasn't the right time for that. Before he could let loose with whatever he had in mind, she said, "Let's go." She didn't shove him out the door, but she might as well have.

Once he was out on the sidewalk, he blinked as if he didn't quite know how he'd got there. Then, slowly—almost the way Stanley Hsu had—he nodded. "Thanks," he said. "I probably would have said something dumb. I'm trying not to do that so much." He paused. "Thanks for everything else, too."

"You're welcome," Lucy said, and then, "What are you eating?"

"Mostly burgers and hot dogs—uh, franks—and stuff," Paul answered. "I've got a room, and it's got a hot plate, but I'm not much of a cook."

"That's about what I thought. Do you want to come home for supper with me? There's always room for one more." Lucy wasn't sure her mother would agree with her, but even if she didn't, Paul would never know it. Mother would feed him till he was stuffed even if everybody in the family went hungry. Pride ran deep in her.

Paul started to nod, but then caught himself. "I'd better not. It's not because I don't want to, but it probably wouldn't be safe for you. If the Germans are still keeping an eye on your dad, and they see me show up . . . That wouldn't be good, not even a little bit."

He was right. Lucy knew it as soon as she heard what he said. "It's not fair," she said, but she also knew fair didn't have anything to do with it. It was smart. It was sensible.

"Take care of yourself, and thanks one more time," Paul said. "I'll probably see you again before too long."

"I guess you will," Lucy said. It wasn't as if they were going out. They had a bond even so. "Where are you staying now?"

"Tenderloin District." He made a face. So did Lucy. The Tenderloin made the Sunset District seem like a Sunday picnic in Golden Gate Park. Paul went on, "I don't think I'd better say just where. What you don't know, nobody can make you tell."

Did he mean the *Feldgendarmerie* or the Triads? Either way, once more he made more sense than Lucy wished he did. He had a way of making sense. She'd noticed that. Most people blathered on and on, but he came straight to the point. Not even Stanley Hsu could match him. The jeweler was just as smart, maybe smarter— Lucy wasn't sure she'd ever met anybody as smart as Stanley Hsu. But he enjoyed talking around things, talking in riddles, perhaps to show off how smart he was. Paul Gomes didn't waste time fooling around. Lucy liked that better.

"I'd better go." Paul made as if to shake her hand, then seemed to think better of it. With a quick little nod, he hurried off toward the west.

Lucy found herself wishing he hadn't thought better of it. *He's shy,* she realized in surprise. *He hides it pretty well, but he is.*

With Paul gone, there wasn't much point to standing in front of the jewelry store. She went on up into Chinatown to her crowded apartment.

Her mother greeted her with, "You're late. How come?" She explained. As she did, her mother's face got longer and longer. "All these people at Curious Notions are nothing but trouble. Nothing but trouble, I tell you."

"Not quite nothing," Lucy said. "Without them, Father might still be in jail."

"Without them, he wouldn't have gone to jail in the first place," Mother pointed out. Lucy made an unhappy face, for that was true, too. But then her mother added, "You should have brought him home to supper. Chicken stew tonight. I could have put on some extra rice to make it stretch. It's about time the rest of us meet this mysterious fellow, don't you think?"

Before Lucy answered, she gave her mother a hug. Then she said, "I did ask him, but he didn't want to come. He said it could bring more trouble down on us if the Germans were watching and saw him here."

"Oh." Mother thought that over. Her mouth tightened. When she nodded, she plainly didn't want to. "I won't tell you he's wrong. I wish I could, but I can't. Should I be glad he's doing us that kind of favor?"

"I don't know," Lucy said. "Would you be glad if he didn't?"

"No-o-o," her mother said slowly. Then she turned away, as if she didn't want Lucy to see what she was thinking. "Go set the table, will you? Supper will be ready in a few minutes."

"Yes, Mother," Lucy said—almost always a safe answer.

Paul wished he knew what was going on inside the *Feldgendarmerie* jail. How hard were the Kaiser's men squeezing Dad? What was he saying? Paul had no way to find out. The people at Curious Notions had made friends with some San Francisco cops. That often came in handy. Paul didn't want to test it now. The Americans might feel they had to turn him in to the German masters. One mistake like that would be his last.

He would have liked to stay in his hotel room all the time. But he couldn't. For one thing, he'd go stir-crazy cooped up in there with nothing to do. For another, who would do anything for his father if he stayed? Dad could be a pain in the neck sometimes—even a lot of the time. But he was family. He would do whatever he could for Paul. Paul had to do the same for him.

And besides, the sooner Dad was out, the less chance he'd spill the secret of crosstime travel. That would be very bad, not just for him, and not just for Crosstime Traffic, either. It would be bad for who could say how many different alternates.

Paul did venture out every so often, then. Whenever he did, he wished he had eyes in the back of his head till he got out of the Tenderloin District. Then, as soon as he came close to Curious Notions, he started wishing for them all over again. He wasn't just watching for cops and crooks there. Anybody who'd ever known him in this San Francisco might betray him.

He wished he dared go into the shop. Had the *Feldgendarmerie* discovered the underground room in which the transposition chamber appeared? That could be bad enough all by itself. But the Germans might still have people there waiting to scoop him up. If they didn't, they might have sensors to let them know he was there. Their best gadgets weren't as good as the ones from the home timeline, but they didn't have to be. Paul had no gadgets of his own right now.

Sighing, shaking his head, he turned the corner—and almost walked into a San Francisco policeman. "Sorry," the cop said politely, tipping his hat. He had a face like the map of Ireland. Then his green eyes narrowed. "The Gomes kid! What are you doing here? Have you lost all of your mind?"

"Hello, Andy." Paul got ready to run like the devil. Andy O'Connell's belly stuck out over his belt. He'd eaten a lot of donuts and burgers and chop suey in his years on the beat. He couldn't run any faster than a dump truck. But he had a big pistol strapped to his hip. If he pulled it out and started shooting, he didn't need to run fast.

He kept staring at Paul. "The Kaiser's bully boys want to lock you up and lose the key. You know that?" He didn't make any move for the gun, or for his handcuffs, or for Paul.

"Yeah, I know that. But I don't know why," Paul said. "I didn't do anything."

"The bulletin says 'suspicion of subversion,'" the policeman told him. "That's what the Germans say when they want somebody and don't want to talk about why. They don't even want us to know why they want you." He spat on the sidewalk to show what he thought of that.

Hope flowered in Paul. He'd always thought Andy O'Connell was a pretty decent guy. He hadn't trusted him far enough to take a chance on him, but now he didn't seem to have much choice. "Is Dad okay?" he asked. "Do you know?"

"I haven't heard that he's not, but I don't know if I would," the cop answered. "You want I should ask around a little? I can do it so it doesn't look funny."

"Would you?" Paul said eagerly. "That'd be great."

"Do my best," O'Connell said. "Meantime, you should make like a tree, and leaf. Find a hole. Jump in. Cover it up over you. The *Feldgendarmerie* wants you, sonny. They want you bad."

"Now tell me one I didn't know," Paul said.

The Irishman eyed him with real curiosity. "What the devil *did* you do?" He held up a hand before Paul could answer. "Don't tell me again you didn't do anything. Nobody every did anything, not since the world was new. I'll ask it a different way. What do the Kaiser's boys think you did? If I know that, it'll help me ask the right questions."

No doubt that was true. But anything even close to the truth would be dangerous to Paul. He said, "I can't tell you, because I don't know. All I know is, they grabbed Dad while I wasn't home." That last was the truth, but only a tiny part of it.

"Uh-*huh*." As cops will, O'Connell had developed a fine-tuned sense of what was so and what wasn't. He didn't come right out and call Paul a liar, but he didn't believe him, either. He shrugged broad shoulders. "Well, like I said, I'll see what I can do. Meantime, you get lost."

"I intend to," Paul said.

"You better," the policeman told him. "There's a reward out for you—you know that?"

Paul nodded. "Somebody told me." He didn't want to name Louie. Anybody who knew anything about him could end up in trouble because of it.

"You're lucky it wasn't somebody who turned you in instead," O'Connell said. "Believe you me, kid, you don't know how lucky you are."

"Some luck," Paul said. "If I were really lucky, the Germans wouldn't be after me." Andy O'Connell just shooed him away. He might have been saying he'd already wasted too much time on him. Paul left. He walked for several minutes before he realized he'd been as lucky with the cop as he had with the short-order cook.

Eight

Whenever Lucy went out these days, she kept looking around to see if she could spot Paul. He'd turned up a lot when she wasn't looking for him. Now that she was, she never got a glimpse of him. Things often seemed to work out like that.

She wondered if he had any clothes besides the ones he was wearing. Once she saw somebody who looked a lot like him in an orange-and-black Seals shirt. She was glad when that turned out to be a stranger. She thought of Paul as a Missions rooter, the way she was. She didn't know whether she was right. They'd never talked about it. But she would have been disappointed to find out he backed the team the rich and famous cheered for.

Work just went on from day to day. She'd learned the things she needed to know to be a good clerk. Now the job was just routine, the way her time at the sewing machine had been. Her supervisor couldn't complain. She did everything that needed doing, and did it well.

Even though she did it well, she wondered what she had to look forward to. Another fifty years of this? That was probably what she would have had if she'd stayed at the sewing machine. She hadn't thought about it so much then. She wondered why not. The work had been a lot harder.

Maybe that was part of the answer. She'd been so busy at the sewing machine, she hadn't had a chance to think about anything. This job made her think, at least some. And it had slow times when she couldn't help thinking. She almost wished it didn't. She would have had more peace of mind.

Sometimes she felt ashamed of herself for worrying. Paul was the one with things to worry about now. The Germans held his father. They seemed to have stopped caring about hers. They weren't after her. They sure were after him. She had a job. He was, she supposed, looking for one. If he wasn't, she didn't know what he'd do for money.

She also had somewhere to go home to. The *Feldgendarmerie* were keeping an eye on his home. For all she knew, the Kaiser's secret police were standing between him and whatever brighter Sunset District he came from.

Lucy snapped her fingers in annoyance. She'd meant to ask him about that the last time she saw him. The visit to Stanley Hsu's must have distracted her. She laughed, not that it was very funny. Here she'd gone all her life without having anything to do with the Triads. She'd hardly even believed in them, any more than she believed in Santa Claus or the Easter Bunny. They turned out to be real, all right. And how had she found out? Because of somebody who wasn't even Chinese. That *was* funny, in a strange sort of way.

Stanley Hsu didn't think so, though. He took this whole business as seriously as life and death. What did he think Paul could tell him? How much difference would it make to whoever in China was trying to stand up against the Germans? And what difference would *that* make to the United States?

Lucy had no idea what living in a free country was like. How could she, when she'd never done it? (For that matter, her great-grandparents hadn't, either.) She didn't think about living in a free country now, not really. She did hope that, if China somehow came out on top, it would be an easier master than Germany was. That was as far as her ambition went. She couldn't get excited about politics. She'd never had any politics to get excited about.

When she walked into the apartment, her brother bounced up and down. "You've got mail!" Michael squeaked. "You've got mail! Open it!"

"Hush," she told him. She couldn't help being a little excited herself, though. She didn't get mail all that often. The advertising mail that came to the family mostly had her parents' names on it. That kind of junk went straight into the trash, anyhow.

She didn't recognize the handwriting on the envelope or the name in the return address. But the return address itself was on Thirty-third Avenue. Lucy found herself smiling. She knew who'd sent it. Paul had to have figured she would.

The letter inside was chatty. It might have come from a tourist, not somebody who'd grown up in San Francisco. He talked about the sights he'd seen: the twistiest street in the world, the Golden Gate and Bay Bridges, the big bronze statue of Wilhelm IV in front of City Hall, and the museum and Japanese garden in Golden Gate Park.

Japanese garden came at the front of one line. *Saturday* came at the front of the next one. *At three o'clock* came at the front of the one below that. Paul hadn't used a secret code, not really. He'd just hoped Lucy would be awake and alert and figure out what was gong on. She was pretty sure she had. She was also pretty sure no *Feldgendarmerie* man could.

Paul had signed the letter with the same name he'd used on the envelope. The Germans wouldn't know who that was, either, if they'd read the letter. Paul had to believe they would. They might think he was a school friend or someone she worked with.

"Who is this guy it's from?" Michael wanted to know.

"None of your business, brat," Lucy said sweetly.

"I'm gonna tell," Michael said, and then, much louder, *"Mommy!"* But Mother backed Lucy. Her mail was her business. Mother didn't say anything about the *brat*. She didn't always seem to realize Michael was one—she was, after all, his mother, too. But he had been snooping, and so she didn't get mad at Lucy.

Saturday afternoon came around much too slowly. When Lucy first got the extra half day off, she'd thought it was the biggest luxury in the world. Now she took it for granted. Things often seemed to work out like that, too. It was a little disappointing—but having to work the whole day would have been a lot worse.

She took the Fulton Street bus to Golden Gate Park and walked to the Japanese garden. She was way early, but she didn't care. Whether she was seeing somebody or not, it was a nice place to spend an afternoon. Everything was in its place, all the plants perfectly pruned. It was beautiful. And it smelled green and growing, too. She didn't notice missing that when she was away from it, but it was very nice when she found it.

She'd just stooped to take a closer look at some ferns growing by the base of a pine tree when someone behind her said, "Hello, there."

Lucy jumped up and turned. "Hello, yourself," she managed.

Paul was smiling, but he stood too straight and moved in quick jerks. He might have been a wire stretched too tight for too long. "You're early," he said.

"I like it here," Lucy said. "Besides, so are you."

"I like it here, too." Even his smile seemed brittle, as if it might break if she tapped it too hard. "I'm glad you worked out what I was saying in the letter. I'm glad you knew it was me."

"Who else?" she answered. "I don't get a whole lot of letters, especially from people I've never heard of. I know you couldn't put your own name on it, but you didn't really need to."

"Okay," he said. "Shall we walk around and look at things?"

"Sure." They strolled the narrow, twisting paths. Most of the people who came to the garden seemed to be from out of town. Some of them were from out of the country. Several spoke German. Any American recognized the rulers' language—and recognized it as a signal to get out of the way, to make sure you weren't noticed.

Whatever Sunset District Paul came from, he reacted the way Lucy would have. He went down a path that took both of them away from those guttural consonants and flat vowels. After a while, his voice as casual as he could make it, he asked, "So—have you heard anything from Stanley?"

Lucy needed a moment to think of the jeweler by his first name. Paul was smart to talk about him that way, though. Plenty of people were called Stanley. Even so, she had to shake her head. "No," he said. "Nothing. You?"

"Also nada," he answered.

She cocked her head to one side. She could see what that had to mean, but it wasn't English—not to her, anyway. All her doubts and curiosity came flooding forward. "Where *are* you from?" she asked.

"I told you before," Paul said. "From here. From San Francisco. From the Sunset District. From Thirty-third Avenue."

"I know what you told me," Lucy said. "I believe all of those except that you're from here. You can't be from here—you just *can't*." She started talking about all the strange things Curious Notions had, and about Paul's own strangeness (especially if he was supposed to come out of the Sunset District), and about her own thoughts about how maybe there were other worlds. The longer she went on, the more foolish she felt. It all seemed so silly, to say nothing of unlikely.

That was what she thought till she turned and looked at Paul's face. He'd gone white as skimmed milk. His voice shook when he asked, "Who told you about this? Who else has heard about it?"

She'd thought of a lot of questions he might ask, but not those. "Nobody," she said. "Not from me, anyhow."

"What does that mean?" He didn't sound shaky any more. He sounded hard and dangerous. "Is *anybody* else saying that kind of thing?"

If she'd said no, what would he have done? Knocked her over the head with a rock and dragged her into the bushes? She wouldn't have been surprised. He looked so intense, he frightened her. But she answered, "The people from the Triads wonder about you, too. They don't see how you can be from here, either."

Paul went even paler. Watching him, Lucy began to realize her crazy idea might not be so crazy after all. "Oh, great. Just . . . great," he said, and she could make a pretty good guess about what he hadn't quite said. He wouldn't have got so upset if she were crazy. He needed a little while to gather himself. Once he did, he went on, "Listen, you've got to promise me something. You've *got* to, Lucy, you hear me?"

"I hear you," she said. "I'm not going to promise anything till I know what it is."

He nodded jerkily. "Okay," he said, though it seemed anything but okay to him. "You've got to promise me not to talk about this business with anybody. Anybody at all. Ever. You don't know how much trouble it could cause."

"I think maybe I do," she said.

But Paul said, "If you think so, you're wrong. Americans here thought they knew what atomic bombs could do, too. It turned out they didn't. They didn't even come close. This would be like that, too, only worse—maybe thousands of times worse."

Americans here. What other Americans were there? But as soon as Lucy asked herself the question, she saw the answer. There were Americans of whatever sort Paul was. Were there other kinds besides his? Were there . . . thousands of other kinds besides his?

Lucy looked around. The Japanese garden seemed to press in on her. She knew that wasn't real, but it *felt* real. All of a sudden, this whole world seemed nothing more than a single grain of sand on the beach. And how many other grains, almost but not quite like it, lay there on the beach beside it? Thousands? Millions? What came after millions?

Quietly, Paul asked, "Do you see?" What must her face have been showing?

"I think maybe I do," she said again, and now maybe she did, or began to. "That's . . . the biggest thing I ever tried to imagine in my whole life."

"Yeah, well, now that you've done it, try to imagine forgetting about it, okay?" Paul said. "Please? It's important. You don't know how important it is."

That was true enough. How could she know such a thing? But she said, "Maybe you ought to tell me, then. I'm stuck in the middle of this, aren't I?"

"I wish you weren't. I wish there weren't any middle to be stuck in," Paul told her. She believed that. If there weren't any middle for her to be stuck in, he wouldn't have been in trouble, either.

If. If. If. Was that how all the separate worlds were different? A different *if* in each one? She almost asked him. Seeing if he could go any paler than he was already might have been fun. She had more urgent things to worry about, though. "Well, there is a middle, and I'm in it, just like you," she said. "The real question is, how do we get out of it?"

"Good question. Real good question. I wish I had a real good answer," he said. "By now, my people will know something's wrong. But they can't do anything about it, not while the *Feldgendarmerie* is sitting in Curious Notions."

"That's where you go back and forth?" Lucy asked.

Paul nodded, then looked as if he wished he hadn't "Don't ask me stuff like that," he said. "Don't ask me *anything*. The less you know, the less they can get out of you."

Lucy wondered what sort of *they* he had in mind. The Kaiser's men? The Triads? Everybody in this whole world? The last seemed the most likely. He really was a stranger here. "You know how to get in touch with me," Lucy said. "How do I get in touch with you if I need to?"

"You shouldn't," he said. "If you find out where I'm staying, other people will, too. You're okay. Other people?" He shook his head. "You know about the kinds of other people who want to talk to me."

She did, too. She didn't care for his answer, but she saw it made sense. He had a way of doing that. She said, "I think I'd better go. There are a lot of things I need to sort out now." She wondered if she'd be able to go to sleep tonight. She didn't see how.

Her face must have given her away again. Paul laughed—not so much because he thought it was funny, she judged, but because he didn't know what else to do. "I wish you wouldn't," he said. Then he let out another laugh. "I may as well wish for the sun not to come up tomorrow, too. I can see that."

"I can't help it," Lucy said. "This is important. You told me so yourself."

"Me and my big mouth," he muttered. But then he waved her away. "Now you know what you always wanted to. I hope you're not sorry later on."

How could I be? Lucy didn't say it out loud. It was another one of those questions where she could already see the answer.

Paul sat at the edge of his lumpy mattress, staring down at the worn carpet. Every once in a while, he would shake his head. He'd just broken every rule drilled into him in Crosstime Traffic training. Somebody in this alternate knew it *was* an alternate, and he'd admitted as much.

Try as he would, though, he didn't see what else he could have done. Lucy had already figured most of it out on her own. That was bad enough. But she'd also said the guys from the Tongs weren't far behind her. She couldn't do anything about what she knew (except take it to the Germans, but she wouldn't do that). They . . . might be able to. Paul didn't know enough to be sure.

He also didn't know whether he dared visit Stanley Hsu's jewelry store again. If he showed up there, would the jeweler and his pals grab him and start trying to pull what he knew out of him? If he didn't show up there, wouldn't Stanley Hsu forget about getting his father out of jail? He was too likely to be wrong—dreadfully wrong—whether he chose to go or to stay away.

Before long, he had the problem solved for him. He was walking up O'Farrell Street when a Chinese man a couple of years older than he was fell into step beside him. "You're Mr. Gomes, aren't you?" the fellow asked in a friendly voice.

Paul hesitated. If he admitted it . . . If he denied it . . .

Whether he admitted it or denied it turned out not to matter. Three more Chinese men fell in around him. "Why don't you come along with us, Mr. Gomes?" said the one who'd spoken before. *Why don't you come along with us so we don't stomp the stuffing out of you?* hung in the air. The fellow still sounded friendly. Why wouldn't he? He held all the good cards.

Or did he? "What if I yell for a cop?" Paul said.

All four Chinese men smiled. They were four of the chilliest smiles he'd ever seen. "Go right ahead," said the one who did the talking. "Be our guest."

He needed a second and a half, tops, to decide that wasn't a good idea. If he yelled for a cop, the Chinese guys might maim him before the policeman could do a thing. Even if they didn't, the cop was liable to hang on to him and find out who he was. As soon as the cop did find out, he was very likely to turn Paul over to the *Feldgendarmerie* for the reward. Falling into the Tongs' hands might be bad. Falling into the Germans' hands *would* be bad. The difference was small, but it was real.

When he didn't yell, his—escorts?—smiled again. "I thought you had some brains," the talking one said.

"Do I?" Paul asked bitterly. The men surrounding him didn't answer. They just kept smiling. In a movie, he could have broken away or knocked all of them flat.

Here on the dirty, sadly shabby streets of San Francisco, one against four looked like bad odds. He asked, "Where are you taking me?"

"You'll see," said the man who'd asked his name. Paul wanted to kick him just for that. He would have bet it was what he'd get for an answer. Then the fellow added, "It isn't far."

"Thanks a lot," Paul said. The Chinese man grinned at him. *He knows what I'm thinking,* Paul realized. *He knows, and he's enjoying it.*

For whatever it was worth, he told the truth. The Chinese men herded Paul to a noodle shop a few blocks away. They were good at what they did. They didn't look as if they were herding him. By the way they acted, they might have been his buddies. They'd plainly had plenty of practice at their game. He wondered where they'd got it. That might have been one more thing he was better off not knowing.

161

In the shop sat Stanley Hsu and another, older, man in what passed for a sharp suit in this alternate. Stanley Hsu stood up in greeting. The older man, who had what seemed like a permanent sour look on his face, didn't. The jeweler said, "I hope you'll let us buy you lunch while we talk."

"Do I have a choice?" Paul asked.

"There are always choices," Stanley Hsu answered. Paul didn't like the sound of that. Stanley Hsu went on, "Why don't you sit down? We'll eat lunch, we'll talk, and we'll see what some of the choices are."

Paul glanced at the rugged young men who'd brought him to the noodle shop. "Is one of the choices making them disappear?"

Stanley Hsu looked to the older man. That told Paul something about who bossed whom. The older man jerked a thumb at the door. The four escorts trooped out without a backward glance. The older man pointed to a chair. Paul sat down.

Stanley Hsu's eyes went to the older man again. The fellow's frown got deeper as he thought for a moment. Then he nodded. The jeweler said, "This is Mr. Lee—Bob Lee."

"Hello," Paul said. That let him stay polite without saying he was glad to meet Bob Lee. Was the Chinese man named for the Confederate general? That would have been funny. Paul wanted to see what he could get out of the men from the Tongs. He asked, "How is my father? Do you know?"

Once more, Stanley Hsu looked toward Bob Lee. The sour look didn't leave Lee's face as he answered, "The Germans are treating him pretty well. They're treating him very well, in fact. We don't know what that means."

One thing it might mean was that Paul's father was telling the *Feldgendarmerie* men what they wanted to hear—or maybe what they needed to hear. But would he do that? Paul hoped not, anyway.

After enough . . . persuasion, anybody might say anything. You couldn't blame someone for that. Before, though? Before was a different story.

The man behind the counter brought everyone at the table big bowls of noodles piled high with shrimp and scallops and crab meat and three or four kinds of mushrooms and even more kinds of vegetables. Nobody had asked Paul if that was what he wanted, but it looked good. The man gave Stanley Hsu and Bob Lee chopsticks. He started to hand Paul a fork. "I can use chopsticks, too," Paul said.

The man blinked, but handed him a pair. Stanley Hsu and Bob Lee looked at each other. Lee rattled off a few words in Chinese. If they didn't mean, *This I gotta see,* Paul would have been amazed.

I'll show 'em, he thought. He'd been using chopsticks in Chinese and Japanese and Vietnamese restaurants since he was a little kid. He dug in. He might not have been quite so neat as the two Chinese men with him, but he had no trouble. The food disappeared. It tasted as good as it looked.

He'd got halfway down the bowl before he noticed the jeweler and the older man staring at him. That was when he realized showing he could use chopsticks might have been a mistake. "You weren't kidding," Stanley Hsu said.

Paul swallowed a mouthful. "Should I have been?"

"I don't know," the jeweler said. "I can't remember the last time I saw . . . someone who wasn't Chinese—or Japanese, I suppose—who could handle chopsticks like that."

"I never have," Bob Lee said flatly. "Never."

This was an alternate. They did things differently here. Not all the things they did differently were obvious. People who weren't Asian went to Chinese restaurants here. Paul had seen that. But evidently they ate with knife and fork when they did. Who would notice something like that . . . till it tripped him up?

"They aren't that hard to learn," Paul said.

Stanley Hsu looked down at the chopsticks in his own hand. "Maybe not," he said, but he didn't sound as if he believed it.

Bob Lee rattled off several sentences in Chinese. Stanley Hsu answered in the same language. They went back and forth for a couple of minutes, though they didn't forget their food. Finally, Bob Lee went back to English: "I think they are easy to learn, too. But I am old enough to be your father—almost old enough to be your grandfather—and I have never seen Americans or Germans take to them the way you do. You have your tools, we have ours—and not everyone in Chinatown uses chopsticks, either."

"You're Americans, too, aren't you?" Paul said.

Stanley Hsu and Bob Lee looked at each other yet again. "Yes and no," the jeweler said after a moment. "We are American, yes, but we are also something different."

"Something more," Lee added. He might have said, *Something better*. He didn't quite, but he might have.

Thoughtfully, Stanley Hsu said, "Young Mr. Gomes also seems to be something more, if not in the same way we are. The way he eats argues for that, don't you think?"

Paul wished he'd never heard of chopsticks. He would have thrown them down and gone back to the fork had he thought it would do any good. Since he thought it would only make things worse, he went on eating the way he'd started. He'd lost his appetite for the seafood, which was a shame.

"Where *are* you from, anyhow?" Stanley Hsu asked him. His tone was just like Lucy's when she'd asked him the same question.

He gave the jeweler the same answer he'd given Lucy, too: "Me? Thirty-third Avenue, in the Sunset District."

Stanley Hsu's head and Bob Lee's went back and forth in exactly the same rhythm: left, right, left, right, left. It would have got a laugh on a TV sitcom. Sitting here where they could do whatever they wanted to him, Paul didn't think they were funny at all. Lee said, "You could be from a lot of different places, Mr. Gomes. Wherever you *are* from, though, that isn't it."

"But it is," Paul said. And it was . . . in a way. "I fool around in Pine Lake Park. I just graduated from Bay High."

"Excuse me," Stanley Hsu said, and disappeared into the noodle shop's back room. Paul heard him talking on the telephone, sometimes in English, sometimes in Chinese. He came out again and sat back down. "We can check on that. If you are lying to us, you will be sorry."

"So much for enjoying my lunch," Paul said. Both Chinese men laughed. Paul didn't think that was funny, either.

He'd finished eating by the time the phone rang. The owner called Stanley Hsu into the back room once more. Again, Paul listened to him talking. The jeweler slammed the phone down. He was scowling when he returned to the table. He pointed a finger at Paul. "Your records at the high school are where they ought to be. You got very good grades."

"See?" Paul said triumphantly. "Uh, and thank you."

"Do not thank me," Stanley Hsu said. "Your picture is not in last year's annual, or the one from the year before, or from the year before that, or the year before *that.* Your name is not in any of those annuals. Records are easy to fix. We know about that." Bob Lee nodded, as if to say he knew it very well indeed. Stanley Hsu went on, "Fixing records does not make things turn true. We want the truth now, please."

Urk, Paul thought. The men from the Tongs were right. Slipping a false record into a file wasn't very hard. That probably would have been enough to keep the Germans happy. It wasn't enough for these men. They knew San Francisco better than the occupiers ever could.

"Well?" Stanley Hsu said.

"Well, what?" Paul answered. "I thought we had a bargain. Get my father out, and then we talk. You don't have any business pressing me till you take care of your half."

"You have gall. I've already seen that," the jeweler said. "How much good it will do you may be another question."

Bob Lee was blunter: "Times have changed since we made that silly bargain. We need the truth from you—no more nonsense."

"The *Feldgendarmerie* would tell me the same thing," Paul said.

Stanley Hsu looked pained. Bob Lee only shrugged. "And what would you tell the *Feldgendarmerie* if they got their hands on you?" he asked. He answered his own question: "You'd tell them whatever they wanted you to tell them, that's what."

"And how is that any different from what you want me to do?" Paul asked.

Lee didn't seem to care. He just wanted answers. How he got them, what he did to get them, didn't matter to him. Stanley Hsu saw the point Paul was making. Whether he agreed with it was probably a different story. But he did see it. He spoke in Chinese. Bob Lee answered with several crackling sentences in the same language. The jeweler said something else. Lee threw his hands in the air as he replied. *You must be out of your mind,* he was saying, or something much like that.

"You've made yourself . . . hard to find," Stanley Hsu said, in English and to Paul. "How do we know you'll keep your half of the deal? Tell us where you are staying—"

"Show us where you are staying," Bob Lee broke in. "We have already seen you can come up with lies that seem like the truth."

"Yes—show us where you are staying," Stanley Hsu agreed. "That would be better. Then the bargain will be safe."

Letting them know where he lived was the last thing Paul wanted to do. They would have a hold on him then. And he was sure they would keep an eye on him 24/7 after that. But he didn't see what choice he had. This was what he got for being alone in a world not his own.

With a sigh, he gave them the address of the cheap hotel where he was staying. They both made faces. Bob Lee said, "I wouldn't go into that part of town on a bet."

"I haven't had any trouble—except from your people," Paul said.

That didn't impress the Chinese men. Stanley Hsu spoke in Chinese to the man who ran the noodle shop. That fellow dipped his head and hurried out of the place. When he came back, he had with him the four young men who'd brought Paul there. Stanley Hsu smiled and said, "They will make sure nothing happens to you on your way back to your room."

"Right," Paul said tightly. They'd make sure he was staying where he said he was. But he was stuck. He could see that. He got to his feet and nodded to the jeweler and Bob Lee. "Thanks so much for lunch." He almost hoped they would get angry. They didn't. They just laughed.

"Let's go," said the young man who'd done all the talking. Paul went. The four of them stayed around him all the way back to that lousy hotel. He was less sorry to have them along in the Tenderloin than he would have been a lot of other places in San Francisco. People here went on and on about how bad the Sunset District was. And it *was* bad, especially compared to the same part of town in the home timeline. But a sea gull flying over the Tenderloin was liable to get its pocket picked.

If Stanley Hsu and Bob Lee were telling the truth, nothing much had happened to Dad yet. Maybe the *Feldgendarmerie* men knew what a valuable prisoner they had. Maybe they didn't want to do anything to spoil their chances of getting the answers they wanted. Paul hoped that was what was going on.

Maybe Dad was talking just enough to keep the Germans happy, and no more. Paul tried to do that with the men from the Tongs. Paul hadn't fallen off the tightrope yet, but he'd sure wobbled in the noodle shop. If they pushed him a little more . . .

He chuckled, which made his escorts give him a funny look. They didn't ask him to explain. That was a relief. He'd wobbled in the noodle shop, yes. But Lucy Woo had pushed him right off the rope and into space. She'd figured out where he had to be from. Stanley Hsu and Bob Lee had all the evidence in front of their noses—more evidence than Lucy'd had. They knew he hadn't gone to Bay High *here*. If they saw all of what that meant, though, they hadn't shown it to Paul.

He stopped in front of his hotel. "Thanks for bringing me back," he said. He wouldn't thank them for taking him away.

They all nodded. They all waited on the sidewalk while Paul trudged up the grimy concrete steps and into the lobby. In the home timeline, most hotels had doors so you could see out. The door to this place could have turned a charging tank to scrap metal. That kind of door was common in this alternate's Tenderloin.

The desk clerk looked up when Paul came in. As soon as the fellow recognized him, he went back to his book. It wasn't quite a comic book, but it had lots of gaudy pictures. The clerk's lips moved as he read. The pages didn't hold many words, but he didn't turn them very often.

OUT OF ORDER, said the sign on the elevator. It had been there a long time. Paul's lips moved when he read it anyway. He wasn't quite silent. The clerk kept his nose in his story even so. Paul went to the stairs and climbed to his room. The stairway smelled of stale tobacco and even staler food. Somebody going down passed him. They looked away from each other, as if neither wanted to admit he had to live here.

Paul carefully locked all the locks on his door after he went inside. You never could tell, not in this part of town. He walked over to the window and looked down at the sidewalk through the dirty glass. The four young Chinese men were still there. One of them looked up. Paul drew back in a hurry. He didn't want them seeing him, though he couldn't have said why. What difference did it make? They already knew where he was.

He felt almost as imprisoned as his father was. That was partly because the men from the Tongs knew he was here, but only partly. Being stuck in this alternate seemed as bad as being in jail. And he feared it might be a life sentence.

Someone from another world! Lucy had never thought that about anyone but her brother before. This was different. Michael was just a nuisance. He didn't really come from anywhere else. Lucy remembered when he was born. She'd been little then, but she remembered. Paul truly was from . . . somewhere else.

That didn't mean he wasn't a nuisance, too. Lucy's life had got very complicated since she met him. Not many of the complications were much fun, either. She had a better job now, but her father had gone to jail and might never have come out again. And she'd had to start dealing with the Triads. She remembered how she hadn't even been sure they were real. Real? They were powerful, more powerful than she'd ever dreamt. They had connections that reached all the way across the Pacific. And they had connections that reached all through San Francisco.

Lucy smiled as she chopped cabbage in the kitchen with her mother. The Triads had far-reaching connections, all right, but so did she. Theirs reached back to China, the land of (most of) her ancestors. But hers . . . hers reached farther still. Hers reached to a world where Thirty-third Avenue in the Sunset District was a nice place to grow up. How could anyone's connections stretch any farther than that?

Her mother said, "Pass the white pepper, please."

So much for distant worlds. "Here," Lucy said. "Not too much, or Michael will squawk about how spicy everything is." She would have squawked herself, up till a couple of years before. These days, she liked things a lot spicier than she had.

With a small smile, Mother said, "I really do know how much to put in, dear." She sprinkled the pepper into a pot where pork bubbled. "Now for that fine cabbage." In it went. So did two kinds of mushrooms. A smaller, covered pot with rice in it bubbled over a low flame on another burner. Lucy's mother nodded to herself. "Supper in about ten minutes."

"Okay." Lucy looked into the pot with the pork and cabbage and mushrooms. Then she noticed her mother was looking at her. Embarrassed, she asked, "What is it?"

"Nothing." Mother laughed—which only flustered Lucy worse—and then went on, "Or maybe everything. I'm watching you growing up right in front of my eyes. You're starting to do things I don't know about and think thoughts I can't follow. What *was* going through your head while you were cutting up that cabbage? Your eyes looked like they were a million miles away."

Farther than that. A lot farther than that, Lucy thought. Mother knew all kinds of things. But if Lucy tried to explain about different worlds, would she follow? Lucy didn't think so. She wouldn't have believed it herself if she hadn't had her nose rubbed in it.

Besides, Paul had asked her to keep his secret. She bit down on that as if on a piece of bone in some meat. Who was more important, Paul or Mother? It was Paul's secret, but even so . . . .

"I don't know," Lucy said. "I'm all confused."

Her mother didn't laugh now. She put an arm around Lucy's shoulder. She had to reach up to do it—Lucy was three inches taller. Mother said, "Whether you know it or not, getting confused some of the time is part of growing up, too. Things are more complicated for you than they were when you were a little girl."

Lucy found herself nodding. Mother was absolutely right about that.

Nine

Paul thought hard about disguises. He had very few clothes to work with. He'd got away from Curious Notions with only what he had on his back. Buying more ate into his cash, so he'd done as little as he could. Luckily, San Francisco's mild climate meant he didn't have to have a lot of different kinds of clothes. Everything could be about the same, and he could mix and match.

He thought about growing a mustache like his father's, but decided it would take too long. He thought about buying a false mustache or a blond wig. The one, though, might not change his looks enough. As for the other . . . He didn't see how he could look like anything but a brunet wearing a blond wig.

If he went out as himself, the men from the Tongs were going to follow him. Since he couldn't do anything about that, he resigned himself to it. He even tried to make it work for him. He stayed in the shabby little room as much as he could stand. When he went out, he went to the most boring places he could find: to the laundry, to a little café around the corner, or to the newsstand to buy a paper. Then he'd head back to his room.

This San Francisco had buses, but it didn't have the BART subway lines. He couldn't disappear into a hole in the ground and lose people like that. All he could hope to do was lull them into thinking he was the dullest person in the world, somebody they could follow if they were half asleep.

He still had enough money to leave town. If this were his world, he would have done it if he saw the chance. As things were, he couldn't. He couldn't leave his father, and he couldn't get too far from Curious Notions. Down below the shop was the only way he could get back to the home timeline.

What were they thinking there? When shipments and messages stopped, they'd figure out that something had gone wrong . . . wouldn't they? But if they did, would they try to send somebody to this alternate to find out what? They might. If they did, though, they were liable to walk right into the *Feldgendarmerie*'s hands.

However much Paul wanted to, he didn't see what he could do about that. He did try to get free of his followers one foggy morning. He went into that café around the corner—he often ate breakfast there. This time, though, he took off his denim jacket, put on a cloth cap he'd stuffed into his pocket, and left without ordering anything.

He kept his head down, walked with a limp, and muttered to himself in what he hoped sounded like an old man's voice. Maybe all that confused the men from the Tongs. Maybe the fog had more to do with it. Whatever it was, it worked. As soon as he rounded the corner, he sped up. He went left and right at random for several blocks. Every so often, he would pause in a doorway to see if he'd shaken off his followers. When he didn't see anyone, he'd move on.

There he was, on his own. The fog lifted. The sun came out. It turned clear and crisp and lovely, the kind of weather only San Francisco can have—and that San Francisco can have any month of the year. Everything was perfect. Well, almost everything.

He realized he had no idea what to do next.

He couldn't break Dad out of jail singlehanded. If he owned

any brains, he wouldn't get anywhere near the jail. The Tongs and the Germans would both be watching it. He thought about going to see Stanley Hsu. The jeweler could tell him what was going on. He thought about it . . . and then shook his head. Here he was, free, and he wanted to go tell the man from the Tongs that he'd shaken his followers? How stupid was that? Stupid enough, for sure.

Then he thought about going to see Lucy. He laughed at himself. He really was dumb this morning. She'd be working. She liked being a clerk better than running a sewing machine. It paid better, too—not well, but better. Even so, it didn't seem right that somebody younger than he was should be working a fifty-five-hour week at a dead-end job.

Nothing about the United States in this alternate seemed right. The country wasn't free. Nobody except the handful of rich people could hope for a decent education—and they had to suck up to the Germans. There was no chance of anything better. Back in an old book he'd read in school, somebody'd called tyranny a boot in the face of mankind forever. The home timeline was lucky. It hadn't worked out like that there. The home timeline had its troubles, but most people were free. Here . . . Here was the boot heel, right in the kisser.

Something else that didn't seem right was leaving somebody as smart and as nice as Lucy Woo stuck in a miserable place like this. Because of what she'd figured out, she was a security risk for the home timeline. But if he ever got the chance, he wanted to show her a Sunset District where even the stray dogs didn't have to look over their shoulders every few minutes.

He walked along for half a block. Then he stopped, kicking at the bumpy, uneven concrete of the sidewalk. He was thinking about what he wanted, not about what Lucy would want. This was her home. Her family was here. Taking her away would be kidnapping, even if it were possible. And she couldn't go for just a visit. That would be—what did Shakespeare call it?—the most unkindest cut of all. She'd know things could be better, and she wouldn't be able to tell anybody. What could be more unfair to her?

And she'd know the whole crosstime secret, not just most of it. That wouldn't do, either.

Could things get better here? Could the United States be free again, after close to a century and a half of getting its nose rubbed in the dirt? Could the Chinese help? *Would* they help, or would they just want to be top dogs instead of the Germans? Those were all good questions. Paul had answers to none of them.

He wondered what Lucy thought. Everything kept coming back to her. That was . . . interesting. He hadn't realized she'd got so far under his skin. He'd never kissed her, never even held her hand. She wasn't under his skin like that, exactly. But he liked her. More than that, he admired her. She had problems bigger than any he'd ever imagined—till now, anyhow. She didn't even know how big some of them were, because they were the problems of this whole alternate. No matter how big and how tough they were, she carried on. She didn't complain or make a fuss. She just did what she needed to do. He admired that, too.

What about me? Paul wondered. *What do I need to do? How do I need to do it?* Lucy seemed to know without even thinking about it. Paul had an idea of what he needed to do: get Dad out of jail and get back to the home timeline. How? That was a different question.

He also didn't know what he ought to do now that he could do it without leaving the Tongs any the wiser. He realized he should have thought that out before escaping his followers. Now he was all dressed up with no place to go. And if he had to get free of them again, it wouldn't be so easy. They'd know he could, so they'd keep a tighter watch on him.

Maybe I ought to go back. Maybe I ought to pretend I didn't know they weren't keeping an eye on me. Paul shook his head. He couldn't stand that. He *had* managed to get away. Not doing something with his new-found freedom seemed a criminal waste.

Casually, his hands in his pockets, he ambled in the direction of Curious Notions. Who could say what might turn up? If he didn't go and take a look around, he'd never find out.

"Lucy, where is Frances Klingerman's personnel folder?" Mrs. Cho asked.

"Isn't it in the maternity file?" Lucy asked. The sewing-machine operator had had a baby boy a week earlier.

"Oh," Mrs. Cho said. "Let me check there." She did, and then nodded. "Yes, I have it. Thank you."

"You're welcome," Lucy said. She made a face behind her supervisor's back. Mrs. Cho knew everything there was to know about the shoe factory's paperwork. She understood company policy and rules and regulations in a way Lucy wouldn't for years and years. Most of the time, she knew where all the folders were, and which papers lurked in each one.

But she didn't know Frances Klingerman had had a baby. She didn't have the faintest idea who Frances Klingerman was. To her, the woman was jut a name on a label on a manila folder. Lucy had worked a few machines away from the new mother. She knew her husband stayed out at night in saloons, and sometimes came home drunk and mean. She knew how the little girl the Klingermans already had was starting to lose her baby teeth. She knew Frances liked to eat sandwiches with really smelly cheese in them for lunch.

Frances Klingerman was a person to her. The woman was nothing but her folder to Mrs. Cho. That seemed wrong to Lucy. What seemed even wronger was that Mrs. Cho could fire Frances Klinger-man or demote her or cut her pay without ever finding out who she was.

Then, all of a sudden, Lucy shivered. If she stayed in the person-nel office till she was as old as her supervisor, wouldn't she learn all the ropes? Wouldn't she find out everything there was to know about policies and rules and regulations? Wouldn't she stop thinking about the people who actually made the shoes—stop thinking of them *as* people? Wouldn't they just turn into . . . folders for her? Wouldn't she turn into Mrs. Cho?

She'd never had a scarier thought.

What can I do about it? How can I help it? Like a trapped ani-mal, she looked around the office. Where was the way out? How could she help becoming what her supervisor already was?

Did they have offices like this in the world Paul came from? If they'd figured out how to make the Sunset District a nice place, wouldn't they also know how to turn work into something people could stand or even enjoy? She sighed. They sure hadn't done that here.

Enjoy it or not, she kept going till the end of the day. Every time she took care of something without even thinking about it, she worried. *Am I turning into Mrs. Cho?* She hoped not. She wouldn't have had to wonder about anything like that if she'd stayed at her sewing machine. Nothing could have made her turn into somebody like Hank Simmons.

She felt even more tired than usual when she started for home. Putting one foot in front of the other took work. But she kept going. She wondered how Paul was doing. Next to the worries he had, hers were small potatoes.

Thinking about Paul also made her think about Curious No-tions. She wondered if *Feldgendarmerie* men still lurked inside.

She also wondered if the Triads had come by to grab whatever they could. How much would the Germans have left? Was there stuff inside the Germans didn't know about? Was it stuff Paul might have told the Triads about?

It won't hurt to take a look, Lucy told herself. *Nobody will pay any attention to me if I just walk by. I'm only another face. For that matter, I'm only another Chinese face. The* Feldgendarmerie *will think I look like every other Chinese girl in San Francisco.*

Talking yourself into doing something dangerous and foolish could be amazingly easy. Lucy didn't worry about that till later—which only went to show how easy it was.

Almost before she knew it, she was walking up the street toward Curious Notions. Paul would have told her she was dumb. Her father would have told her she was dumb. Even Michael would have told her she was dumb. She didn't want to think about what her mother would have told her. She walked up the street anyhow.

And she turned out not to be the only one drawn like a moth to the flame. Paul stood across the street from Curious Notions, leaning against a telephone pole. He seemed casual enough, till she saw his face. He eyed the shop he and his father had run the way a hungry dog eyed at a steak.

He eyed Curious Notions—and didn't even notice the two big, beefy cops sneaking up behind him. The cops looked like something out of a bad movie. They were so obvious, people should have been pointing at them or running away from them. And people were.

Everybody except Paul, whose attention was elsewhere.

"Look out!" Lucy yelled. "They're after you!"

Paul jumped a foot in the air. When he came down, he took off as if he had wings on his shoes.

"Stop!" one of the policemen yelled.

"Stop in the name of the law!" the other one added. They both pounded after him. They didn't draw their guns. Lucy thought that was interesting. They wanted him, all right, but they wanted him alive.

She put her head down and kept walking. The policemen hadn't noticed who she was. They'd been watching Paul as hard as he'd been watching Curious Notions. They had no idea who'd shouted the warning.

One of them blew a whistle—*Tweeeeet!* The long, shrill blast of sound did nothing to slow Paul down. The cop blew again anyway—*Tweeeeet!* Paul scooted around a corner. Big black shoes thumping on the pavement, the policemen gave chase. He was speedier than Lucy had thought he would be. The two cops weren't going to catch him unless he fell down and sprained his ankle—or unless they started shooting.

Before long, Lucy heard sirens. More policemen were coming. She hoped Paul would get away. She couldn't do anything more for him right now. It was only luck that she'd been able to do what she had. She walked faster. Some helpful soul was liable to tell the cops what the girl who'd shouted out that warning looked like. Better if she wasn't there when that happened.

When she got back to the apartment, she told her mother what she'd done. That turned out to be a mistake. Lucy should have seen it coming, but she hadn't. "That boy has caused nothing but trouble," Mother said. "You shouldn't have anything to do with him."

"I don't have anything to do with him, not like that," Lucy said.

"A good thing, too." Mother pointed to a big pile of shrimp on the counter. "You can peel those out of their shells."

"Okay." Lucy didn't want to quarrel about Paul. And, while peeling shrimp was work, eating shrimp was pure pleasure. She pointed to them, too. "Where did they come from? They're always so expensive."

"Your father did some work for Charlie Antonelli, the shrimper up at Fisherman's Wharf. Mr. Antonelli paid him back with shrimp instead of money."

"Father should work for him more often," Lucy said, and her mother laughed. Maybe she wasn't going to nag about Paul. Lucy hoped not, anyway.

Mother had boiled the shrimp. They were a lovely white and orangeish pink, not the greenish color they had when they were fresh. Most of the shell, along with their little legs, came off easily. Lucy used her fingernail to take out the black vein along each shrimp's back. She got meat under it, but she didn't care.

The tail was separate. Sometimes you could peel that off, too, and leave the meat on the shrimp. Sometimes the tail broke off, with the little bit of meat still inside. Lucy would crack the tails with her fingers and get the extra meat out. When she did, she'd pop it into her mouth. That was the bonus the person who peeled the shrimp got.

Michael came into the kitchen when the job was almost done. "Can I help?" he asked.

"Mother told *me* to do it," Lucy said, and she ate the meat out of another shrimp tail right in front of his nose.

"Mommy!" Michael said—the magic word.

"Let him have a few to do, Lucy," Mother said. Michael looked so smug, Lucy wanted to drop a shrimp down the back of his shirt. If Mother hadn't been standing there watching, she might have done it. But then who could guess what her little brother would do to her to get even?

Michael didn't just eat the meat out of the tails. He ate a couple of whole shrimp, which was cheating. When Lucy told on him—and she did—Mother only wagged a finger at him. She had an indulgent little smile on her face. Michael could get away with stuff where

Lucy couldn't because he was a boy. It wasn't fair, which didn't mean it wasn't true.

Supper was wonderful. They all had as much shrimp as they wanted. "Hooray for Mr. Antonelli!" Lucy said. Not even Michael argued with that. Lucy asked her father, "What did you do for him?"

"I put a radio direction-finder in his boat," Father answered. "I hate to say it, but it's a lot better than an ordinary compass."

"Why do you hate to say it?" Michael asked.

"Because Chinese people invented the compass, a long time ago," Father said. He made a sour face. "The direction-finder is a German gadget. It's a good one, though. It does just what it's supposed to do."

"How did you get hold of a German gadget to put on Mr. Antonelli's boat?" Lucy asked. Michael looked angry, maybe because she'd beaten him to the question.

"Well, sometimes you get to know people who will sell you things if the price is right, and who won't ask a lot of questions about what you want to do with them." Father winked. "The Germans are just like any other people. Some of them will do things like that. For this, though, it would have been too expensive. Getting my hands on the drawings was more complicated, but a lot cheaper. Then I made it myself. All the parts are right off the shelf. That's one of the things I like about it."

"Wow," Lucy said.

Father only shrugged. He was a modest man. If he'd been less modest, he might have had more money. "It's not that hard," he said. "Anything ordinary people use, I can deal with and not have too much trouble." He cocked his head to one side. "That was what drove me crazy about your friends from Curious Notions. Some of the things they had . . . Well, they worked. I saw them work. I'm still not always sure about how or why, but they did."

I know why they were strange. I know why they were different. Lucy wanted to tell her father. She wanted to, but she didn't. Letting him know would make him happy—if he believed her and didn't think she'd gone crazy. But letting him know could endanger Paul. The *Feldgendarmerie* had already grabbed Father once. They might come back. They might not just throw him in jail this time, either.

Lucy didn't like keeping secrets from her family. She wasn't keeping Paul's secret only from her family, though. She was keeping it from the whole world.

One of the things Paul had learned in Crosstime Traffic training was to act as normal as he could. That wasn't always easy, but it was good advice. As soon as he got away from the first two San Francisco policemen, he stopped running. People stared at someone dashing down the sidewalk. They remembered him. Some of them would give him away if the cops came by a little later on.

But somebody sauntering along the street without a care in the world . . . Who noticed somebody like that? He might be on his way home from work, or off to visit a friend, or maybe just heading to the grocery store around the corner. Whatever he was doing, there were hundreds more just like him.

A police car drove up the street past Paul. Its red dome lights spun and blinked. Its bell clanged. The cops inside had to be on the lookout for him, and for nobody but him. They didn't give him a second glance. The car shot past and was gone.

For once, coming into the Tenderloin was a relief. Policemen who came here had more criminals than him to worry about. He wouldn't even have minded running into the young men from the Tongs. *They* wouldn't give him to the *Feldgendarmerie*.

What they might do to him themselves was an interesting question. They couldn't be happy with him for giving them the slip. He might have made a good-sized mistake of several different flavors by showing he could get away.

But he didn't see any of his watchers when he got to the cheap hotel where he was staying. Had they fanned out all over San Francisco looking for him? If they had, they wouldn't be very happy to find out he'd returned right under their noses. No, he probably hadn't been very smart to show what he could do. He couldn't stand being watched all the time, though.

Too late to worry about it now. He went up the worn, grimy steps and into the worn, grimy lobby. The desk clerk sent him an incurious glance, then went back to his picture-filled story.

Paul clumped up the stairs to his room. The elevator, he was convinced, would never be repaired. And when were the walls of the stairway last painted? They were a very peculiar color, halfway between dirt and fog. It was a color that had given up on itself a long time ago.

The carpet in the hallway wasn't as old as that sad, sorry paint, but Paul would have bet it was older than he was. The locks and dead bolts on his door, on the other hand, were shiny new. He took out his assortment of keys and worked them one by one. At last, with all of them unlocked, he turned the knob and went into his room. He let out a sigh of relief. This wasn't much of a home. Such as it was, it was his castle.

Bob Lee sat on the edge of the bed.

Paul's jaw dropped. "What are you doing here?" he demanded. "How did you get in?" He still had the key ring in his hand. It felt useless for anything except perhaps throwing at the intruder.

"Gomes, you are a lot of trouble," Lee said.

That didn't answer either of Paul's questions. Paul got the idea the Chinese man wasn't going to tell him anything more, either. "Get out," he said. "Get out or I'll . . ."

Lee laughed in his face. "You'll what? Call the police? Go ahead. I'll give you a nickel for the phone. Throw me out? You can try." A small automatic pistol appeared in his right hand. One second, it wasn't there. The next, it was. The man from the Tongs looked as if he knew what to do with it.

As steadily as he could, Paul said, "Shoot me and you'll never find out any of the answers you want."

"Not from you, maybe." Bob Lee shrugged. "I know where someone else who's got them is stashed." He had a smile only a reptile could love. But the pistol vanished as fast as it had appeared. "You have some explaining to do. How did you get away from my . . . associates? They said you must have used some of your special tricks, because they were watching you all the time."

Now Paul laughed. Bob Lee's eyebrows rose a millimeter or two. Paul said, "If I had as many special tricks as you think I do, would I be in the mess I'm in?"

"Who knows?" Lee's voice was hard and flat. "Anyone can have things go wrong—anyone at all. Now answer my question. How did you get away?"

Paul thought about jumping him. Then he thought better of it. He said, "No special tricks, not like you mean," and told what he'd done at the café.

The man from the Tongs studied him. At last, Lee gave a reluctant nod. "Okay. I believe you. I think you caught them napping. I don't think you'll catch them napping again. You'd better not, or I'll have some new associates." He didn't say what would happen to the ones who'd been watching Paul. Paul didn't think they would just get a lecture.

He said, "What are you going to do with what you get from my dad and me? I can tell you, it won't be as much as you think it is. We don't work miracles."

"Close enough," Bob Lee said. "Some of the things you were selling . . ." He eyed Paul like an eagle eyeing a rabbit. After a moment, he went on, "What will we do? Some people have been in the driver's seat here for a long time. Now, maybe it's the turn of some other people." He didn't quite point a thumb at his own chest, but he might as well have.

"How will you be better than the Germans?" Paul asked. "*Will* you be better than the Germans?"

For a split second, naked surprise showed on Lee's face. Plainly, being better than the Germans had never occurred to him. It probably hadn't occurred to anyone else in the San Francisco Tongs or back in China, either. All they thought about was being on top. Paul wasn't surprised. He couldn't say he wasn't disappointed.

At last, Lee answered, "We won't be the Kaiser. We won't be the *Feldgendarmerie*. Is that enough?"

"What do I know? I'm just the goose with the golden eggs, remember?"

Lee's laugh was anything but amused. "Some goose."

"Have it your way." Paul shrugged. "Looks like you will anyhow. But if you put the Emperor of China where the Kaiser used to sit and the men from the Tongs move into the *Feldgendarmerie* offices, what's really changed? Why should anybody who isn't part of your gang even care whether you win or lose?"

Would Bob Lee even understand what he was talking about? A lot of people who made revolutions made them for their own sake and thought no more about it. Lee, meanwhile, studied him again, this time with a different kind of surprise.

"You think about these things, don't you?" Lee said.

"I hope so," Paul answered. "Do you?"

"I also hope so," the older man said. "I know this, though: whatever I think doesn't matter till we overthrow the Germans. If we don't do that, if we can't do that, nothing else matters. Nothing at all."

Paul would have liked to tell him he was wrong. He would have liked to, but he couldn't. He said, "I'll tell you what matters to me. Getting my father out of jail matters to me, that's what."

Lee rose. "I think maybe we have to do that. If he talks to the Germans and you talk to us, nobody is better off. So all right, we take care of it."

He walked out of the room with no more good-bye than that. He wouldn't be trying to free Paul's father as a favor now. He'd be doing it because he saw an advantage for himself in the doing. That meant he was much likelier to get the job done.

Lucy kept walking past Curious Notions every so often. No one in that neighborhood knew who she was. She strolled right by San Francisco policemen and *Feldgendarmerie* officers. Neither Americans nor Germans gave her any special notice. Why should they have? Whoever she was, she obviously wasn't Paul Gomes.

Sometimes the *Feldgendarmerie* men had their big Alsatians with them. The dogs took no notice of Lucy, either. She was glad of that. They were even meaner than most of the Germans who led them.

Little by little, the Germans and their American stooges began to pay less attention to Curious Notions. Or maybe they just paid less obvious attention to the store. All Lucy knew was that she saw them less often. No, she knew one other thing, too: she didn't miss them a bit.

She'd just walked past a *Feldgendarmerie* sergeant with an Alsatian when the dog began to bark. The noise sounded like ripping canvas. Lucy jumped. When she turned around, the sergeant was tugging on the leash for all he was worth. "*Nein,* Fritz!" he shouted. "*Nein!*"

Fritz wasn't interested in Lucy. He was trying to get a marmalade cat. And the cat seemed ready for him. Its ears were flat against its skull, its back arched, the fur on its tail puffed out till it looked like a bottle brush. Its green eyes blazed. A snarl showed off needle teeth. That the Alsatian would have made a mouthful of it seemed to bother it not a bit. It would go down swinging.

"Fritz!" the *Feldgendarmerie* man yelled again. He gave the leash a yank that must have almost choked the Alsatian. With a last growl and then a yelp, the dog came. The sergeant tipped his cap to Lucy. In accented English, he said, "Sorry if he scare you, miss. Dogs and cats, *ja?*"

"Dogs and cats," Lucy agreed. She liked cats better herself. The sergeant led the dog away. Lucy knelt by the red tabby. She didn't hold her hand out. The cat had been ready to fight. It might bite or claw her. She just waited to see what it would do next.

It eyed her. When she didn't do anything, it started licking a paw and using the wet fur to wash its face. Then it washed its side for a while, and then started nibbling at the tufts of hair between its back toes. It also gnawed at one of its hind claws. She could hear the noise of its teeth. It sounded like a man biting his nails.

After the cat finished taking care of its person, it looked up. It seemed mildly surprised to find Lucy still there. Now she did stretch out her hand towards it. She was ready to snatch it back as fast as she could. But the marmalade cat leaned forward till it seemed about to topple over. It didn't, of course. It sniffed her fingers, then rubbed the side of its head against her hand and started to purr.

"Hello!" Lucy said softly. "Hello!" She scratched behind its ears and stroked its nose. It purred louder. After a minute or so, though, it shook its head till its ears rattled. Then it trotted off, tail held high, as if it had just remembered it was late for dinner with a friend. It didn't look back once.

Lucy wished she could go where she pleased when she pleased. She wished she could make friends and forget about them, both in the blink of an eye. She wished she were a cat, in other words. She wasn't, and she couldn't do any of those things. She could only wish.

When she got home, she went into the kitchen to help Mother with supper, the way she usually did. Instead of handing her a knife or a spoon or an eggbeater, Mother said, "There's something in the mail for you."

"Is there?" Lucy said—that was always a small event, a break from routine. "Who's it from?"

"I don't know. No return address." Her mother paused and then added, "Whoever it is, he has very nice handwriting."

"Oh." That disappointed Lucy, though she tried not to show it. She'd hoped the mail came from Paul, and his handwriting was pretty ordinary. You could read it, but you couldn't say it was anything special.

The envelope sat on the dining-room table. The handwriting *was* nice. It was so neat, it was almost elegant. The paper was much finer than what she usually saw, too. She thought she knew who'd sent the note even before she opened it. And she turned out to be right.

If I could have the pleasure of your company at seven o'clock on the evening of the seventeenth, I would greatly appreciate it. Under the single sentence, Stanley Hsu had signed his name with a fancy flourish. The seventeenth was . . . day after tomorrow. The jeweler had made sure the invitation would get to her on time.

She stuck it in her purse. She didn't want Michael finding it and reading it. She didn't know what sort of rude, nasty thing he would say, but she was sure he'd come up with something.

"Well?" Mother asked when she went back into the kitchen.

"It's from Mr. Hsu," Lucy answered. She wished for one more thing—that she had nothing to do with the Triads. She was no more likely to get that wish than to turn into a cat. "He wants to see me night after next."

"Does he say what it's about?" Mother asked. Lucy shook her head. Mother said, "You've got to go."

"Yes, I know." Lucy sighed. "I wish I didn't."

"You can't help it," her mother said. "He's being polite about things, but that can change." She snapped her fingers. "It can change like *that*. You don't want it to change. Believe me—you don't."

Lucy sighed again. "I believe you. I'll go." She reached for a knife and started chopping up vegetables. Mother set a wok on the stove and put a little—just a little—oil in it. The vegetables and a bit of leftover chicken would go onto rice for supper.

Lucy liked the wait before she saw Stanley Hsu about as much as she liked waiting before the dentist called her in. Her teeth were good. She'd had only two cavities. But getting them fixed hadn't been any fun at all.

Work was slow. That gave her more time to think, and to wonder, and to worry. She would almost sooner have been back at her sewing machine. But no sooner had she thought that than she heard Hank Simmons bellowing at somebody. Maybe he had reason to bellow, maybe he didn't. He always did it, though, whether he had reason to or not. All of a sudden, being right where she was didn't seem so bad.

The evening of the seventeenth was cool and foggy. Car horns were everywhere, warning people—and threatening them, too. Lucy stepped off corners very carefully. Twice she came close to getting run over anyhow.

Because of the fog, she almost walked past the jewelry shop, too. She stopped two paces past it, feeling foolish. She would rather have kept on walking. Maybe her feet were trying to tell her something. Whether they were or not, though, she couldn't afford to listen to them. She opened the door. The bell above it rang.

"Good evening, Miss Woo," Stanley Hsu said from behind the counter. "And how are you today?"

"I'm all right," Lucy answered, "or I will be when I find out what you want from me." She knew she was supposed to be polite to the jeweler. He was an important man with even more important connections. But it wasn't easy.

His smile said he didn't even notice her rudeness. No—it said he noticed, but he was too nice a fellow to care. That kind of smile was almost always a lie. He said, "I have someone here I would like you to meet. Excuse me for one moment." He ducked into the back room.

When he came out again, Paul Gomes' father came out behind him. Seeing a smile so much like Paul's come out from behind that big mustache was a jolt. "Good to see you again, Miss Woo," Lawrence Gomes said. "Good to see anybody but *Feldgendarmerie* men again—you'd better believe it is."

"It's great to see you free," Lucy said. "Does Paul know you're out yet?"

Paul's father glanced toward Stanley Hsu. Now the jeweler

looked faintly embarrassed. "There is one slight problem with that. We hoped you might be able to help us, Miss Woo."

"What is it?" Lucy asked.

"Paul . . . seems to be missing. We don't know where he is. Do you, by any chance?"

Helplessly, Lucy shook her head. "No."

Ten

Paul's escorts started sticking to him like glue. Whenever he came out of the lobby of his miserable hotel, they walked up to him as if they were old friends. Once, just once, he tried going out the back way, the way the trash went out. Two of them were waiting for him in the alley. They didn't seem surprised to see him. He wasn't very surprised to see them. He walked down the rubbish-strewn alley as if it were the street. They tagged along.

When they got to the sidewalk, the rest of the young men from the Tongs fell in with them. The one who did most of the talking for them said, "Your old man's just about sprung, I hear."

"Good." Paul tried not to get too excited at the news—or at any news he just heard. Seeing was believing. Until he saw, he wasn't going to start jumping up and down. It was too easy for people to lie to him to get him to do what they wanted.

For that matter, even after his father got out of jail—if he did— their troubles weren't over. How were they going to get back into Curious Notions? How were they going to get back to the home timeline? How were they going to keep the Chinese and the Germans from figuring out at least the basics of the crosstime secret?

Good questions were so much easier to find than good answers. He'd noticed that before.

A San Francisco policeman walked by on the other side of the street. He was swinging his nightstick by the leather thong and whistling at the same time. He paid no attention to Paul—he was too busy showing off and having a good time.

"Dumb flatfoot," one of Paul's escorts said.

"Would you rather run into a smart one?" Paul asked.

The young Chinese man didn't bother to answer, not in words. By the way he threw back his shoulders and stuck out his chin, he didn't think there were any smart San Francisco cops. Paul's guess was that he was wrong. Paul also guessed his escort wouldn't listen if he pointed that out. One of these days, the fellow from the Tongs would probably find out the hard way.

"Find out the hard way," Paul muttered. He'd found out too many things about this alternate like that. How many more would he have to bang his nose into before he got back to the home time-line? That led straight back to the even more basic question he'd asked himself before—*would* he get back to the home timeline?

Up the street toward him came a middle-aged Asian man who reminded him of Bob Lee. It was dislike at first sight, as far as he was concerned. The man strode along as if he owned the sidewalk. He didn't get out of the way for Paul's escorts, and they didn't get out of the way for him.

That was liable to mean trouble. Such faceoffs could end up as badly here as in the home timeline or almost any other world. That Asian man was asking for a trip to the hospital if he thought he could take on so many by himself.

Then, just before he would have bumped into Paul and his escorts, the man spat out a sentence in harsh Chinese. The young men around Paul stopped as if they'd run into a brick wall. Paul took one more step forward, and found himself out in front of the pack.

The man pointed to him. "You," he said in tones that put Paul's back up right away. "You come along with me."

"What? Why?" Paul yelped.

"Triad business, that's why." The man added another sentence in Chinese. Paul understood not a word of it, but it kept his escorts frozen in their tracks.

Hesitantly, the one who did most of the talking for them said, "But we haven't seen you around here before, sir." It was one of the politest protests Paul had ever heard—a lot politer than he would have expected from the young men who led him around.

It didn't impress the stranger. With a sniff, he said, "Well, of course you haven't. I just got here from Hong Kong—he's *that* important." He jerked a thumb toward Paul.

"Oh," the escort said, his eyes wide. "Do you want us to come with you, then, make sure nothing happens to him?"

An impatient shake of the head answered him. The middle-aged man said, "He's not going anywhere I don't want him to." He slapped his vest pocket. He didn't come right out and say he had a gun in there, but Paul believed it. So did the young men from the Tongs. They didn't argue any more. The man pointed at Paul again, then jerked his thumb back over his shoulder. "Get moving, kid. We don't have all day."

Paul got moving. As he went, he said, "Will somebody for once tell me what the devil's going on?"

"Haven't you figured it out?" The Chinese man steered him around a corner. The fellow paused for a moment before following— he wanted to make sure the escorts weren't coming along in spite of what he'd said. They must not have been, for he caught up to Paul with a smile on his face. It made him look younger and not nearly so unpleasant. "It took me long enough to get here from Berlin—and from Crosstime Traffic."

Now Paul was the one who stopped dead. "From . . . Crosstime Traffic?" he whispered.

"Yup," the Chinese man said cheerfully. "I'm Sam Wong, by the way. Call me Sammy—everybody else does. A dollar for your thoughts." He paused to take a longer look at Paul. "You okay, kid? You're a little green around the gills."

"I don't know." Paul felt dizzy. He wasn't surprised Sammy Wong could see it in his face. Too much was happening too fast "Wait a minute." He tried to gather himself. "You're from—"

"The home timeline? You better believe it," Wong answered.

He knew the right things to say. Nobody in the home timeline said *a penny for your thoughts* the way they did here. Nobody in the home timeline had even seen a penny since Paul's great-grandfather was a boy. Sammy Wong knew there *was* a home timeline, which gave him a head start right there. And he knew there was such a thing as Crosstime Traffic.

All of which proved . . . what? If the *Feldgendarmerie* had squeezed Dad, or if somebody else form the home timeline had goofed and got caught, who could guess what the locals knew?

"I'd better believe it?" Paul said. "How can I? How can I be sure, I mean?"

"Oh." Sammy Wong winked at him. "I get it. You don't think I'm the genuine article. Well, you can find out. Ask me anything."

"Like what?"

Wong shook his head. "No. If I tell you what to ask me, you'll figure I told you to ask that because somebody briefed me on it. You pick the questions."

That made sense. Paul thought. What were some things nobody from this alternate was likely to know? "Who won the Super Bowl last year?"

"The Bengals. Second year in a row," Sammy Wong answered at once.

He was right. But that was the sort of thing clever people might brief an agent about. Paul needed something else. He snapped his fingers. "How much does a Whopper combo cost, and who sells it?"

"You get 'em at Burger King, and they run about five benjamins."

Paul grinned with relief. "Okay. I'm convinced. And I'm mighty glad to see you, too."

"Yeah, well, somebody had to come pick up the pieces. Happens they stuck me with it," Wong said. "What *did* go wrong here? You guys vanished off the face of the earth."

"They decided our electronics were too good to be true," Paul said bitterly. "I was afraid that would happen, and I was right. They got Dad. Only reason they didn't get me, too, is that I wasn't home when they came."

"That would have made things harder," Wong said. "More complicated, anyhow. For now, it looks like the Chinese are going to be able to get your father out of jail."

"Great!" Paul said—the escort hadn't been lying, then. The older man didn't seem so delighted. After a moment, Paul saw why: "Oh. Then they'll have him instead."

"Right the first time," Sammy Wong said. "And maybe they'll play nice if you sing for them. . . . I suppose that was the deal?" He waited. Paul nodded. So did Wong. "Okay. Figured as much—it was the only card you had. Can't blame you for playing it. But they might decide to hang on to you and your old man once you do sing. This is their big chance, or they hope it is."

"Uh-huh," Paul said. "Wouldn't do them as much good as they think."

Wong shrugged. "I don't mind giving them some help, as long as I can do it without giving away the crosstime secret."

Paul almost said the secret was already lost. Lucy had it, sure enough. But if he told that to this fellow who'd never met her, what was Wong liable to do? Get rid of her. Crosstime Traffic people could be ruthless when they had to. That was part of their job. Paul didn't care about their job. He didn't want anything happening to Lucy.

He did say, "The Tongs are close. I'm not sure how close the Germans are." Sammy Wong needed to know that. Paul went on, "Don't bet that the Germans aren't, especially now that they've got their hands on Dad. But it was what we were selling that made people sit up and take notice. Like I said, it was too good. People knew it couldn't be from here."

Frowning, Wong said, "I don't know what to do about that. If we just sell ordinary junk, who'll buy from us? Where will we get the money we need to buy produce? The home timeline has to eat, you know." He was smooth. He didn't say anything like *Crosstime Traffic has to turn a profit*. That was there, but he didn't come out and hit Paul over the head with it.

As a matter fact, Dad had used exactly the same argument. Paul hadn't been able to tell him he was wrong, either. Nor could he tell Wong *he* was wrong. All he could do was ask, "So what happens next?"

"I think we put you on ice for a while," the Crosstime Traffic man answered. "We've still got to work out how we're going to set all this to rights." He muttered something to himself, then spoke out loud: "It's not going to be as easy as anybody back at the home timeline thought."

His idea of how to put Paul on ice was . . . different. After the *Feldgendarmerie* raid, Paul had tried to find the most obscure hidey-hole he could. Sammy Wong, by contrast, walked over to the Palace Hotel on Market Street and booked him in there. It was the fanciest, most expensive hotel this San Francisco boasted.

Sammy Wong turned out to have the room next door. Grinning,

197

he said, "When somebody goes missing, the cops'll turn the Tenderloin upside down. Nobody'd think to look here."

"Easy for you to say," Paul answered. "I couldn't have afforded this for a week, not with the money I had."

"That does make a difference," Wong admitted. "You're here now, though. Enjoy it. Call room service. Order yourself prime rib or a lobster. Why not? It's on the company."

The bed was big enough to get lost in. The bathtub was big enough to swim in (though nobody here had ever heard of a Jacuzzi). Room service seemed wonderful. Paul decided that, if he had to hide out somewhere, this knocked the socks off the miserable joint where he had been staying.

Whenever Lucy was out on the street, she looked for Paul. She knew the Triads had lots of people doing the same thing. So did the San Francisco police. And so did the *Feldgendarmerie*. Her odds of finding him first—of finding him at all—weren't good. She looked anyhow.

It's for his own good, she told himself. Anyone else who caught him would want to pull information out of him. Whoever did wouldn't be gentle about it, either. Lucy wondered what she'd do if she spotted him first. Tell him to run away and hide, she supposed. But how could he have disappeared so completely?

Had he somehow gone back to his own world? How? He'd said the only way there was through Curious Notions. He couldn't have got back in the shop . . . could he? She didn't see how. The *Feldgendarmerie* hadn't forgotten about it. They weren't that dumb. Germany wouldn't have stayed top dog for as long as she had if the people in her secret police were fools.

Lucy wondered if Stanley Hsu and his friends had figured out that Paul might have vanished from this world altogether—and that his father might do the same. She didn't say anything to the jeweler about that. She wondered if Lawrence Gomes would mention it. She didn't think so. If that possibility wasn't his ace in the hole, she would have been amazed.

One evening, she was washing dishes and her little brother was drying them. Michael hated drying dishes, which meant he did a lousy job of it. It also meant he looked for any excuse not to dry them. Even talking with his sister was better than doing what he was supposed to do—especially if he could annoy her. He did his best, saying, "You haven't heard from your boyfriend lately."

Lucy was washing a big serving platter. Mother would get upset if she smashed it over Michael's head. *Too bad,* she thought. She looked down her nose at him instead. "I haven't got a boyfriend," she said loftily.

"You know the one I mean—the guy from that place with the neat electronics." Michael was going to take over Father's shop one of these days (*if I don't strangle him first,* Lucy thought). He'd already learned a lot about the things Father repaired.

What he'd learned about people, on the other hand, would fit on a pinhead, and a little pinhead at that. Lucy sometimes thought *he* was a little pinhead. She said, "Paul's not my boyfriend. You'd better remember that. And you'd better remember he got Father out of jail, so you don't want to make rude remarks about him. You *do* want to dry that platter. Don't just stick it in the drainer."

Michael made a face at her. He dried the platter, but wanting to was a different story. Then he made another face, not the same one this time. "If he's not your boyfriend, what is he?"

"He's none of your business, that's what," Lucy snapped. Michael grinned. He'd made her angry, which won him a point. For a little while, Lucy was hotter than the water in the sink. Then she said, "He's just a friend. That's not the same as a boyfriend. You'll find out what the difference is when you get bigger."

Her brother made yet another face, one both disgusting and disgusted. At ten, he was sure girls were poisonous. He was sure he'd feel that way forever, too. He wasn't as smart as he thought he was. He wasn't smart enough to realize he wasn't as smart as he thought he was, either.

When he stopped making gagging and choking noises to go with the horrible face, he said, "If he's just a friend, how come he never comes over here?"

Because it might bring the Feldgendarmerie *down on him. Because it might bring the* Feldgendarmerie *down on us, too.* Lucy smiled sweetly. "Because then he might meet you, and he'd never want anything to do with me again after that."

"You're mean!" Michael could dish it out better than he could take it. He fired the big gun: "Mommy!"

"What's going on?" Mother called from the living room. A warning note rang in her voice.

Michael's explanation differed from Lucy's by about 180 degrees. They both got louder and louder, trying to shout each other down. Michael snapped the towel at Lucy. That could have hurt, but he missed. She splashed him with dishwater. He screeched so shrilly, even dogs would have had trouble hearing him.

"What's going on?" Mother said again, this time from the doorway. Again, the stories she heard might have happened on two different planets. She set her hands on her hips. "That will be enough from both of you. One more peep from this kitchen out of either one of you and you'll both be sorry."

Lucy finished washing the dishes. Michael finished drying them. They made faces and sent rude gestures at each other till they were done. Neither said a thing. They got their messages across just the same.

When Lucy came out of the kitchen, her father looked out from behind his newspaper. That was enough to make her stop in surprise. Once he started looking at the paper, he was usually gone till he got done. Then he surprised her again by saying her name.

"What is it, Father?" she asked.

"What do you know about Curious Notions?" Charlie Woo asked in turn. "Will they be opening up again? I want more of a chance to find out how they do what they do."

I know how they do what they do. They bring things in somehow from another world. No wonder you couldn't figure out how their gadgets work. But Lucy didn't think she could tell him that. He might believe it. He knew those gadgets weren't like any *this* world made. They hit him the same way Paul's claim to come from Thirty-third Avenue in the Sunset District hit her. They didn't fit. They *didn't* fit. But the reason they didn't fit was Paul's secret. And he'd made it very plain that he wished she didn't know it, let alone anyone else.

She might have told her father anyway, except for one other thing. Paul had also made it very plain that knowing his secret was dangerous. If he hadn't, what had happened to him and to his father and to Curious Notions would have. Lucy didn't want her father to know the secret because it might be dangerous to *him*. The Germans had already jailed him once just for being near the edges of it.

So all she said was, "I don't think they're going to be opening up again any time soon. The *Feldgendarmerie* let Mr. Gomes go, but they haven't let him get back to work."

"I wonder why not," her father said. "If they want to catch him doing something, they should give him the chance to do it. If they leave the place closed, they'll never find out what he was up to."

Lucy blinked. She hadn't thought of it like that. Most of the time, it would have made good sense. But one of the things Mr. Gomes could do—or she supposed he could—was disappear from this world and go back to his own. And if he did, how could the *Feldgendarmerie* go after him?

"I didn't know you could think like a *Feldgendarmerie* man," she said.

Her father made a face nastier than any of the ones Michael had aimed at her. "You say the sweetest things," he muttered.

"I didn't mean it like *that*," Lucy told him.

That horrible face melted into a tired smile. "I know you didn't, sweetheart," he said. "But I've met the Germans up close, and you haven't. I don't want to think like them, believe you me I don't."

She started to say she'd met the *Feldgendarmerie,* too, when they let him out of jail and brought him back here. Something in his eyes told her that would be worse than just wasting her breath. It would be saying something not only stupid but naive. No one could know the German secret police who hadn't been in jail, who hadn't been grilled. Father had. She hadn't. It was as simple as that.

He went back to his newspaper. She went to her room. He hadn't rubbed her nose in the mistake she almost made. That wasn't his style. But he'd made sure she knew about it. And she did. She didn't think she'd ever be foolish that particular way again.

The next couple of days, Mrs. Cho was grumpy. She was worse than grumpy, in fact—she was downright mean. Lucy wondered if her supervisor was having a hard time at home and taking it out on her. If it wasn't something like that, then the Triads weren't happy with her. She hoped it was Mrs. Cho's problem.

But it turned out not to be. When she got back to her desk

from lunch on the third day, she fond a note on it. *Please see me this evening—S.H.*, it said in Stanley Hsu's elegant script. Lucy wondered who'd put it there. Mrs. Cho? Somebody from outside the shoe factory? She realized she'd probably never find out.

She tore the note into little pieces and threw it in the trash. She wished she could ignore it along with ripping it up. But she couldn't, and she knew it.

She did her best to look on the bright side of things. She usually did, even if it didn't always help. Maybe the jeweler or Mr. Gomes had learned what had happened to Paul. Maybe he'd even be there. She didn't really expect he would, but she could hope.

Mrs. Cho kept right on being nasty the rest of the day. Did that mean she wasn't the one who'd put the note on Lucy's desk? Or was she just trying to show Lucy that the Triads were still mad at her? Lucy gave up trying to figure it out. She'd get some answers—or she hoped she would—when she saw Stanley Hsu.

"Hello, Miss Woo. How are you today?" he said when she walked into his shop. His manners were perfect for setting rich customers at ease. That made them feel a little phony, a little oily, to Lucy.

"I'm all right," she said. "What do you want from me? What do you need from me?"

"I was wondering—and Paul's father was wondering—whether you'd heard from him," Stanley Hsu answered. "The two of you seem to have struck up quite a friendship. If anyone has seen him, you're likely to be the one."

"I haven't," Lucy said. Stanley Hsu looked disappointed. Mr. Gomes came out of the jewelry store's back room. He looked disappointed, too. Lucy didn't think he was faking that, though she felt less sure about Stanley Hsu. If Paul's father was still worried about him, what did that mean? Probably that Mr. Gomes didn't

203

think Paul had gone back to their own world. If he believed Paul had, he wouldn't seem so worried . . . would he?

"Do you have any idea where he might have gone?" Stanley Hsu asked.

Lucy shook her head. "I was hoping you would." She wasn't going to say a word about that other Sunset District. She didn't know what Paul's father had told Stanley Hsu. She could tell she'd end up in trouble if the man from the Triads found out she knew things he didn't. Mr. Gomes might end up in trouble, too.

Stanley Hsu just said, "No, we don't."

Paul's father added, "This whole business is just a mess. When the Germans grabbed me, Paul managed to stay free. And now he's missing, but I'm out." He nodded to Stanley Hsu, to let him know he knew whom he ought to thank for that. The corners of his mouth turned down in a frown. With the big, droopy mustache he wore, it looked as if he were frowning twice. "Once we get back together, we can . . . figure out what to do next."

Had the jeweler heard that little hesitation there? Lucy sure had. What had Mr. Gomes started to say? Something like *We can go back to where we belong*? That would have been her guess.

"Paul hasn't tried to get in touch with you?" Stanley Hsu persisted. "No notes? No letters? No phone calls at work?"

"No, Mr. Hsu. Nothing," Lucy said truthfully. She suspected the jeweler already knew the answer was no, but was going through the motions—maybe for Mr. Gomes' sake. She also suspected Stanley Hsu knew exactly what her mail was, and exactly who called her. If Paul had done any of those things and she'd said no . . . She didn't think she would have enjoyed that.

"What are we going to do?" Paul's father aimed the question at Stanley Hsu, not at Lucy.

The jeweler looked annoyed—not at Lawrence Gomes, but

because he had no answer for him. "We're looking," he said. "That's all I can tell you right now. We are looking. We can do a better job of looking than anyone else in this city. That includes the police and the *Feldgendarmerie*. We have more eyes than they do, and better eyes. The Kaiser's men and their stooges have to pay bribes. People help us because they want to."

How true was that? If the Triads asked you to keep an eye out for somebody, would you tell them no? Lucy didn't think that would be smart. The Triads didn't have the law on their side, the way the cops and the Germans did. But they could take revenge that had nothing to do with law. And the *Feldgendarmerie* had been trying to knock them out ever since Germany conquered the USA. That was a long time ago now, and they hadn't done it yet.

"If one of us has to be in jail, it should be me," Mr. Gomes said. A father was supposed to say that if he feared his son was in trouble.

But Stanley Hsu said, "He's not in jail in San Francisco, not with the police and not with the *Feldgendarmerie*. We would know. I can guarantee that. I don't think he's in jail anywhere else—not unless he left San Francisco on his own. If the Germans or their flunkies have tried to smuggle him out, we would know *that*."

He sounded very sure of himself. Lucy believed him, too. She wasn't so sure about Paul's father. "Well, where is he, then?" he exploded. "In the Palace Hotel?"

Lucy burst out laughing. That was the most ridiculous thing she could imagine. Stanley Hsu gave Mr. Gomes a thin smile. "You are a man of wit, sir."

"I don't care about wit right now," Paul's father said. "All I care about is getting my son back again."

"We want the same thing you do," the jeweler said, his voice smooth as glass.

No, you don't! Lucy wanted to shout it, but she kept quiet. What the Triads wanted to do was get their hands on both people from Curious Notions. Once they had them, they thought they could get answers out of them. Didn't Paul's father see that? But even if he did, what could he do about it? The Triads were his only hope of seeing Paul again. If he didn't play along with them, he had no hope at all.

"Do you need me for anything else?" Lucy asked Stanley Hsu.

He shook his head. "No, Miss Woo. I do thank you for stopping by. And if you should hear anything from Paul, please let us know."

"I will," Lucy said. *If I have to, I will. If I think you know anyway, I will. Otherwise? Otherwise, don't hold your breath.*

"It could be very important," Mr. Gomes said.

"If I have anything to tell, I'll tell it." Lucy was more willing to tell Paul's father than she was to tell Stanley Hsu. She wondered why. Whatever she told Mr. Gomes, the jeweler would find out in short order. She still felt there was a difference. Maybe it was that Mr. Gomes had the right to know about Paul, where Stanley Hsu didn't.

She was glad to get out of the jewelry shop. The door hadn't quite swung shut before the two men inside started shouting at each other. Lucy wondered what it was all about. She could think of several possibilities. Maybe Mr. Gomes saw more than he'd let on in front of her. She hoped so. He would almost have to, wouldn't he? But the less he showed he knew, the more choices and chances he might have later on. He might give Stanley Hsu a surprise if one of those chances came up.

Or he might not. The jeweler was a slick operator. And he wasn't on his own, the way Paul's father was. He had the resources of the Triads behind him. Those resources reached all the way back to China. What could Mr. Gomes put in the scales that would balance them?

Lucy realized that wasn't just a rhetorical question, as she'd thought at first. The gadgets Curious Notions sold showed that Paul and his father knew things people in this world didn't. That they were able to get from their world to this one showed the same thing. What else did they know that they weren't letting on? Lucy would have bet they had other secrets to use when they needed them. In their shoes, she would have.

She tried to imagine what some of those secrets might be. She didn't have much luck, and started laughing at herself. They wouldn't be much in the way of secrets if she could figure them out, would they?

When she got home, her mother said, "You're a little late."

Lucy shrugged. "I know. I'm sorry. I found out I had to make a stop."

"Oh." Mother let the word hang in the air. "At the jeweler's?" She didn't give any hints about what she thought of that.

"Yes, at the jeweler's," Lucy said. "He wanted to know if I had any idea where Paul was. So did Paul's father."

"I believe *that*," Mother said. "And do you?"

"No. I haven't heard from him for a while," Lucy answered.

Mother didn't say anything for a moment. The knife in her hand flashed, slicing mushrooms almost thin enough to see through. At last, she asked, "Is that good or bad?"

"I don't know," Lucy said. "I just don't know."

Living in a luxury hotel was fine for a little while. It might have stayed fine longer if Paul had been able to go out when he wanted to. But Sammy Wong wanted him to sit tight. Paul couldn't blame the man from Crosstime Traffic for that. He understood it. But it made the luxury hotel feel like a luxury jail.

"Why don't we do something?" Paul asked him. "If the Tongs have my father, why don't we get him away from them? As soon as we do that, we can go to Berlin and get back to the home timeline."

"It's not quite so simple, I'm afraid," Wong answered. "I can get you away, and him, too—that's no problem." Paul stirred. It looked like a problem to him. Before he could say anything, the older man went on, "Getting you people away isn't the only reason I'm here, though. I'm here to try to make sure the Tongs and the Germans don't get their hands on the crosstime secret. That's number one."

"Nice to know I'm excess baggage," Paul said.

Sammy Wong grinned at him. "You're high-quality excess baggage, anyhow."

"Thanks a lot."

The Chinese man nodded, as if to say, *Sure. Any time.* Maybe he didn't notice the sarcasm. Maybe he did, but didn't want Paul to know he did. That struck Paul as more likely. It also made him want to strike Sammy Wong, preferably with a blunt instrument.

Instead, he went back to his room next door. It was fancy enough—no two ways about that. The carpet was thick enough for his shoes to disappear when he stepped down on it. The TV had a big screen—though the color wasn't as good as it would have been in the home timeline, and the picture was grainier.

No matter how big the TV was, it didn't show much he wanted to see. Newsmen going on about how wonderful the Kaiser was and how everything the Germans did was perfect weren't his idea of excitement. Quiz shows with excitable hosts were just as idiotic here as they were in the home timeline. Comedies struck him as anything but funny. Either the jokes were dumb or they were based on things you had to be from this world to get—or both.

That left sports. Soccer wasn't his cup of tea for killing time on TV. They played baseball and basketball here, too, but he also couldn't get thrilled about teams that weren't his own and players he'd never heard of.

He was, in a word, bored. In two words, very bored.

He even started to hate room service. The food was always good. But it always came from the same menu. You could tell it always came out of the same kitchen. No matter what he ordered, it seemed . . . familiar. A hamburger and greasy French fries from some mom-and-pop—Louie's, say—would have tasted like heaven.

Every time he looked out the window, the skyline reminded him that this wasn't *his* San Francisco. For the USA in this alternate, it was a first-rate city. But this USA was a second-rate country, and this San Francisco felt second-rate to him. The town he was used to *bounced*. This one . . . lurched.

Paul thought about asking Sammy Wong for permission to go out, just for a little while. He thought about it—and then he laughed at himself. He knew what the man from Crosstime Traffic would say. Wong would say no, that was what. He might say more than just no—he might say it so it sounded louder and more impressive than just no—but no was what it would boil down to.

And Paul didn't feel like hearing no. When he had to stop himself from kicking in the TV instead of just turning it off, he decided he had to get outside for a little while. *Only for a little while,* he told himself. Seeing more of the world than he could from his window, eating a hamburger from a place where he'd never been—he did know he shouldn't go back to Louie's or anywhere else in the neighborhood of Curious Notions—struck him as the most wonderful thing in the world.

Part of him knew that what he was thinking about wasn't the greatest idea in the world. The longer he stayed in the Palace Hotel, the less he cared about that part. Was he an animal in a cage? If he was, why hadn't Sammy Wong taken him to the zoo?

He knew why. In the zoo, people would look at him. Wong wanted to put him on ice and keep him on ice. Paul understood his reasons well enough. They made good sense. But their making sense wasn't enough to keep him from climbing the walls.

Only for a little while. The more that handful of words echoed inside his head, the better they sounded. After one last bowl of cioppino that tasted just like the other four bowls of cioppino he'd ordered, *only for a little while* sounded too good to resist.

Paul waited till after midnight. He wanted his keeper (that was how he was thinking of Sammy Wong by now) to be asleep. And he wanted the streets of San Francisco to be nice and quiet. If nobody was around when he took his little jaunt, nothing could go wrong.

He shut his door as quietly as he could. He walked down the hall to the elevator. A real, live elevator operator ran it. "Lobby," Paul said, and tipped him a nickel when he got out. The doorman didn't seem to think anything of someone heading out in the wee small hours. He opened the door with one hand while lifting his top hat from his head with the other.

It was chilly. It was foggy. Paul's breath came out in clouds. The street lights might have been ghosts of themselves. He stuck his hands in his pockets and ambled along. He could have been anybody out there, anybody at all. It felt wonderful.

Most of the shops and restaurants were closed. He did get that hamburger, though, at a place full of tough-looking men and the women who kept them company. Nobody gave him a second glance. He ate fast and got out, coughing from the cigarette smoke that hung in the air. People here smoked a lot more than they did in the home timeline. Maybe they didn't know how dangerous it was. Maybe they just didn't care.

He heard a soft clicking on the sidewalk behind him. *Stray dog,* he thought. A moment later, the dog came up beside him. It was almost the size of a Shetland pony. The instant he recognized it as an Alsatian, he realized it wasn't a stray. And he realized he was in trouble.

A hard hand fell on his shoulder. "You are Paul Gomes," a German-accented voice said. "Come with me at once. You are under arrest."

Eleven

Somebody on one of the other shifts had lost a worker's folder. Lucy poked through all the logical places it might be. When it didn't turn up in any of them, she had to start thinking about illogical places. She checked the file for fired employees. It wasn't there. She checked the file for deceased employees—and there it was.

She couldn't imagine why anyone would have put it there. The woman whose file it was remained very much alive. Lucy worked a few stations away from her, and still saw her every day. But how things could get misfiled no longer surprised Lucy. She'd seen worse than this. She pulled out the file—at least it was in the right place alphabetically—and took it to Mrs. Cho.

"Here you are," she said, not without pride.

Her supervisor checked the name, then smiled. "Oh, good. I was afraid it was gone forever. That would have been a nuisance. Where did you find it?"

"Somebody put it in with the dead ones," Lucy answered.

Mrs. Cho laughed. "Haven't run into that for a while." The laugh and the smile that went with it vanished as if they'd never been. "If I knew who, I can think of a folder that would belong in the fired file."

She wasn't kidding. Lucy could tell. Mrs. Cho put up with inexperience and fumbling around. You had to, or every new worker

212

would drive you nuts. But she would not stand for incompetence from people who should have known better. If they didn't shape up to suit her, they were gone. Sometimes she didn't even give them the chance to shape up. One mistake of the wrong kind was plenty.

"What now, Mrs. Cho?" Lucy had learned she should always look for something to do. It didn't have to be important. As long as it made her look busy, that was fine. The one thing the people over her couldn't stand was to see her sitting around and twiddling her thumbs.

Before her supervisor could answer, the front door flew open. It swung through an arc of 180 degrees and slammed into the wall. Half a dozen big men in trench coats and high-crowned caps that made them look even bigger charged into the room. Three of them carried pistols. The other three had submachine guns. "Hands high!" one of them shouted.

People dropped what they were doing—literally. Papers cascaded down onto the floor and splashed across it. Several clerks screamed. Everyone's fingers pointed straight toward the ceiling. All the other people in the big room looked as scared as Lucy felt.

"What is the meaning of this?" Mrs. Cho tried to sound as tough with the *Feldgendarmerie* men—they couldn't be anything else—as she did with the people who worked for her. She didn't have much luck. Her voice wobbled and squeaked.

"*We* ask the questions," said the German who'd ordered hands raised. "Where is"—he paused to check a paper he pulled from his pocket—"Lucy Woo?"

Even before he spoke her name, Lucy knew it was coming. She had not a prayer of running or hiding. Every eye turned toward her. In a very small voice, she said, "Here I am."

The secret policeman looked at her. He looked at his five strapping friends. He was as big as any of them. Lucy barely came up to his shoulder. He started to laugh. "They sent lions after a mouse," he said.

I'll bite you if I can, Lucy thought. Shouting defiance at the Germans wasn't smart, though. All she said was, "I haven't done anything."

That set the *Feldgendarmerie* men laughing again. "The next person I hear who says, 'Oh, yes, I did what you say I did,' will be the first. If you listen to the ones we grab, they are so innocent it's a miracle God doesn't carry them off to heaven." Now his laugh took on a sinister ring. "God takes care of the innocent—and we take care of the rest. Come with us, if you please."

Mrs. Cho began, "Lucy is a very good worker and a very nice girl. She—"

With a wave of his submachine gun, the secret policeman cut her off. "If she is as sweet as you say, we won't keep her long. *If.*" He bore down heavily on the word, then gestured with the weapon again. This time, he used it to point toward the door. Helplessly, Lucy went.

She wondered if they would put handcuffs on her. They didn't bother. That almost made her angry. They didn't think she was dangerous enough to worry about. It felt like an insult. The only trouble was, they were right.

They bundled her into an enormous car. It had to be enormous to hold all of them and her as well. It roared down the street. The driver leaned on the horn. That special scream meant everybody had to clear a path for the German car. People on foot and on bicycles and in other cars got out of the way in a hurry.

"I didn't do anything. I really didn't," Lucy quavered.

"Ha!" said the secret policeman who seemed to do the talking for this bunch. "You know Lawrence Gomes and his son. Don't try to tell me any different, or you'll be sorry. We got what we needed out of the older one. Now we're finding out what the younger one knows."

Lucy tried not to flinch in dismay. Paul, in the hands of the *Feldgendarmerie*? She didn't want to believe it. She tried not to believe it. Maybe this fellow was lying to make her sing. That seemed the sort of thing the secret police would do.

But then she remembered that Paul *was* missing. His father and Stanley Hsu didn't know where he was. One logical reason they wouldn't was if he was in some *Feldgendarmerie* jail.

Maybe this one, Lucy thought as the car pulled up in front of a building with the red, white, and black German flag floating above it. The door opened. Three of the *Feldgendarmerie* men got out. "Now you," said the fellow who did the talking. Lucy obeyed. What else could she do? The rest of the secret policemen piled out behind her.

They could have safely brought a criminal mastermind into jail with that kind of firepower. For a terrified sixteen-year-old girl, it was overkill. They used it anyhow. Up the steps she went. One of the spike-helmeted guards at the top opened the thick, heavy door. In Lucy went. It closed behind her with a soft thud. She wondered if she would ever come out again.

Not for the first time, Paul wondered if the Germans were afraid of killing the goose that laid the golden eggs. That was the only reason he could see that they weren't tearing chunks off of him. So far, the questioning had been on the mild side, as *Feldgendarmerie* questioning went. Of course, he had no guarantee it would stay that way.

The cell was about three meters on a side. The cot in one corner had its legs sunk into the concrete of the floor. It wasn't going anywhere. Aside from the cot, the cell held a toilet and a cold-water sink. That was it. The secret policemen hadn't given Paul a chance to shave. His beard, four days old now, was starting to itch.

He was starting to itch all over, in fact. With the best will in the world, you couldn't stay clean with only a cold-water sink and no soap. Maybe the *Feldgendarmerie* men thought he'd lose heart if he got dirty and scruffy. If he did, he intended to do his best not to let them know it.

Maybe they thought he'd lose heart if he got hungry, too. They fed him twice a day. It was slop. People in the home timeline complained about the lousy food prisoners got. Sometimes they wrote letters to the newspapers. They started e-mail campaigns on the Net. They staged public protests. If they'd had to eat these nasty stews, they would have decided what prisoners in the home timeline got wasn't so bad after all. This was better than starving, but not by much.

Worst of all was the boredom. Nobody else was in a cell Paul could see. Everything was quiet except for the clump of guards' boots against the floor. Paul could pace up and down or he could lie on the cot and grow moss. No TV. No radio. No nothing. Those horrible meals soon became the high points of his day. That was a really scary thought.

And then there were the times that weren't so boring. Those usually came in the middle of the night. He wondered if the *Feldgendarmerie* had watched too many old movies. They couldn't wake him up by shining a bright light in his face, because they never turned off the lights. But they did make a habit of waking him out of a deep sleep.

The door to the cell would fly open. *"Raus!"* they would shout. "Prisoner Gomes, come with us at once!" Paul was a sound sleeper. If they hadn't screamed his own name at him, he would have had trouble remembering who he was when he first woke up. They wanted him groggy and stupid when they questioned him. They had ways of getting what they wanted, too.

They'd slam him down into a hard chair in a dark room. *Then* they'd shine the bright light at him. They'd throw questions at him. Where did Curious Notions get its goods. What happened to all the produce it bought? What did he know about the Tongs? (Except they called them Oriental subversive organizations—regardless of the alternate, cops talked like that.)

Paul told them as little as he could. He pleaded ignorance. He was just a kid—how could he know anything important? They were walking around the edges of the crosstime secret. Unlike the people from the Tongs, who were looking for allies wherever they could find them, the *Feldgendarmerie* men didn't quite seem to know they were on the edge of it.

Or maybe they were just holding back. Bright lights and shouted questions were as far as they'd gone up till now. They hadn't tried hot things or pointed things or sharp things. They hadn't tried electricity. They hadn't tried drugs.

Good luck is where you find it, Paul thought after one of those sessions. Even as it was, he felt his brain had been turned inside out. But it could have been worse, and he knew it.

Once, the German asking the questions told Paul, "This is not what your father says to be the case."

"Why don't you ask him about it, then?" Paul answered. As far as he knew, he had told the truth here. The *Feldgendarmerie* man wanted to know the prices he'd been paying for Central Valley produce. That seemed harmless enough.

"I am asking *you*," the German said. Did his voice lack some of its usual snap? Paul thought so.

He said, "That's how I remember it. If Dad knows something I don't, it's news to me. Maybe he's the one who remembers wrong. Like I say, you can ask him about it."

"We have transcripts of what he said," the German replied. "He . . . is not available for questioning right now."

"Why not? What did you do to him?" Paul enjoyed being able to ask questions instead of answering them. He knew the Tongs had got his father out of jail. He didn't know how they'd done it, but Sammy Wong had assured him that they had. He wondered if the man on the other side of the bright light would admit it.

He should have known better. The German said, "That is none of your business, and of no concern to you."

"He's my father," Pal protested. "Of course it's of concern to me. You've got a lot of nerve, telling me my own father is none of my business. What did you do to him? Did you make him disappear?"

Did you make him disappear? was a polite way to ask, *Did you kill him?* Plenty of people "disappeared" from German jails. Paul happened to know Dad hadn't, or not that way. But the man questioning him didn't know he knew. If Paul could yank the fellow's chain, he would. Why not? The *Feldgendarmerie* man had sure been doing his best to yank *his*.

The German muttered something in his own language. Paul understood German. He thought the man said, *Miserable kid*. That made him feel better than he had since the *Feldgendarmerie* nabbed him. The secret policeman went back to English: "Your father has not disappeared. Not in the way you mean."

"Oh, yeah? Prove it," Paul said. "Let me see him. Then maybe I'll believe you."

More mutters in German. This time, Paul couldn't make out what they were. Then the secret policeman spoke to his pals in the room: "Take him back to his cell. He's being very uncooperative."

One of the other *Feldgendarmerie* men spoke in German: "You ought to use the wire and the thumbscrews. The punk would sing like a nightingale then."

Paul didn't want them to know he could follow their language. Keeping a blank look on his face was one of the hardest things he'd ever done. They could torture him whenever they wanted to. What would stop them? Not a thing.

But the man doing the questioning said, "*Nein*. Not yet, anyhow. Things are more . . . delicate than you realize, Horst." That also came in German. Not showing relief was as hard as not showing fear. Paul didn't know why things were delicate, but he was sure glad they were.

The *Feldgendarmerie* men hauled him back to the cell. The door clanged shut. Compared to the bright light glaring into his face, those empty cells across from his didn't look so bad. He wondered what was going on outside the jail. By now, Sammy Wong would know he was missing. Wong would probably know why, too. Would Dad? Would Lucy? What were they doing to get him out? Were they doing anything? Or were they saying, *Serves you right for being dumb* and leaving him in here till he rotted?

They wouldn't do that. Would they? With nothing but bars as far as his eye could see, Paul began to wonder. Maybe this view wasn't that much better than the one in the room where they questioned him after all.

Lucy was both sick of answering questions and surprised the Germans hadn't done anything but ask them. Oh, they'd yelled and shone bright lights in her face and told her they would do horrible things if she didn't come clean. They'd told her that, yes, but they hadn't done them.

In her bare cell, Lucy shook her head. They hadn't done them *up till now*. That didn't mean they wouldn't. They were Germans, after all. Was there anything they wouldn't do?

At least the people at work knew what had happened to her. For one thing, that probably meant her folks would find out about it. For another, it might mean she'd get her job back if the *Feldgendarmerie* ever let her out of jail. Mrs. Cho would know why she wasn't coming in now. She'd know Lucy wasn't out somewhere goofing off and having a good time.

That made her laugh. No, she wasn't having a good time at all.

When they took her away for another round of questioning, they started yelling at her again. "You must know more than you admit about Curious Notions! You must!" shouted the man behind the lamp. She'd never seen his face. "They named your father a supplier! Why would they do that?"

To get you out of their hair, Lucy thought. And look how well that worked! She said, "We don't have anything to do with them as far as business goes." Then she remembered something Paul told her in Golden Gate Park. "If you don't believe me, you can ask Captain Horvath. He knows we are what we say we are."

She wasn't sure how much weight a mere San Francisco cop carried with the *Feldgendarmerie*. But a police captain wasn't mere, was he, even if he was only an American? Fatty Horvath had a good reputation in Chinatown. And he had done something to get Lucy's father out of a mess a lot like this one.

"Horvath? Who is this Captain Horvath?" the *Feldgendarmerie* man behind the lamp demanded. Lucy's heart sank.

But one of the other Germans in the room said, *"Amerikanischer Polizeikapitän."* Lucy could figure out what that meant. The *Feldgendarmerie* man went on in his own language. Lucy recognized more words here and there, but not enough to let her figure out what he was saying. Was he telling the fellow behind the lamp that Horvath was a big wheel, or that he was full of hot air? Lucy's nails bit into her palms in frustration. She couldn't tell.

Her questioner said, "Tell us more of this Paul Gomes. Tell us everything you know. Tell us in great detail."

Fright flared in Lucy. *Did* the Kaiser's men have Paul? It seemed much too likely. She said, "Well, I don't have much to tell you. I've only met him a few times." She wished she could say she didn't know him at all, but they wouldn't believe that. "He seemed like a pretty nice person. He wouldn't shine a light in my face and yell at me." That wasn't much in the way of defiance, but it was all she had in her.

It didn't impress the *Feldgendarmerie* man. "My job is not to be nice. My job is to get answers. And I will get answers. I do not care if Paul Gomes is nice or not. I want to know what you know about him. Believe me, I have ways to get what I want. Talking freely is better and easier."

She did believe him. She was just glad he hadn't done anything worse than shine a light in her face and yell at her. If she didn't give him some of what he wanted, he was liable to. She wondered what she could say that might satisfy him without hurting Paul. "Well, he told me he's from the Sunset District," she said.

"This we already knew. We have checked his school records," said the man behind the lamp.

You don't know as much as you think you do, Lucy thought. Paul probably came from the Sunset District, all right, but not from *this* Sunset District. If the secret policeman understood San Francisco, he would have seen that right away. Somebody like Paul just couldn't come from a place like that. But if he had records there good enough to fool the *Feldgendarmerie* . . . That said something about how well his people were organized, and how many of them there were.

221

"Tell me more," the German said. "Tell me quickly. Do not sit there making up your lies."

"I'm not lying. I just told you the truth. You said so." Lucy tried to sound angry instead of scared. It wasn't easy, not when she *was* scared. She tried again: "I know Captain Horvath likes him, and some other important Americans." In fact, she didn't know they liked him. But she did know the people at Curious Notions had influence on them. That was as good as the other.

No matter how good it was, it didn't impress the *Feldgendarmerie* man. "Important Americans?" he jeered. "There are no important Americans." He had a nasty laugh. "There will never be any important Americans."

One of the other men spoke to him in German again. They went back and forth for a couple of minutes. Lucy wondered what they were talking about. Her, probably. Doing it in a language she couldn't understand was rude. Somehow, she didn't think that would worry them.

Her questioner returned to English: "A while ago, *Polizeikapitän* Horvath and some others urged us to let your father go. Is this not so? Did they not do it because of Paul Gomes and his father?"

"I don't know anything about that," Lucy said, which was technically true. She hadn't asked Captain Horvath or anyone else why he'd asked the Germans to let her father go. She added, "I thought you let him go because you couldn't show he'd done anything wrong."

The *Feldgendarmerie* man laughed again, even more nastily than before. "That is not enough reason to let anyone go. Believe me, it is not. The guilty are often good at covering their tracks."

"If you go on like that, you can show anybody's guilty of anything," Lucy said.

"You begin to understand," her questioner said. What she began to understand was how much trouble she was in, or could be in. The *Feldgendarmerie* man went on, "Did you not tell one Margaret Ma at the zoological garden that you are fond of Paul Gomes? Is this not why you seek to cover up for him?"

Lucy needed a second to remember that Margaret was the name Peggy came from. She'd never called her friend anything but Peggy as long as they'd known each other. Had she said that to Peggy? She couldn't remember. But if Peggy had told the secret police what she thought they wanted to hear, who could blame her? Anything to make them go away.

"Well? Speak!" the *Feldgendarmerie* man snapped.

That made Lucy want to go *Woof!* She didn't think it would be a good idea. "I do like him, but not like *that*," she said, which was more or less true. Paul fascinated her, but more as a puzzle than as anything past a friend. So she told herself, anyhow. She went on, "And I'm not trying to cover up for him. But if you ask me about things where I don't know anything, how can I tell you anything?"

"Ha! A likely story," the German jeered. Then he spoke in his own language to the other *Feldgendarmerie* officers in the room. They hauled Lucy out of her chair with arrogant, effortless strength and took her down the hall. Back into her cell she went. The door slammed shut. They must have closed it extra hard. The clang of metal on metal sounded dreadfully final.

Paul blinked and narrowed his eyes against the glare of the lamp. The Kaiser's men let him get away with that much. If he tried to turn away from the bright light, they jerked him back towards it. They got less gentle each time, too. He'd given up. They were liable to tear his head off if they got the chance.

"Sssso," said the man behind the lamp, the one whose face he'd never seen. He stretched the word out into a long, snakelike hiss. "You are acquainted with a certain Lucy Woo, is that not true?"

Alarm trickled through Paul. "I've met her," he answered cautiously. "I can't say that I know her real well." Like so much of what he said in this alternate, that was truth and lie mixed together. He hadn't met her all that often, and he didn't know her all that well, not the way he knew his friends in the home timeline. But what he did know, he liked. She had brains and she had spirit. And she *was* cute: not spectacular, but cute.

"This is also what she says of you," the *Feldgendarmerie* man told him.

Did that mean they had her? Did it mean the German wanted him to think they had her? Or did it just mean they'd asked her some questions? One thing it had to mean was that the German wanted to see how excited he'd get. He shouldn't get excited, then, or shouldn't show it if he did. All he said was, "Well, there you are."

"*Ja.* Here I am. And here *you* are. You are plainly guilty of enough things—starting with illegal import and export and going on from there—to send you to prison or a penal colony for many years." The German paused. "Not that many people last many years in a penal colony, of course." He paused again. "If you begin telling us the truth, perhaps—perhaps, I say—we can go a bit easier on you."

"I have been telling you the truth," Paul said. *Some of it, anyway.* Inside, he was calling himself forty-seven different kinds of idiot. That was probably only half as many as Sammy Wong would call him. And Paul would have been happy—would have been delighted—to smile and nod and agree to every single one.

He knew what kind of mistake he'd made. He also knew it was one of the commonest for people from Crosstime Traffic. Because they had higher technology than the locals, and because they could usually leave an alternate if they got in trouble there, they often thought nothing could happen to them.

Not many people last many years in a penal colony, of course. If the Germans sent him to Patagonia or New Guinea or Siberia or even the Mojave, how would Crosstime Traffic ever find him again? If they did find him, how would they pull him out? If they couldn't pull him out, how long would he last?

This was real. The German on the other side of the lamp wasn't playing games. He'd do what he said he'd do—and he'd be sure he was doing the right thing while he did it, too. The Kaiser might pin a medal on him for it. Why not? He'd deserve one. He was serving his country the best way he knew how.

Paul braced for the next question. Instead, the *Feldgendarmerie* man spoke to his pals: "Take him away. We will try something else tomorrow."

They had him on the ropes. He knew it. He knew it much too well. And now they were letting him off? He didn't care what they'd try tomorrow. That was what he told himself just then, anyhow. They were giving him a day to recover. He felt like singing as the secret policemen hauled him back to his cell.

He wasn't so cheerful once he'd sat on the edge of the cot for a little while. His imagination started to work. Something else tomorrow? Hot things? Sharp things? Pointed things? Electricity? Wondering was almost a worse torture than what might happen to him. Almost.

He didn't have a good night at all.

Four big guards stomped up to Lucy's cell. "You will come with us," one of them said. "Immediately."

What choice did she have? If she said no, they'd drag her or carry her. Any one of them could have, let alone all four. She kept what pieces of dignity she had left. When they unlocked the door, she strode out with her head high. She might have been a cat going to the vet's. She felt like yowling like a scared cat, too, but she didn't. The guards might think she was afraid, but she didn't want to prove it.

They didn't take her to the room where they'd been questioning her. She wondered whether that was good or bad. *I'll find out,* she thought, and shivered.

"In here," the guard said. He opened an ordinary door. The room beyond it seemed ordinary, too, if bare. It held a cheap table and two even cheaper chairs. The walls and ceiling were painted a plain white. A grayish carpet that had seen better days covered the floor. Only the wire mesh over the small window reminded her she was still in a jail.

All the guards trooped out. The room had only the one door. She wasn't going anywhere till they let her. She sat down on one of the chairs, wondering what they had in mind. Whatever it was, it wasn't as bad as she'd expected—not yet, anyway.

Ten minutes later, the door opened again. In came Paul Gomes. Lucy stared at him. He was grimy and worn looking, and he needed a shave. He was well on his way to growing a beard, in fact. She brushed a hand back over her hair, realizing she wasn't at her best herself just then.

She also frantically tried to think. Had the *Feldgendarmerie* had him all the time he was missing? She thought the Triads would have known about it if the Germans had. She thought so, but she wasn't sure. The Germans hadn't run things for so long by not being able to keep secrets.

"I'm sorry you got dragged into this," Paul said as his burly escorts left the room. The door closed behind them. "You had nothing to do with it, not really."

As he spoke, he pointed to the ceiling and cupped a hand behind his ear. Lucy nodded to show she got it. The *Feldgendarmerie* was listening to whatever they said. The secret police had to be hoping they'd talk too much. That meant they had to be careful not to.

"It's good to see you," Lucy said. Then she'd remember she'd told her questioner she didn't know Paul very well. She quickly added, "It's good to see anyone who's not yelling at me and thinking I did things."

"Boy, do I know what you mean." Paul might have overacted a little, but not much. As he talked, he winked at her. "It's especially bad since we *haven't* done anything." He paused. "You're right. It is nice to see anybody who doesn't think you're a criminal."

Lucy smiled at him. He was getting things in between the lines, too. He didn't want the Germans to think the two of them were friends. That would give the *Feldgendarmerie* one more weapon. Didn't it have enough already?

"I never thought that." Lucy smiled at him. In fact, they grinned at each other, right there under the Germans' noses. She went on, "I do think it's terrible that you've had so much trouble."

"Well, it doesn't seem like I'm the only one," Paul answered. "It's just too bad, that's all. You know what I'd like to do when this is all over, to try to make up for some of the trouble we've caused you?"

"What?" Lucy thought he was an optimist for believing this would be over any time soon, if ever. But if you weren't an optimist when you were in trouble, wouldn't the weight of it squash you flat?

"I'd like to take you to dinner and a movie, if that's okay." He sounded nervous in a way that had nothing to do with being stuck in the Germans' jail. Lucy remembered thinking he was shy.

She nodded. "I'd like that." Would anything more come of it? *Could* anything more come of it? She had her doubts, even if she wished she didn't. The distance between that other San Francisco, the one with the nice Sunset District, and this one felt enormously wide. But dinner and a movie could be fun by themselves.

"The *Feldgendarmerie* hasn't been too rough with me. I hope they haven't with you." Paul yawned.

"No, not too bad." Lucy yawned, too. She wondered why. It was early in the day. She saw Paul sag down in his chair the instant before blackness also washed over her.

"You idiot." Sammy Wong looked as disgusted as he sounded.

Paul stared up at him. He remembered yawning, and then nothing else—till the man from Crosstime Traffic appeared in the room. It might have been magic. It might have been, but it wasn't. Across the table from him, Lucy Woo slumped in sleep. Paul's left arm burned. "You drugged us," he said. "You drugged us, and then you gave me the antidote."

"Hand the clever fellow a prize!" Sammy Wong kept right on glaring at Paul. "I drugged this whole building. Neofentanyl's good stuff. No odor, no taste, goes through the ventilating system like that"—he snapped his fingers—"and knocks you out for eight hours unless you get a shot. To the Devil with me if I know why I bothered giving you one. After that stunt you pulled, I should have just left you here."

He wasn't wrong. Paul stared down at the cheap gray carpet, feeling ashamed. "I did something stupid. I know that. I've had enough time to think about it in here. I'm sorry."

"Not sorry enough." His rescuer didn't seem to want to let him off the hook. He had trouble blaming the man from Crosstime Traffic, but even so . . . .

He looked up. "Haven't you ever done anything stupid in your whole life?"

"Not *that* stupid." Sammy Wong sounded very sure of himself. He turned toward the door. "Come on, kid. Let's get out of here. That eight hours is all very well, but the Kaiser's boys are going to start wondering what's up when the phone rings here and nobody answers."

"Okay," Paul said. "Wake Lucy up, too." He nodded toward the sleeping Chinese girl.

"What?" Wong stared at him. "Are you nuts? No, I won't wake her up. That's dumber than sticking your nose out of the hotel. Now get moving. We're wasting time."

"No," Paul said. "It's not fair to leave her here. Crosstime Traffic got her into this mess. The least we can do is get her out."

"She's a local," Sammy Wong said. "The crosstime secret comes first."

What would he do if I told him she knows it? Paul wondered. But he clamped down hard on that. The older man might want to shut Lucy's mouth for good. Paul did say, "This room is bound to be bugged."

"Won't pick up a thing." Again, Sammy Wong sounded sure as could be.

"Okay." Paul believed him. "But she's helped me a lot. I owe her one. You can't just leave her here with the *Feldgendarmerie*."

Wong blew out a long, exasperated breath. "Why not? If you're gone and she's still here, they'll figure she didn't have anything to do with you."

"If I'm gone and she's still here, she'll figure I walked out on her," Paul said. "If I go and she stays, the Tongs will figure we're not to be trusted—and won't they be right? They've still got Dad somewhere, remember? Finding me was easy. What about him?" He waited. Sammy Wong looked even more sour than usual. He made a good match for Bob Lee. Paul added what he hoped was the clincher: "Besides, *nobody* deserves to be in a *Feldgendarmerie* jail, and she's only sixteen."

"If I let her out, she can't just go back to her family," Wong said. "The Germans would jug the lot of them."

"She can't stay here, either. She *can't*," Paul said. They glared at each other. Impasse. Paul sighed. "If you can't see your way clear to letting her out, I'd better stay here, too. Fair's fair."

Sammy Wong's eyes got wider than Paul thought they could. "What?" he yelled. "I can't do that! I couldn't do it before, and I especially can't do it now!" He was almost hopping up and down, he was so excited. "What will the Germans think? They all decided to take a nap at the same time?"

"I don't care." Paul had made up his mind. He didn't know whether he was right or wrong. A lot of the time, that didn't become clear till later on anyhow. "If she doesn't go, I don't go."

"I ought to bop you over the head and drag you," Wong said savagely.

Paul tensed. "You can try." Could the man from Crosstime Traffic do it? Maybe. Paul had had self-defense courses, but he'd never be a black belt or anything like that. He told himself he'd put up the best fight he could. And even if he lost . . . "Good luck explaining why you're lugging me down the street on your back."

Wong said several things in Chinese that didn't sound like compliments. Then he said several things in English that *weren't* compliments. Paul just smiled. Wong yelled, "You won't work for Crosstime Traffic again!" Paul's smile got bigger. That threat hurt. He refused to let Sammy Wong see how much. Besides, some things were more important.

"How soon do you think it'll be before somebody phones?" Paul asked.

Some of the things the older man called him made what he'd said before sound like a love letter. Paul looked down at his wrist. He wasn't wearing a watch, but the message came through loud and clear. "Here," Wong snarled, and the one word sounded worst of all. He took out a hypo and jabbed it into Lucy's arm.

Twelve

When Lucy woke up, she needed a moment to realize she *had* awakened. She'd gone to sleep or passed out or whatever it was so fast, she hardly even knew she'd done it. But the Asian man in the room with her and Paul sure hadn't been there what seemed like only a few seconds before. He looked mad enough to bite nails in half.

"Hi," Paul said. "This is Sammy Wong. He's one of my friends from the Sunset District."

"Oh. Hello," Lucy managed. Did that mean what she thought it did? Was this furious-looking Mr. Wong from whatever *other* San Francisco Paul came from? If he was, Paul had said so in a way he wouldn't know about. She nodded to the older man. "I'm pleased to meet you."

"I'm not pleased to meet you, not even a little bit," he snapped. The glare he sent Paul could have melted iron. "Come on. Let's get out of here."

That made Lucy squeak in surprise. "What about the Germans?" she asked.

"What about 'em?" Sammy Wong said. He walked to the door and opened it. Lucy and Paul followed him.

Feldgendarmerie men sprawled in the corridor. They weren't dead—their chests were going up and down. But they'd passed out as fast as Lucy and Paul had. One of them had held a cup of coffee. He'd spilled it on himself, and all over the floor.

More Germans had dropped in their tracks, all through the jail. "How did you *do* this?" Lucy asked.

Sammy Wong gave her a smile that was anything but friendly. "I'm magic."

She was tempted to believe him. She was also tempted to kick him for not telling her what she wanted to know. Paul suffered from that disease, too. But this Sammy Wong didn't suffer from it—he reveled in it. He hustled her and Paul along as if every second counted. And every second probably did.

The guards outside the jail hadn't been flattened by the magic, or whatever it was. When one of them asked Wong, *"Was ist hier los?"* he answered in fluent German. It wasn't the bits and pieces of the language that most Americans picked up. He spoke German like a German—like a high-ranking German, in fact. He pulled papers from his pocket to back up his words. When he finished, all the guards came to attention and clicked their heels. *"Jawohl!"* they chorused. Wong led Paul and Lucy down the stairs and down the street.

"What did you tell them?" Lucy whispered once they were out of earshot.

He looked at her. "That I was the Kaiser's cousin, and I wanted to play hopscotch with the two of you."

She did try to kick him then. He sprang out of the way—he might have been good at hopscotch. Paul said, "He told them he was going to use us for bargaining chips to try to trap some of the men from the Tongs."

Lucy hadn't known Paul understood German that well. It didn't surprise her. By that time, nothing much would have surprised her.

Had Sammy Wong really turned out to be the Kaiser's cousin, she would just have nodded and filed the news away, like a folder back in the office.

Would she ever see the office again? How could she, when she'd just broken out of the *Feldgendarmerie* jail? The Germans and their American stooges were going to start turning San Francisco upside down and inside out.

"What happens now?" she asked, still in a very small voice.

"Now we have to get Dad out of his mess," Paul said.

"And then we have to get out of here," Wong added.

Paul's *we* plainly included Lucy. Wong's *we,* even more plainly, didn't. Lucy called him on it: "What happens to me now? What happens to my family?"

He scowled. Instead of answering her, he rounded on Paul. "We ought to leave her in the lurch. You know it bloody well, too." He sounded as furious—and as sure he was right—as anyone Lucy had ever heard.

Paul didn't even blink. "Go ahead," he said calmly. "But if you leave her, you leave me, too."

"Wait!" Lucy exclaimed.

He shook his head. "I'm not waiting for anybody. We've been through too much together. I'm not going to let anything bad happen to you if I can stop it."

"You blockhead." Sammy Wong still sounded savage. "Half of what's happened here—more than half—is your own stupid fault."

"Some of it is, yeah. I made plenty of mistakes," Paul said with a shrug. "More than half? No way, José." Lucy had no trouble figuring out what that meant, but nobody in this San Francisco would have said it. Paul went on, "I'll tell you what the real trouble is—what we were selling. It was too good. It got us noticed."

Wong said something about what they'd been selling that should have made the sidewalk catch fire. "*Elliott* didn't have any trouble," he finished.

Paul ignored the bad language. "No. You're wrong," he said, replying to the older man's last sentence. "Elliott didn't *see* any trouble. We had it from day one. That means it was here waiting for us ahead of time."

"Any old excuse in a storm," Sammy Wong jeered.

"Okay, think like that. Go ahead. But we can find out." Paul turned to Lucy. "How long has your dad been wondering about Curious Notions and what it sold?"

"Quite a while now," she answered. "At least two or three years. Maybe longer—I'm not real sure."

"You see?" Paul said to Sammy Wong.

"I see somebody who got himself in trouble and who's looking for a way out," Wong said.

"I got myself into some of this trouble, yeah, but not all of it," Paul said. "And the trouble between the Tongs and the Germans has been here since . . . for longer than we've been alive."

Sammy Wong didn't notice that he'd changed course there. Lucy did. He'd probably been about to say something like *since before we got here*. But if he did say that, it would give away that he and Wong had come from a different world. He might also have given away that Lucy already knew they were from that other world.

"When we get home—" Wong didn't just change course. He broke off, and went back to nasty muttering in English and Chinese.

He led Lucy and Paul south, away from Market Street—off to an area not too far from where Lucy worked. Paul said, "Where are we going? This isn't the way back to the Palace Hotel."

Lucy started howling laughter. She couldn't help it. It poured out of her, peal after peal, till she couldn't even walk any more. She stood there, doubled over, tears running down her cheeks. Paul and Sammy Wong stared at her as if she'd lost her mind. So did people walking by on the street. "You were . . ." she started, and then had to stop, because another spasm seized her. Finally, she got it out: "You were staying . . . at the . . . Palace Hotel?"

"Yeah, we were." Paul reached out. She had to lean on his arm to straighten up. He still looked puzzled, and almost angry, too. "What about it? You scared me half to death there."

"When you disappeared—I guess that's when Mr. Wong found you—the Triads were trying to figure out where you'd gone." Lucy spoke carefully. Her ribs and stomach hurt from laughing too much. "Your father didn't know, either. When he and Stanley Hsu were talking, he got rude and said he thought you were staying at the Palace. Oh, my." She wiped her streaming eyes on her sleeve.

Paul thought about it. Then he said, "I guess maybe you had to be there."

"I guess maybe you did," Sammy Wong said. "Come on. In here." *Here* was a not very fancy house in a not very fancy neighborhood. It had two bedrooms, a bathroom, a tiny living room, and an even tinier kitchen. Wong sighed. "I'll sleep on the sofa. I didn't expect to have more than one person along." He sent Paul one more sour stare.

"Life is full of surprises," was all Paul said.

"If you sit tight, that'll sure be one," Wong snapped. Paul turned a dull red.

"We're all on the same side here—I think," Lucy said. "Can we try to get along till we figure out what we ought to do next?" She had no idea what that would be. She had to hope Paul and Sammy Wong did. *They'd better,* she thought. *They can do almost anything. But when it comes to knowing what they* should *do, they're no better than anybody else—worse than some people.* The thought was oddly cheering.

"You make good sense," Paul said. "You usually do, I think."

"Thank you," Lucy said. She looked toward Sammy Wong. The other man from that other Sunset District still seemed anything but happy, but he nodded. That made Lucy feel a little better. If only she'd had the faintest notion where they were going from here, she would have felt better yet.

Somebody shook Paul awake in the middle of the night. A bright light shone in his face. Panic threatened to grab hold of him. But it wasn't the *Feldgendarmerie*. It was Sammy Wong in a flannel night-shirt. In its own way, that was almost as scary a sight as a big, beefy German in a trench coat.

"Listen, kid, we've got to talk," Wong said in a voice that brooked no argument.

"Go ahead. I'm listening," Paul said around a yawn. His wits slowly started to work. He pointed back behind Wong. "You closed the door."

"You bet I did. This is Crosstime Traffic business, not stuff for the locals."

Paul didn't like it when Wong talked about Lucy that way. She *was* a local, of course, but it made her sound like part of the background in a movie. "Well, go on," he said.

"You really know how to complicate things, don't you?" Wong said.

"Things were complicated before I got here," Paul said. "I keep telling you that, but you don't want to listen to me."

"Okay, fine. I'm listening now. Things were complicated before you got here. I even believe you, for whatever you think that's worth." Sammy Wong's voice dropped to an angry growl: "But you sure haven't done one stinking thing to make 'em any simpler, have you?"

Paul bit his lip. He couldn't very well argue with that. If he said he'd just tried to stay out of jail and stay out of trouble, the man from Crosstime Traffic would ask him how much luck he'd had—either that or he'd just laugh himself silly. Quietly, Paul asked, "Where *do* we go from here?"

Wong pointed a stubby, accusing finger at him. "You made me show some of my cards getting you out of jail. The Germans will be having kittens trying to figure out how I did that. And now we've got your stray kitty in the next room." He jerked his chin toward the bedroom Lucy was using."

"It's not like that," Paul said wearily. He also thought for a moment about the marmalade cat that had started to adopt Curious Notions. He hoped it was all right, and that someone else was giving it handouts these days.

Sammy Wong snorted. "Yeah, yeah. But even if it's not, it's every bit as much trouble as if it were. The Germans and the Triads and her folks will all be wondering what's happened to her." Paul would have put Lucy's folks first, but he saw Wong's point.

"If we'd left her in jail, they'd know what was happening to her. And so would I." He glared at Wong. "I bet you've broken all the mirrors in your house so you don't have to look at them."

With a shrug, the older man answered, "When you've got a mug like mine, looking in the mirror never was much of a thrill." That made Paul glare in a different way. Wong ignored him and went on, "You really do complicate my life. You complicate things for the company, too. Lucy knows too much." A stab of fear shot through Paul. Sammy Wong ignored that, too. He said, "Now we've got to do something with her. Probably with her whole blinking family, too."

For a second, Paul thought he'd said *do something to her*. He braced himself to jump the man from Crosstime Traffic. He knew that would likely get him nothing but a set of lumps, but he was going to try it. Even if he did knock Wong cold, he'd stay stuck in this alternate forever—or till Crosstime Traffic brought in somebody else and hunted him down. All the same . . .

Then he heard what Sammy Wong had really said. He gaped. "What—what can we do with them?" he stammered.

"Get 'em out of this alternate, if we can," Wong answered. He pointed at Paul again, this time with his thumb upraised to make his hand into a gun. "Kid, you would not believe the kind of forms you're gonna have to fill out when you get home. Would not *believe*. Serves you right, too. When we have to extract somebody from an alternate, and especially when we have to extract a bunch of somebodies . . . You miserable nuisance."

Paul went right on gaping. "You mean—we do that?" He shook his head in disbelief. "In all the training we got, they said we never do stuff like that. Never, with a capital N, no matter what."

"Yeah, well, there are plenty of good reasons for that, too. I bet you can figure out most of 'em for yourself." Sammy Wong proceeded to spell out what he meant in spite of what he'd just said. Grownups did that too often, as far as Paul was concerned. "Biggest one is, we want people to act like we never do it. If they thought there were times they could smuggle a boyfriend or a girlfriend—'cause that's what it's usually about—back to the home timeline, they'd do it too often. People in the alternates would start wondering what was going on. And besides, not everybody from the alternates can fit into the home timeline. Most of the time, moving people is a lot—a *lot*—more trouble than it's worth. Every once in a while . . ." He shrugged. "Every once in a while, you have to fill out all those stupid forms."

"The Woos could fit in," Paul said eagerly. "This alternate isn't as far along as we are, but it's pretty well up there. They work hard. They speak English. They're even Americans, sort of."

"Yeah, sort of," Wong said. "And sort of not, too. To be *real* Americans, they'll have to stop looking over their shoulders all the time. But I won't say you're nuts—not on account of that, anyway." By the look on his face, not all was forgiven or forgotten. Oh, no. He went on, "Now we've just got to make it happen."

He made it sound easy. Paul wished *he* thought it were. "How?" he asked.

"Way I see it, we've got four problems," the man from Crosstime Traffic said. "We've got to get your dad away from the Triads. We've got to make the Woos disappear. We've got to get to the transposition chamber. And we've got to do all that so nobody—not the *Feldgendarmerie*, not the Triads, *nobody*—is any the wiser about what we really are and where we're really from. Am I forgetting anything?"

"I don't think so." Paul knew he sounded troubled. "That seems like enough all by itself."

"One step at a time, that's all." Wong reached out and clapped Paul on the shoulder. Paul would have thought he'd resent the attention. Instead, he was oddly glad to have it. The man from Crosstime Traffic went on, "Anyway, I wanted to make sure we were on the same page. Now go back to sleep."

"Yeah, right," Paul said. Sammy Wong laughed. Ten minutes later, Paul was snoring.

Mr. Wong went out early in the morning. Before he did, he sat Lucy and Paul down on the sofa. He said, "*Stay* here, you two, okay?" He pointed to Paul and spoke in tones of heavy menace: "This means you."

Lucy thought Paul would get mad. Instead, he just nodded and said, "Okay." Lucy wanted to scratch her head. Paul didn't usually take something like that from anybody. But she didn't think he was lying.

Evidently, Sammy Wong didn't, either. He nodded back and walked out the door. When Lucy looked over at Paul, she found he was looking at her, too. "Hi," she said.

"Hi, yourself," he answered. After a moment, he added, "I'm sorry we got you into this mess."

She started to tell him it was okay, but she didn't. That went too far. "At least you're trying to get us out of it," she said. Yes, that was better.

"Now I think we are," he said, and glanced toward the door through which his—acquaintance? colleague? what was the right word? not *friend,* plainly—had just left. He hesitated again. His words came out in a rush: "How would you like to see what that other Sunset District is like?"

"That . . . other Sunset District?" Lucy said slowly. She'd figured out that Paul had to come from a different world. He'd admitted it, too. Now she discovered the difference between believing it and *believing* it. "You really can do that? You really *do* do that—go back and forth, I mean?"

"We can. We do. We have to," he said. "We're going to get you and your family out of here. Once you get used to things where I come from, I think you'll like it a lot better than you like this San Francisco."

This San Francisco. The words brought home his strangeness all over again. She wondered if he was strange because he was crazy. She shook her head. Crazy people didn't have the kinds of things Curious Notions sold. Crazy people didn't get you out of the Germans' jail, either. "Can you really do that?" she whispered.

"I hope so. We're working on it," Paul answered. "Um, one other thing." He looked a little embarrassed, or maybe more than a little.

"What is it?" Lucy asked.

"When you find out about other alternates—worlds where things didn't happen the way they did in this one—act surprised, okay? You're not supposed to know anything about that. You're not supposed to know big time."

That was one more bit of slang nobody from *this* San Francisco would have used. Lucy didn't have any trouble figuring out what it meant, though. "I'll remember," she promised.

"Okay," Paul said. Lucy wondered how many different worlds—alternates, he called them—there were where people said that. Then she wondered how many there were where people *didn't*. And then she wondered which number was bigger. She had so many questions, so few answers. But now, if everything went right, she'd have the chance to find some of them, anyway. No sooner had that thought crossed her mind than Paul said, "Ask you something?"

Lucy laughed. "Sure. Go ahead. But I was just thinking about all the questions I want to ask you."

"About alternates and things?" he asked, and Lucy nodded. He managed a laugh, too, but it sounded self-conscious. "That isn't the kind of thing I was going to ask you."

"Well, what is?"

"When we get this mess straightened out—*if* we get it straightened out—and you're all settled in the home timeline and everything, you still want to go to that movie with me?"

"Yes, I would like to," Lucy said seriously. "It will probably take a while for us to get used to how you do things there, and it would be nice to know somebody who already knows his way around." She frowned. That hadn't come out quite the way she wanted it to. It sounded as if his knowing his way around was the only reason she would want to go out with him. She tried again: "It would be nice to be friends with somebody who already knows his way around." There. That was better.

Paul tipped an imaginary cap. "Happy to play tour guide for you, ma'am. All tips gratefully accepted."

"You're ridiculous," she said. He bowed sitting down, as if she'd paid him a compliment. One of her nine million questions came to the surface: "What are movies like in the—the home timeline, did you call it?"

"That's right. But that's one more thing you can forget you ever heard, too, okay?" Paul thought for a little while. "They're mostly dumb, but they're not dumb the same way they are here. Here they're kind of sappy, at least to me. Boy finds out he's really a duke's nephew so he can marry the countess he's in love with, that kind of thing."

"Sure," Lucy said. She'd seen at least four movies with plots like that. They were a way to kill a couple of hours. Her whole family could go for eighty-five cents—three quarters, plus a dime for Michael till he turned twelve. That was a pretty good deal.

"Well, when we make movies, what we mostly do wrong is use too many special effects—too much trick photography, you'd say," Paul told her. "We can do more of those, and fancier ones, than you can here. And sometimes, if we see lots of things blowing up or funny-looking people from other planets or ghosts or werewolves or whatever, we don't care if there's any real story behind them. But what you remember is mostly the spectacular stuff, not the people."

"People are what matter," Lucy said.

"They ought to be, anyhow," Paul agreed.

"How much does it cost to get into a movie in the, uh, home timeline?" she asked.

"Usually about 800 dollars," he answered. She gave him a nasty look, sure he was pulling her leg. He held up his right hand—he might have been taking an oath. "It really does, so help me. But a dollar there isn't like a dollar here. It isn't even like a penny here. Dollars are teeny-tiny small change. Benjamins start to be real money. A benjamin is a hundred dollars, so a movie costs eight benjamins or so."

Lucy thought about that. "So one of your benjamins—what you call a hundred dollars—is worth about three cents of our money?"

"Three cents, a nickel—something like that." Paul sounded as if it didn't matter much. To him, it didn't: "What difference does it make, as long as people have the money they need to buy what they want? And they do, or most of them do. They're better off than people are here."

She wondered if she ought to believe him. To try to find out, she asked, "Can they afford the things you were selling in Curious Notions?"

Instead of answering right away, Paul broke out laughing. "Lucy, that stuff is junk in the home timeline. We make it for the export market. We don't use it ourselves. We've got better—lots better—at home. You'll see."

Lucy had trouble believing that. To her father, what Curious Notions sold was far ahead of the state of the art. The Triads and the Germans felt the same way. Junk? But the way Paul said it make her take him seriously. And if he and Sammy Wong and their people could travel back and forth between worlds, what could they do when they stayed at home? Maybe, before too long, she'd find out.

The front door opened. In came Wong. He was carrying a great big sack. By the way he handled it, it was bulky but not heavy. When he dumped it on the floor, four tightly rolled sleeping bags spilled out. Lucy caught his eye. He nodded back to her. "Three for your family—and one for your dad, Paul."

"How do we get him back?" Tension tugged at Paul's voice.

Sammy Wong grinned. "I think I've got something worked out."

Not long before, Paul had been wild to go out on the streets of San Francisco. Now he wished he could stay in. Whenever he saw a cop, he wanted to run. He didn't—he knew better—but he wanted to. He and Lucy had to be hotter than a two-benjamin pistol. But as long as he acted as if he belong here, knew where he was going, and knew he had a right to get there, nobody paid much attention to him. Evening twilight helped make him harder to recognize from any distance, too.

Even though he had the address, he almost walked past Stanley Hsu's jewelry shop. It didn't go out of the way to call attention to itself. He paused with one foot in midair when he spotted the plain door with the right number on it. Then he opened the door and went inside.

The jeweler was working on something—an earring, Paul thought—behind the counter. He looked up when the bell above the door rang. "Young Mr. Gomes!" he said. "It really is you. I tell you frankly, I had trouble believing it."

"I'm here." Paul rubbed at his left upper arm. "Where's Dad?" A scrabbling noise came from overhead. "And what's that?"

Stanley Hsu shrugged. "A repairman on the roof. My landlord warned me he would be there. *Not* a *Feldgendarmerie* man, believe me. As for your father . . ." He went into the back room. When he came out, Lawrence Gomes was with him.

"Good to see you!" Paul exclaimed. A little to his surprise, he found himself meaning it. He and Dad were like cats and dogs a lot of the time. But they were still family. That counted. And, in this dangerous alternate, they were both from the home timeline. That might have counted for more.

Stanley Hsu studied Paul. "How on earth did you get out of the *Feldgendarmerie* jail? Do you have any idea how upset the Germans are?"

"I'll tell you something, Mr. Hsu—I'm not very happy with the Germans, either," Paul said. With luck, the jeweler wouldn't notice that he hadn't answered his questions.

But Stanley Hsu did. Paul wasn't very surprised. The jeweler didn't miss much. He said, "And is it true that you brought Miss Woo out with you? I gather she is also among the missing from the jail?" Paul's father stirred at that. For a wonder, though, he kept his mouth shut.

"I don't know where Lucy is." Paul kept his eyes on some carved jade not far from Stanley Hsu. As long as he was looking at something like that, his face was much less likely to give him away in a lie.

Whether it did turned out not to matter much. Stanley Hsu's smile stopped short of his eyes. "Do you really expect me to believe that?" he asked. "She could not have escaped if you did not. Will you try to tell me anything different?"

More rattling and scraping from the roof made Paul look up. The jeweler ignored the racket. He was good at ignoring anything that didn't matter to him. That was part of what made him so formidable.

He went on, "We still have a bargain to finish, too, don't we? Now you and your father are both free of the Germans. That means we have some talking to do, eh? I look forward to asking you a lot of questions."

Paul believed that. He also knew he could afford to answer none of them—not with the truth, anyway. What had Dad said to the Tongs? For that matter, what had Dad said to the *Feldgendarmerie*? Dad was looking back at him, but Paul couldn't tell what his expression meant.

Dad yawned. So did Stanley Hsu. They both crumpled to the floor. The jeweler banged his head on the counter as he went down. Paul hoped it wasn't . . . too bad.

A couple of minutes after that, Sammy Wong walked in the front door. He wore denim overalls and carried a tool chest. Except for the derby perched on his head, he could have been a repairman in the home timeline. "They out?" he asked.

"You better believe it." Paul pointed behind the counter.

"Okay." Sammy Wong went over there and gave Paul's father the antidote for neofentanyl. As Lawrence Gomes grunted and sat up, Wong began breaking into jewelry cases and putting some of the best pieces in the toolchest.

"Hey!" Paul said. "What are you doing that for?"

"Let 'em think it's robbery," the man from Crosstime Traffic answered. "Let 'em think the whole thing with Curious Notions was just a setup to rip them off. They'll want to kill us, of course, a millimeter at a time." He sounded much too cheerful about that. "They'll want to kill us, but they won't believe in crosstime travel, any more than they believe in Santa Claus."

"He's right," Paul's father said as he climbed to his feet. He nodded to Sammy Wong. "Nice scheme. Do we know each other?"

"I don't think so." Wong gave Paul's father his name and went on stealing jewelry. Paul didn't need long to decide it *was* a good scheme. The Tongs might decide they'd been conned. That was okay, as far as Crosstime Traffic was concerned. While the Chinese in San Francisco might tear things apart looking for robbers, they wouldn't look for people from a different alternate.

Sammy Wong straightened. "Have enough?" Paul's father asked. Wong nodded. Dad said, "Cool. Let's get out of here."

"Second the motion," Paul added.

"No arguments from me," Wong said. Out the door they went. Paul worried. The police, the *Feldgendarmerie,* and the Tongs all knew what he and his father looked like. The cops and the Germans just wanted them back. Sammy Wong was right: the Tongs would want them dead.

The Chinese man from Crosstime Traffic strode along as if he hadn't a care in the world. So did Dad. Paul did his best to imitate them. He'd seen for himself that acting normal helped fool anybody who might be after you. It wasn't easy, though. He kept wanting to run, and to look down at the sidewalk so nobody could get a good look at his face.

When they turned on to Market Street, Paul let out a sigh of relief. True, Market was the main drag, and had more cops on it than other streets did. But it was also packed with people. As long as Paul didn't do anything to draw policemen's eyes, why should they notice him? He kept telling himself the same thing over and over.

They didn't. He and his father and Sammy Wong got back to the little house south of Market with no one the wiser. They had one problem solved, maybe even one and a half. Too many still lay ahead.

"We have to be careful around here," Lucy told Sammy Wong. "We don't want anyone from the shoe factory to see me."

"No, that wouldn't be so good," Wong agreed. "Okay, you lead the way around it so nobody's likely to spot us." Once they got up on Market Street, he nodded to her again. "Very neat. Very smooth. You know your way around, all right."

"I'd better," she said. "This is my city, after all." *How much longer will it be my city? How different will that other San Francisco be? Is that other San Francisco real?* Sometimes, when she was feeling what she'd once thought of as sensible, she had trouble believing it. But nothing that had happened to her lately was even close to sensible. When common sense stopped making sense, you stopped using it, didn't you? That was only . . . sensible.

She tugged at a wisp of hair that had got loose. She was wearing it pulled back into a ponytail, not falling free on both sides of her face. She had on more makeup than she usually used, too. It made her look older, and not much like the self she was used to.

She remembered the not-quite-hidden-enough glances Paul had sent her way before she went out the door. She thought they meant he found the changes interesting. She hoped so.

Then she stiffened and worried about things that mattered right this minute. Here came a *Feldgendarmerie* man. People got out of his way, where they wouldn't have for any American. He walked past Lucy and Mr. Wong without even seeing them. Sure as sure, to the Germans all Chinese looked alike.

The streets around her father's shop had a funny kind of familiarity. When she was little, she'd come here all the time. Since she'd got a job of her own, though, she'd gone there instead. So she mostly remembered what things had looked like a few years before. Some of the shops had new owners now. Some had closed. A few had opened. Things weren't quite right, but she wasn't always sure just how they were wrong. She kept blinking and looking around, trying to figure out what had changed.

"You're not going in," Sammy Wong reminded her. "Too big a

chance they'd recognize you. That's one place they will be watching, to see if you show up."

"I know," Lucy said. "It's okay. We'll do it just the way you planned."

"Good." Wong eyed her. "You're a solid kid. Paul was right about that much."

With a shrug, she answered, "I know what needs doing."

"I think maybe we both just said the same thing." Wong chuckled. "One thing the *Feldgendarmerie* won't be looking for is an old guy bringing in a radio to get it fixed." The radio he was carrying really didn't work. Lucy liked that. It showed attention to detail.

There was the shop. It looked exactly the way it was supposed to. The dragon with the electric-plug tail sprawled across the window. Sammy Wong steered Lucy to the little café across the street. The fellow behind the counter was new. She'd never seen him before. Better yet, he'd never seen her before. He didn't know she was Charlie Woo's daughter. She ordered fried rice with pork and sat down where she could keep an eye on her father's shop.

A man in the café seemed to be watching the shop more than he was eating. Maybe she was imagining that. Then again, maybe she wasn't. The man didn't pay any attention to her.

She knew what Sammy Wong would be doing across the street. He'd wait till he was the only customer—he probably wouldn't have to wait long. Then he'd show her father the TV pictures he'd shot of her. The camera was smaller than her closed fist. The screen was just a little square of plastic with some switches and controls on the back. Nobody in this San Francisco had anything like either one. They'd helped convince her that other Sunset District really was out there . . . somewhere. If they didn't convince her father of the same thing, nothing ever would.

Mr. Wong came out of the shop as she finished the fried rice.

He looked down the street, as if towards a friend, and nodded twice. Lucy got up and left the café. This was the part that made her nervous. She crossed the street and walked by in front of the shop. She didn't go in. She didn't even look in the window. She just wanted to show Father she really was okay. But if that man in the café realized who she was . . . That wouldn't be good at all.

She came up to Wong. "Everything all right?" she asked quietly.

He nodded one more time. "They'll be there. Now let's us disappear."

They didn't go right back to the house south of Market. They made sure nobody was following them first. But Sammy Wong was grinning before very long. So was Lucy. They'd sneaked right under the Germans' noses, and they'd got away with it. How could anything go wrong now?

Thirteen

It was after dark. Streetlights near Curious Notions were few and faint. That was true of street lights in most parts of this San Francisco. Cold, clammy fog rolled in off the bay. Paul was nervous even so. If somebody spotted him now, everything could still go horribly wrong.

And it wasn't just him. His father was there, too, and Lucy, and her folks. Sammy Wong didn't think anybody had followed Lucy's father and mother and little brother to their meeting with him. He was just about sure nobody'd followed them all from the meeting to the now very crowded little house where everyone had stayed.

Didn't think. Just about sure. When you were talking about most things, those little phrases didn't matter so much. When you were talking about freedom, about getting back to the home time-line . . . Paul wanted to be sure. He couldn't. Knowing he couldn't ate at him.

"Go on around the corner," Wong said. "I'll be with you in about ten minutes. Then we'll all go back to Curious Notions. And then we'll go."

He made it sound very easy. Paul hoped it would be. He had trouble believing it. Nothing in this alternate had ever been easy. But then he shook his head. He'd got out of the *Feldgendarmerie* jail. That had gone as smoothly as anyone could please. This could, too. And from could to would wasn't far. *Only ten minutes away,* he thought.

Before they all walked into Louie's, Paul made sure no cops were in there stuffing their faces with burgers and fries. *That* would complicate things, and things were complicated enough already. But, except for Louie, the place was empty. It wasn't the sort of night that brought customers out in droves.

The Greek fry cook looked up from a crossword-puzzle magazine when the bell over the door jingled. He did a better double take than any Paul had ever seen on the movies or TV. Those were rehearsed. This one was the real McCoy.

"You!" Louie said hoarsely. "Both of you! What are you, nuts? You aren't just hot. You glow in the dark." He said something in Greek that sounded as if it glowed in the dark. Then he pointed at the Woos. "I don't know who the Devil you people are, but you've probably got everybody and his brother after you, too."

Lucy's father gulped and made as if to get out of the hamburger joint in a hurry. Her mom set a hand on his arm. "It's all right. I think it's all right, anyhow," she said. "They wouldn't bring us to anyone who'd sell us out."

"They've been wrong before," her father pointed out.

Louie said something else explosive in Greek. "That's for the cops," he added in English. "It goes double for the *Feldgendarmerie.*"

The San Francisco police and the German secret police weren't the only ones who wanted Paul and his dad and the Woos. Nobody said anything about that. What Paul's father did say was, "As long as we're here, we might as well have some baklava."

Hamburgers and franks were one thing. Baklava was something else. Baklava hit Louie where he lived. He made a small ceremony of cutting big slices and putting them on half a dozen paper plates. Lucy exclaimed in delight when she dug in. So did her brother. Paul wondered if they'd ever had it before. He would have bet they hadn't.

Dad set a twenty-dollar bill on the counter. That was a lot of money here. When Louie started to make change, Dad said, "Don't bother."

The cook glared and went on pulling money out of the cash box. "I pay my way. You don't need to give me nothin' to keep my mouth shut."

Paul was afraid his father had made a bad mistake. Whatever Louie didn't have, he had pride enough for three men. But Dad saved things, saying, "That's not why I did it. Call it a good-bye present. We're not going to be around much longer."

"You sure won't, not with all the people you got mad at you," Louie said. But he tucked the twenty away. "Okay, pal, since you put it that way. Thanks."

What if something went wrong inside Curious Notions? What if Wong didn't come back? *Then we won't be around here much longer. Dad would be right. But so would Louie.* Paul didn't want not to be around Louie's way.

His stomach had started churning overtime when the door to Louie's finally opened. In strolled Sammy Wong. "Let's go, folks," he said. "Everything's just the way it ought to be."

Everybody hurried out into the night. Louie lifted his cap off his head in a sort of salute. "Can this be real?" Lucy's father muttered. Paul didn't think he was supposed to hear that, but he did.

"Hang on for one second." Wong paused in a particularly dark stretch of street. "You need the antidote, so the anesthetic inside the shop doesn't knock you out."

He gave everybody a shot. Lucy's little brother yipped when he saw people getting stuck. She knew how to keep him from doing anything more than yip. "Are you going to be a baby, Michael?" she said. "*I* can get a shot without making a fuss." And she did. After that, you could have set Michael on fire and he wouldn't have let out a peep.

"Here we are." Sammy Wong opened the front door to Curious Notions. Paul tried to smell neofentanyl in the air. He couldn't, of course. It had no odor. That was one of the things that made it so useful. The other was that it would stop a charging elephant in its tracks. Paul remembered yawning in the *Feldgendarmerie* jail. Then he remembered waking up when Sammy Wong gave him the antidote. In between? As far as he could prove, there was no in between.

"Down to the basement," Paul's father said briskly. "And then down to the subbasement." By the way he said it, it might have been his plan.

Paul found one more thing to worry about. What would the German secret police think when they found the subbasement? Nobody could put the file cabinet that hid the trap door back where it belonged. He shrugged. After so many enormous worries, that was a small one.

Down to the basement they hurried. Michael went last so he could slide down the banister instead of walking down the stairs. Paul didn't think he would have done that in the dark when he was eleven years old. Lucy's kid brother was a piece of work, all right.

Sammy Wong shone a flashlight on the file cabinet. "Let's do it," he said.

Another flashlight beam stabbed out from behind Paul. "You will put your hands up at once, all of you," a German-accented voice said. "In the Kaiser's name, you are all under arrest." Spinning, Paul saw a tall man in *Feldgendarmerie* uniform wearing a pig-snouted gas mask. He had a flashlight in his left hand. His right held a pistol aimed at Wong.

The German paid no attention to Michael Woo, who stood right beside him. Michael might have hit him or kicked him in the shins. Instead, he did something even better. He reached up and yanked off the German's mask.

After an outraged yelp, the *Feldgendarmerie* man sucked in a breath of air. That was all he needed to do. His eyes rolled up in his head. He didn't even yawn, the way Paul had. He just crumpled to the floor. The pistol fell from his hand and skittered away, luckily without going off.

Lucy ran over to Michael. She gave him a big, smacking kiss. He yelped louder than the German had, and did kick her. She yelped, too.

"Come on," Paul said. "Let's get out of here as fast as we can, before anything else happens."

Not even his father argued with him. Dad went over to the file cabinet and shoved it out of the way. By then, Sammy Wong had his little automatic out. "I'll go first," he said. "The stuff wouldn't have got into the subbasement till now. If they've found it and they've got somebody waiting down there . . ."

But they didn't. It was empty. Plainly, no one had been in there since the *Feldgendarmerie* seized Curious Notions. Paul hurried to the computer set off to one side from where the transposition chamber would appear. "Wake up," he told it, and the screen came to life. Lucy exclaimed at that. So did her father.

"Voice signature recognized," the computer said. "Go ahead." Lucy and her father did some more exclaiming. Paul only half heard them. He spoke the code phrase that meant everything was okay and nobody was holding a gun to his head. Then he called for a chamber as fast as the home timeline could send one. His words showed up on the screen as he said them. Even Michael Woo exclaimed at that. Again, Paul hardly noticed. He hoped the Crosstime Traffic people were monitoring this chamber's equivalent in the home timeline.

Wong scattered a little bit of white powder on the floor in one corner of the room. He dropped a gold coin near it. "What's that for?" Paul asked.

"Let the Germans think we were smuggling," the older man answered. "That's a *normal* kind of thing, just like stealing jewelry is a *normal* kind of thing. If they think it's smuggling, they won't think about alternates. Them not thinking about alternates is what we want." The transposition chamber appeared out of nowhere. The door opened. Wong asked, "Paul, did you warn the home timeline about neofentanyl?"

"Oops," Paul said.

Oops it was. The chamber operator passed out as soon as she got a whiff of the air in the basement. Enough neofentanyl had come in through the trapdoor to knock her for a loop. Sammy Wong picked her up off the floor and gave her the antidote. She was not happy, to say the least.

"Never mind that," Paul's father said as he and everybody else hurried into the transposition chamber. "You can yell at us later. Just get us out of here now."

The door slid shut. After that, nothing seemed to happen. "Is it all right?" Lucy asked. "Are we supposed to feel something?"

"It's fine," Paul answered. "It'll feel like it takes about fifteen minutes. When we get to the home timeline, though, the clocks will say the same thing as they did in the alternate we just left."

"That's weird," Michael said.

"That's impossible," his father said.

Paul only shrugged. "It's what happens, honest."

"Won't be long, any which way," *his* father said, and he was right. When the door opened again, they were back in the home timeline.

This new San Francisco endlessly fascinated Lucy. It was the city she knew, and yet it wasn't. Most of the streets had the same names as the ones in her San Francisco. They went the same places as the ones she'd always known. She could find her way around. South of Market here was the same place as it was there.

But finding her way around didn't mean a thing. The streets were the same, but most of the buildings were different. A few old ones, like City Hall and some of the churches, were the same. Somehow, that only made them seem stranger, not more familiar.

For those were the buildings that had ruled the skyline in her San Francisco. Here, they huddled in the shadows of structures she'd not only never seen but never even imagined. Paul called them skyscrapers. That word had fallen out of use in the English she knew. It seemed to fit them, though. They did leap far, far up into the sky.

Some of them had elevators you could ride all the way to the top. One had a restaurant up there, a restaurant that revolved once an hour. She could eat a hamburger and fries and a milkshake and look out at the whole city. She knew she would remember that for the rest of her life.

But the people in this San Francisco were even more interesting than the scenery. Men's clothes weren't *too* different from what she was used to. The things girls and women wore, though . . . They

showed more skin, and skin in odder places, than she'd thought anybody could or would. They weren't embarrassed about doing it, either. It was as normal to them as her clothes had been to her.

By her standards, just about everybody was rich. That wasn't
because everyone had millions of dollars, though everyone did. A
million dollars here were only ten thousand benjamins, and ten
thousand benjamins were worth about what she'd made in a year at
the sewing machine. But people here all had cars—those who
wanted them, anyway—and radios and televisions and telephones
they carried around with them and those marvelous machines called
computers and all sorts of other things she hadn't dreamt of. Paul
hadn't been kidding. The things they knew about here put Curious
Notions to shame.

She discovered supermarkets. So many things, all right there
together! People filling shopping carts full of whatever they
wanted. They didn't seem to worry about the prices. That told Lucy
they had plenty of money, too. If they hadn't, they would have complained more or bought less.

Signs above some of the vegetables said they came from one
alternate or another. Lucy pointed at Paul when she noticed those.
"So that's why you dealt with those farmers from the Central Valley," she said.

He nodded. "That's right." When he was in her alternate, he'd
sounded just a little funny. Here in what he called the home timeline, everyone talked the way he did. Lucy was the one with a tiny
trace of accent. If she was going to stay here, she'd have to lose it
to fit in. That shouldn't be too hard.

"What about the Central Valley here?" she asked. She hadn't
seen it yet. She hadn't seen anything but this amazing new San
Francisco.

"It grows things, too," Paul answered. "But this is a crowded place. We need more food than we can grow ourselves. We need more of lots of things than we can get from this world."

"And so you get them from other . . . alternates," Lucy said. "That's what you were doing with Curious Notions."

"That's right," Paul said again. "Crosstime Traffic does that kind of thing on lots of different alternates. We don't take a whole lot from any one of them. That wouldn't be fair. We interfere as little as we can, too. Doing more wouldn't be fair, either."

"But you got my family and me out of there," Lucy said.

Paul seemed embarrassed. He was—but not, Lucy realized, on her account. No—he was embarrassed all on his own. "That's one more thing we don't usually do. We wouldn't have if Dad and I hadn't pulled you into what was really our problem. Getting away ourselves and leaving you stuck there wouldn't have been right, either."

"What are the Germans and the Triads doing there?" Lucy asked. Just putting the question that way felt funny. The Germans had been the central fact in politics in her alternate since the middle of the twentieth century. The Triads had been around in her San Francisco even longer, though she hadn't bumped up against them till she got to know the people from Curious Notions. Now both were a mile beyond the moon.

"It's easier to monitor the Germans," Paul answered. "They think we were running drugs. There's a huge price on my head, and on Dad's. The Tongs have to be more secret. From what people have picked up, though, they've got a price on us, too—and on you, I'm afraid."

That sent a shiver through Lucy. She needed a moment to *remember* the Triads in her San Francisco were a mile beyond the moon. Then she thought of something else. "Are there Triads here? In this San Francisco, I mean?"

"Well, yeah. There are." Paul nodded. "They're—mostly—legit, though. And I promise they don't have thing one to do with the Tongs in your alternate."

"That's good." Lucy meant it. She also wondered whether he was right. If the Triads were anything, they were sneaky and patient. Crosstime Traffic might have people working for it who were working for them, too. But that was the company's worry. It—probably—wasn't hers.

And she had trouble worrying about anything here in this amazing temple of food. She pointed to a bin of *very* strange fruit. They were about the size of her fist, bright yellow, and covered all over with not too pointy spikes about half an inch long. (People here would have said *a little more than a centimeter long*. Everybody here used the metric system, the way the Germans did in her alternate. One more thing she had to get used to.)

That was also a worry for another time. She pointed to the yellow . . . whatchamacallits. "What *are* those things, and which alternate do they come from?"

He laughed. "Most people call 'em hand-grenade melons. As a matter of fact, they're from here—from New Zealand, I think. They probably have 'em in your alternate, too, only not for export."

"Oh." Lucy had seen food from China and Chile and the Philippines and Canada and all over Europe and some places that weren't even places in her alternate—Indonesia, for instance, wherever that was. "Everything's for export here, isn't it?"

"Just about," Paul answered. "We—the United States—export a lot ourselves—grain and meat and soybeans, mostly."

Lucy nodded. She believed him. In her alternate, the United States had trouble feeding itself. Maybe this USA did, too, but if it did, it was for different reasons. She wondered how many people lived here. This San Francisco was more crowded than the one she'd known. And this United States hadn't had a lot of its biggest cities blown off the map by German atomic bombs. She gathered they'd worried about the Russians instead. That seemed ridiculous to her.

When she and Paul left the supermarket, he asked, "What shall we do now?"

"I don't know." Lucy stood in the parking lot and thought for a little while. (That the supermarket *had* a parking lot told how important it was.) The breeze off the ocean ruffled her hair. Even though this San Francisco was such a crowded place, exhaust fumes didn't fill the breeze. Cars were cleaner than they were in her alternate. Lucy didn't know how the home timeline managed that, but it did. All of a sudden, she snapped her fingers. "Yes, I do so know. Take me to the zoo!"

"I'll do that." Paul grinned at her. "The bus'll go through the Sunset District, too, so you'll see I wasn't fooling you about it."

"Okay." She grinned back. The grin slipped a little when she found out the bus fare was $145 for each of them. Even though she was starting to know better, that still seemed like a lot of money to her. When she worked it out, though, she decided it wasn't really a whole lot more than the nickel she was used to paying. And the buses here were much nicer than the ones in her alternate. They didn't stink. They didn't roar and lurch. They even had comfortable seats.

Paul hadn't been kidding about the Sunset District. A lot of the houses were old. Some of them might have been old enough to date from before her alternate and the home timeline split apart. All of them, though, were beautifully kept up. They had fresh paint. Their lawns were green as the emeralds in Stanley Hsu's shop. The cars in front of them were bright and shiny and clean.

"My house is just like one of these," Paul said. "Too bad we're not going down Thirty-third Avenue, or I'd show it to you. Oh, well—you'll get over there one of these times."

"Yes, I guess I will," Lucy said. "It's not like we haven't met each other's parents and everything."

"Uh—yeah." Paul turned red. *Isn't that interesting?* Lucy thought.

The zoo was just where it would have been in her alternate. There was still a lot of ivy, and a lot of birds flew around. They were all pretty much the same birds, too. But the zoo sure wasn't the same. No crumbling concrete here. They'd spent a lot of dollars—a lot of benjamins—fancying this place up. The enclosures all looked as if they came from the lands where the animals inside them lived. The displays in front of the enclosures weren't just signs. They were TV screens, and told all kinds of things about the beasts and birds on display.

Not everything had changed, though. That was what Lucy thought, anyhow, when a boy threw peanuts to a bear. The same thing could have happened in her alternate. But this kid got in trouble. A guard came up to him and led him out of the zoo. There were DO NOT FEED THE ANIMALS signs at the zoo in her alternate, but nobody paid any attention to them. Things were different here.

"This is what a zoo is supposed to be like," Lucy said.

"You think this is something, you ought to see the one in San Diego," Paul told her. "They have all kinds of animals there that are extinct in the wild. Tigers and rhinos, even."

The zoo in Lucy's San Francisco had had tigers and rhinos, too. None of the signs there had said they were extinct in the wild. As far as she knew, they weren't in her alternate. Maybe not quite all the differences in the home timeline were for the best.

She and Paul walked past an enclosure that held slim yellow

cats with black spots. "We do have cheetahs here," he said. "None of those left in the wild, either."

"Cheetahs never prosper," Lucy agreed gravely. Paul nodded. He took a step, and half of another one. Then he stopped and gave her a horrible look. She winked at him. He tried to stay disgusted, but couldn't do it. He started to laugh.

"You're going to fit right in here," he told her. "You're out of your tree."

"Thank you," she said.

They stopped and got something to eat. For reasons Lucy couldn't figure out, people here called wieners hot dogs. No matter what people called them, they were still wieners. Lucy slathered hers with sauerkraut and mustard. Paul put onions and pickle relish on his. They wrinkled their noses at each other's choices. Paul said, "I think you like sauerkraut because the Germans were running things in your alternate."

"Maybe," Lucy said. "But plenty of people here must like it, too, or the stand wouldn't put it out." Paul changed the subject, which made her decide she was right.

She frowned a little as she sipped from her Coke. The straw was made of see-through plastic. In her alternate, it would have been waxed cardboard. That wasn't what puzzled her, though. The soda tasted almost the same as it did in her San Francisco, but not quite. It tasted almost as good, too—but, again, not quite.

When she asked Paul if he knew what the difference was, he said, "Yeah. Here they sweeten it with corn syrup. In your alternate, I think they still use real sugar."

"Why don't they here?" Lucy asked. "Is sugar extinct in the wild, too?"

That made him laugh again while he shook his head. "No. Corn syrup's cheaper to use, that's all."

"But it's not as good!" Lucy said.

"That counts, but so does the other," Paul said. "I guess the people who decide what goes into Coke figured they made more money with corn syrup than they lost flavor, and so they kept on putting it in."

Lucy took another sip. This Coke wasn't *bad*. If you didn't know how it was supposed to taste, you'd think it was fine. She suspected the people in the Triads would think the same way the Coke-makers here did. A little bigger profit margin did count. But so did having something really good, not just good enough. Lucy thought so, anyway.

They rode the bus back toward the apartment Crosstime Traffic had got for her family. It was bigger than the one the Woos had had in Lucy's San Francisco. It had a TV and a computer and a fasarta and all the other things people in the home timeline took for granted. In Lucy's alternate, even the richest German noble couldn't have had most of them.

The apartment wasn't far from the western edge of this San Francisco's Chinatown. Lucy had been there a couple of times. It amazed and fascinated her. It was so much more *Chinese* than the one she'd grown up in. In her San Francisco, Chinese was a secret language only the Triads and a few other people remembered. Here, people spoke it on the street. There was a Chinese-language newspaper. There was even a Chinese-language TV station in this San Francisco, with most of the shows in Mandarin and some in Cantonese.

Lucy wasn't alone in being of Chinese blood but speaking only English. That came as a relief. But here she found herself wanting to learn some Chinese, too. In her alternate, that hadn't even crossed her mind.

Paul got off the bus with her and walked her to the apartment. He stayed on the sidewalk when she started up the stairs. She turned back to him from about halfway up. "Thanks . . . for every-thing," she said. "I had a terrific time today."

"Good. That's what you're supposed to do," he answered. "I'll see you again before too long." With an awkward little half-wave, he headed back toward the bus stop.

"Yes. You will." Lucy nodded. Except for her family, Paul was the only person she saw here who knew about the alternate where she'd grown up. A whole world, and it was gone forever. Part of her missed it, the part that misses an old house even after you've moved into a better one. Most ways, this was a better world—but it wasn't the one she was used to.

She slid the security cardkey into the lock in the apartment building's front door. A light flashed green. She turned the knob. The door opened. She closed it behind her. The card was just a flat piece of plastic. She wondered how the lock knew it was supposed to go in there.

Electronics, she thought. That meant a lot more here than it did in her alternate. Would she ever catch up with people who were born here and had had all these things their whole lives? She sometimes doubted it. Those were the times she got homesick. That other San Francisco might not have been so much, but she'd belonged there. It was *hers*. Here, she felt like a stranger, a tourist. But she wasn't going home again.

She didn't have to walk upstairs, the way she would have in her old apartment building. The elevator here was fast and silent as a dream. When she walked down the hall to her apartment, the carpeting muffled her steps. The cardkey that had let her into the building also let her into the apartment. It wouldn't let her into any of the others, though—she'd experimented. How did it know which was which?

Michael was playing a game on the TV screen. Lucy had

never imagined such a thing, but her little brother took to it like a duck to water. The game involved killing dragons and the evil wizards who rode on them. Had dragons been real, they would have been extinct by the time Michael got done slaughtering them.

He's the one who'll do best here, Lucy thought suddenly. *He has the fewest things to unlearn.*

Father sat in a chair with his back to the chaos on the television set. He looked up from the book on his lap and managed a smile for Lucy. "How was your day?"

"It was great. We went to the zoo. It's a lot fancier—it's a lot *cleaner*—than the one in our San Francisco," she answered. "And the bus went through the Sunset District on the way there and back. It really is a nice place here." She pointed to the book. "What are you reading?"

"Well, it *says* it's a basic guide to repairing small appliances." Father's face was unhappy. "I'm following about one word in three. I think I need something more basic than basic."

"They've talked about classes for you," Lucy said. "They aren't born knowing this stuff here. If they can learn it, you can, too."

"Maybe. I hope so. But they've got a forty-year head start on me," her father said.

"It'll be all right," Lucy said stoutly. "Nobody expects you to understand everything all at once."

He looked more unhappy yet. "No, I suppose not. But *I* expected to. I've been fixing small appliances since I was younger than Michael is. How much more was there for me to know?" His laugh was harsh. "Well, I've found out. I don't want to be useless here, or on charity. I want to earn my keep." He slammed the book shut with a noise like a gunshot. "Right now, I don't know if I ever can. I just don't know."

Behind him, Michael whooped, "Die, villain!" He had no worries. Lucy wished she could say the same.

Ignoring her little brother as best she could, she said, "You'll do it, Father." She meant it—she had confidence in him. "We'll all do it, sooner or later. Things are new here, that's all. We haven't been here very long. We can learn."

"Maybe. I hope so." Her father didn't sound sure. That worried her. But this new San Francisco had to be harder for him to get used to than it was for her, just as it was harder for her than for Michael. He'd had longer to become a part of the San Francisco they'd left behind.

So had Mother, come to that. But she didn't seem to be having too bad a time. She didn't feel the need to know *why* things worked, the way Father did. She just needed to know *how* they worked, and she was fine. When Lucy walked into the kitchen to see if she needed a hand, she found her chopping green onions in the food processor and heating something in the microwave. Till she came here, she'd never seen a food processor or a microwave. That didn't mean she couldn't figure out what they were good for.

"Want any help?" Lucy asked her.

"Not me." Her mother shook her head. "I'm doing fine." She paused. "I heard what you and your father were talking about in there. I think you're right. I think we'll all do fine after a while."

The telephone rang. There were telephones in the San Francisco Lucy had left, but there hadn't been one in the Woos' apartment there. In *this* San Francisco, phones were everywhere, either in buildings or carried around. Wherever you went, you heard snatches of other people's conversations. Paul carried a telephone. He'd got a couple of calls while they were at the zoo. Lucy wasn't sure she liked that. The phone here rang again. "I'll get it," she said, and dashed off to do just that. "Hello? . . . Oh,

Paul. Hello!" Maybe carrying a phone around wasn't so bad after all.

When Sammy Wong told Paul he'd never work for Crosstime Traffic again, Paul had done his best to convince himself it didn't matter. The way his heart thudded when he and his father walked into the Crosstime Traffic San Francisco office said he'd lied to himself. He wanted to go out to the alternates again. He wanted to make a career of it. If he couldn't, if he was stuck in the home timeline . . . That would be pretty hard to take.

His father looked nervous, too, though he tried to hide it. Dad had been going out to the alternates for years. What would *he* do if his bosses said he couldn't any more?

Paul sighed. *When I told Lucy how good the home timeline was, this is the stuff I didn't talk about. But it's here. It's real.*

All the security procedures were real, too. They had to show their IDs. They had to get their retinas and their fingerprints scanned. They went through metal and explosives and biohazard detectors. Terrorists were also real. They liked to strike Crosstime Traffic operations. Why not? The company was big and rich. They'd hit Romania not so long before. They could hit the USA, too.

"Go ahead," a guard said after everything checked out okay. "Your action hearing is set for room 582." He didn't call it a disciplinary hearing, but that was what it was.

A board of three women and two men sat waiting for Paul and his father. The chairwoman said, "These proceedings will be videorecorded for the archives and for further review if needed. Do you understand and agree?" She sounded bored. How many times had she said the same thing?

Dad nodded. Paul said, "Yes."

A man with a white handlebar mustache said, "Summarize the events in San Francisco in alternate 3477 from the time of your arrival there to the time of your departure. Keep your summary focused on the problems you ran into."

"Be brief," the chairwoman added.

· Paul and his father looked at each other. Paul said, "The biggest problem we had was that two sets of locals were already much too curious about Curious Notions."

"No," Dad said. "The biggest problem was that we didn't know they were till too late."

"For whatever it may be worth to you, we have had some things to say to the person who operated the shop before you took it over," the chairwoman said.

So Elliott did get in trouble, Paul thought. He couldn't feel too sorry for Elliott. If the other man had warned Dad and him . . . Well, how much would have been different? Some, maybe.

"We still need to know what you did, though, and why," said the man with the white mustache. He was plainly number two on the board. "We need to know how the locals closed down the shop, why you failed to block that, and what you told them while they held you."

"They came in with submachine guns and yelled, 'Hands high!'" Paul's father answered. "The only way I could have blocked that was with a tank."

"We didn't give away the crosstime secret, either, and the Germans and the Tongs were both sniffing after it," Paul added. He didn't say anything about Lucy. But he hadn't given her the secret. She'd figured it out on her own. And besides, she was here in the home timeline. No matter what she knew, she wasn't going to spread it.

"What about your interrogations?" the chairwoman asked.

Dad said, "I told more lies than a software salesman."

"I don't think the *Feldgendarmerie* ever thought crosstime travel was really and truly possible," Paul said. "They would have asked different questions—they would have asked harder questions—if they had. The Tongs came a lot closer, but they don't have anywhere near the know-how the Germans do."

"The way we escaped will keep the Germans and the Chinese in that alternate from figuring out we came from a different one," his father put in. He was ready to take credit for that even if it hadn't been his idea.

But the chairwoman called him on it: "By the reports I've read, Special Operative Wong had more to do with your escape than you did. Do you disagree?"

Dad looked as if he wanted to. He also looked as if he knew he couldn't get away with it. Reluctantly, he shook his head. Paul said, "No, we don't. It's true."

"All right." The man with the white mustache looked at Paul. "And what have you got to say for yourself about wandering away from the . . . the Palace Hotel?" He had to check a monitor set into the table to get the name right.

Paul's heart sank. If they were going to blame him for that . . . But they had a right to. "What can I say?" he answered harshly. "I blew it. I was going stir-crazy, and I went out, and I got nabbed. Nobody's fault but mine. I was really, really dumb."

He and his father got a few more questions. Then the members of the board put their heads together and muttered among themselves. The chairwoman looked up and said, "Please wait outside for a few minutes."

Dad managed a nod. Paul just walked out. In the hallway, Dad said, "The condemned men ate a hearty meal." Paul turned away. He couldn't stand jokes just then.

He waited what seemed like forever. By his watch, it was sixteen minutes. The door opened. "Please come in," said one of the women on the board.

In they went. The chairwoman looked from Dad to Paul and back again. "You both made mistakes," she said. "Your testimony and the reports of others all show that. But the situation *had* been developing before you arrived, and you both showed energy and imagination in trying to deal with the emergency. We don't expect you to be perfect. We do expect you to try. We got that from both of you." Her eyes swung to Paul. "We also expect you won't go wandering off again when you're not supposed to. Special Operative Wong seems to believe you won't."

"He does?" Paul knew he squeaked. He couldn't help it. He'd thought Sammy Wong would nail his hide to the wall. "I won't, ma'am. I promise!"

"That should do." The chairwoman gave him and his father a wintry smile. "You are both cleared to resume crosstime duty, you"— that was aimed at Paul—"as your education permits. Any questions? No? Very well, then. That will be all."

Out in the corridor, Dad stuck out his hand. Paul grabbed it and shook it. They both let out identical sighs of relief. Paul took his phone off his belt. He didn't need its memory to punch in the number he wanted. He knew it by heart. "Hello, Lucy? It's me. We're okay—not great, maybe, but okay. . . . Yeah, both of us. And about that movie tonight . . ."